WITHOUT CONSENT

A NICOLE LONG LEGAL THRILLER
BOOK 2

AIME AUSTIN

AIME AUSTIN
www.AimeAustin.com

Without Consent

This edition published by
Moore Digital Media
1125 N Fairfax Blvd. #46071
Los Angeles CA 90046

Cover Designer: Wicked Good Book Covers
Without Consent/Aime Austin. — 1st ed.

eISBN: 978-1-64414-092-5
ISBN: 978-1-64414-093-2

THE NICOLE LONG LEGAL THRILLER SERIES

Outcry Witness

Major Crimes

Without Consent

The Murders Began

ALSO BY AIME AUSTIN

The Casey Cort Series of Legal Thrillers

Judged

Ransomed

Caged

Disgraced

Unarmed

Kidnapped

Reunited

Contained

Poisoned

Abused

"How do you say no to God, right?"

—Phil Saviano

"To all those who have suffered from my shortcomings and mistakes I both apologize and from them beg forgiveness."

—CARDINAL BERNARD LAW

ONE
JUSTIN PATRICK MCPHEE
NOVEMBER 27, 2008

One look at the kitchen sideboard laden with Polish treats and I knew that our mother had something in store. Something my sisters and I probably wouldn't like. It was the twenty-fifth anniversary of our father's—her husband's—death. That day had coincidentally fallen on Thanksgiving Day, one none of us ever spent with our mother. Unspoken guilt about the milestone anniversary had brought us all home.

I took a deep breath and braced myself for whatever my mother had in mind. My older sister wasn't nearly as patient.

"Mom, why is all this food here? You know I'm going to Adrian's family's place for Thanksgiving." My sister Stacey Burgos had the same pout on her face she'd perfected at sixteen. "You said you had something important to tell us."

Stacey may have had an age-inappropriate purse to

her lips, but she also had a valid point. There hadn't been a turkey in this house since 1983. Nevertheless, the sideboard had an assortment of everything needed for a feast *except* a bird. Pierogies of every kind graced my mother's china serving plates. There were sides of sour cream, applesauce, and onions. On the biggest platter, fried carp. In the tureen, a thick and creamy mushroom stew.

"Everything goes down better with food," my mother said as she fluttered around the kitchen, eventually pulling a strawberry rhubarb pie from the oven to cool on the counter. I tried not to startle at the implication of anything "going down." Thanksgiving was a time for family gatherings, not announcements. I tensed my jaw because my family wasn't much on the gathering part of holidays, at least since Dad had died. In our family *not* being together had become the tradition.

"Mama, Mom!" Stacey protested some more. "Pierogies are not food. They're little bricks of dough I'll never digest. Or when they finally *do* digest, they'll sit on my hips for the rest of my life." Maybe my older sister was doing an imitation of her sixteen-year-old self deliberately because she'd been complaining about the damage our mother's hearty cooking had been doing to her hips for the last twenty-five years. I had no opinion on her body's size, but the way her husband, Adrian, looked at her, I didn't think he cared one iota about the width of her hips.

"But rice and beans are okay?" our mother asked while loading up Stacey's plate. We'd always been served in order of age. Any attempt at making our own plate was

swiftly shut down. "Neither is traditional," Mom continued. Adrian was Puerto Rican. Stacey had gone down to
the island with a friend in college over spring break and
had come back with a boyfriend who was now her
husband and father to her three children.

"You were invited," Stacey huffed, replaying the script
she and Mom ran through a few times a year. "You're
always invited to hang out with the Burgos clan. They'd
love for you to come. You know that."

"Stacey. Mom said she needed to tell us something.
Can we get to that? I, for one, am glad to have a pierogi."
Krystyna Balfour, my youngest sister, dared defy my
mother. We shared a knowing look before she rose and
helped herself to a half dozen of the dumplings. She took a
seat at the round kitchen table where she liberally added
sour cream, then covered that with onions and crispy bits
of chopped bacon. My younger sister's husband was Irish
like our dad had been.

We both knew from experience that the Balfour clan's
dinners weren't going to grace any best-food lists anytime
soon. Though I usually followed Stacey's lead, and my
mother's marching orders, this time I mimicked my
younger sister and helped myself. Anything to get to the
part of the meal where I was going to have to swallow
something unpleasant with my fish. More than I hated
surprises, I disliked the wait for them. The fear and dread
of something unexpected always opened a bottomless pit
in my stomach.

"Do you want some beer, Justin?" Mom asked. Her

voice was bordering on sweet. My mother was anything, everything, but sweet.

I nodded because I always needed more social lubrication, not less. She lifted the bottle opener from the fridge and pried the top from a glass longneck bottle she'd brought from the second refrigerator in the laundry room. I took a sip when she handed it to me.

"Not a Strohmeyer brand," I noted.

"They poisoned those children, Justin. I read the stories in the papers. A boycott was the least I could do to support you." My cold lawyer's heart melted a little at my mom's gesture of kindness.

"Morro!" Stacey yelled. On my right I saw my dog tilt his nose to the ceiling and his throat budge as he swallowed a pierogi whole. It both was and wasn't his finest moment. I couldn't help laughing.

"You have to admire his stealth," Krystyna said as she chuckled around the food filling her cheeks.

"Don't laugh with your mouth full, you could choke," Mom admonished. She waved Stacey down to the table again, and once my sister sat, Mom shoved a plate of dumplings in front of her. My oldest sister had never had much willpower, and before I could blink, she was tucking into the food.

Satisfied that we all had plates in front of us, Mom poured herself some kind of apple or pear *kompot* and sat in the fourth chair. The fifth was empty. Years ago it had been my dad's chair. Now it was most often occupied by mom's...boyfriend...lover...partner...guy, Beau McInnis.

They hadn't married and I never knew exactly what to call him. At least he wasn't here to dial up the awkward.

"I'm so glad to have all my babies here," my mom said. She had that tone that was hovering somewhere along the about-to-cry spectrum. I shifted in my chair. Hers was the one voice that could always stir up my emotions. I didn't like them stirred.

Stacey eyed her watch. If I were to guess, she was wondering if her rambunctious children had set their house on fire. "Before you go down memory lane or anything, what did you want to tell us?"

Mom sighed. I could see that she'd probably prepared some long speech in her head. She huffed another breath, cupped her hands, and pulled them toward her heart.

"*Moje dzieci.*"

"Not the Polish." Krystyna's sigh was almost as big as Mom's. After a long pause, Mom put her forearms on the table, intertwined her fingers, flicked her thumbs back and forth until the right rested on the left. Finally, she spoke.

"I'm thinking of selling the house."

All three of our forks clattered to the table. Morro went from a doze, to standing at attention, his tail stiff with concentration. Shocked didn't even cover the range of emotions coursing through me. I couldn't have named one of them, but they were having an effect. My heart pounded in my chest. My hands started to sweat.

"You said once if not a thousand times, Mom, that you'd have to be carted out of this house in a coffin," I reminded her. That was not a picture I liked to imagine, but the image of a "for sale" sign was somehow worse than death.

"Where are you going to go? Florida?" Krystyna asked, her lip curled at the cliché inherent in the question.

"Beau and I were thinking of Arizona, actually."

"Seriously. Mom. You're going to hang out with old people in a desert?" Stacey protested. "What about the kids? Your grandbabies. Surely you don't want them to grow up without you?"

"I said Arizona, not Mars. There are nonstop flights between here and Phoenix. Plus Adrian's parents moved here all the way from Puerto Rico. It's not like they don't spoil the girls already."

"I thought you'd be the one who taught my son Polish," I blurted out. A second later I wanted to stuff all the words back in my mouth. It didn't work that way.

"Son? Justin. What are you smoking?" Krystyna's eyes bored into mine. "You're damned near forty and don't have any kids."

The way our dynamic worked is that I'd normally snap back at my younger sister. Say something snarky. Stacey would side with her. Mom would come to my defense and we'd hash it out from there. For the first time in a long time, I didn't have it in me to do the familiar, drawn-out routine.

I let Krystyna hang, could see her thinking of possible comebacks to mine. When I didn't speak, I threw off the whole dynamic. My mom and sisters shifted, looked from one to the other, deciding who would be the one to make the next move, get us back on our usual track. Krystyna spoke first.

"Are you dating someone? You never date anyone. Well, not really. Not for more than a week or three."

The room got very quiet when I didn't answer. My sisters were suddenly intensely curious. Mom's face was a mixture of relief and scrutiny. We'd had a closer relationship than she'd had with either of my sisters—moms and boys and all that. I knew she could read me like a first-grade primer.

"Who is she, Justin?" Mom asked. "Are you planning on getting married to her? Making me a grandmother? You haven't brought anyone around."

When I was a kid, I thought Mom could read my mind. To this day, I wasn't so sure she couldn't.

"I don't know how the relationship is going to go," I whispered. They all leaned in close to hear me say, "There really isn't one...a relationship, that is."

"With who?" Stacey asked, her face the picture of disbelief.

"You remember Casey Cort? I mentioned—"

"The one you did the case with?" Stacey interrupted with a question.

"Sure—"

"So funny." Stacey snapped the fingers of her right hand. "I'd been meaning to ask you about her, but I kept forgetting. I thought I saw her at the West Side Market a few months ago and she looked mighty pregnant."

"She *was* pregnant. She had a baby, Simon—"

"How old is he, this Simon?" Mom was leaning forward, her abandonment of us in Cleveland for warmer climes forgotten for a moment.

"Six months. Six months and three weeks."

"That's very specific," Krystyna observed.

"I think the baby may be mine." It was the first time I'd really admitted it to myself without a lot of alcohol in me. The first time I'd said it out loud to someone who wasn't a canine.

"Think? What do you mean, think?" My mother's eyes bored into mine.

"I don't think, Mama, I know," I admitted.

"I have a grandbaby? You have a whole child that...you didn't tell your family about? That's a very big secret to keep. What in the world is going on with you? That you'd keep a baby from me, his grandmother. From his aunts and uncles and cousins. Are you that ashamed of us or something?"

"I'm not ashamed." That was a lie. I wasn't ashamed of them, though.

"Then why haven't you ever brought a girl around? Over twenty years of possible girlfriends and I've never met a single one."

"Why would you think I'm ashamed?"

"Maybe because I have an accent. Because our house isn't some Lakewood mansion." My mother's insecurities started piling up like the maple leaves from the tree in our yard.

"Casey's nothing like that, Mama. She grew up on

West Avenue. Went to St. Joseph. Her father is from Poland."

"Then what is it? Why are we not good enough for you?"

"Mama, it's not about that. You guys are great. Any girl, um, woman I was with would be lucky to have you"—I paused and looked both my sisters in the eye—"to have you all in their life."

"What's the problem?" Krystyna probed.

"She's with someone else."

"Already? You aren't hamsters. She would have only gotten pregnant fifteen months ago. How in the hell did she find another guy so soon?" My mother didn't swear about much, but she was riled up like I knew she'd be when I'd avoided telling her about any of this over the last year.

"Well...it's complicated," I hedged, suddenly very ashamed of everything that had happened between the Sunday she'd gotten pregnant and now.

"This isn't Maury Povich or Ricki Lake," Krystyna argued. "It's not that complicated."

I know we're all seeing the same image in our minds: a lone woman up on stage surrounded by five or ten men, who paternity tests had just determined they *weren't* the father.

"It is, kind of, actually. She didn't know who the father was."

"Well, I know she definitely went to St. Joe's," Stacey said as she sat back in her chair. She pushed away from the table and got up to get her own beer from the fridge. I hated to be the cause of so much day drinking.

"It's not quite like that," I said in defense of the bad-Catholic-girl stereotypes.

"Then how was it?" Stacey asked after taking a long pull from her bottle.

"I told her we couldn't have a relationship. Ron—he's a lawyer, a big firm partner—pursued her. Promised her everything she ever wanted. Marriage, a baby, a house in Shaker with a white picket fence."

"Why couldn't you have a relationship?" Stacey had gone from disbelief to fully perplexed. "Scratch that. If she had your baby, you did have a relationship. It's not like you had a one-night stand, right? You guys worked on that big case together, and some other ones besides."

"It was not a one-night thing. I asked her out for surf and turf at Red's last January and one thing led to another."

"Another thing led to a baby," Krystyna said. She wasn't doing a great job of hiding her smirk.

"That...I didn't mean for it to happen," I said. Though in the quiet and dark of night, when Morro was quietly snoring next to me on the bed in the spot Casey had once occupied during our Sunday night...romps...I wondered how we'd both managed to mess up something as simple as birth control at our ages.

"What happened when she told you she was pregnant?" my mother asked.

"She wanted us to be together," I admitted, "and I told her flat out, it wasn't going to happen."

"And why not, Justin, if it's not us you're ashamed of, then what is it? If you liked her enough to...well, work with her and do that other thing. Did you not like her enough to be with her?" I could see the gears turning in my mother's head and not liking what came out. "Please tell me I raised you better than this. Better than to think women are good for only one kind of thing. You have sisters..."

I shook my head. I mean, I was a guy and did kind of put women into one of two categories. But Casey had never been in either. She'd been in a category of her own, even if I'd always insisted we were just "casual."

"Casey would never be with me." I looked between three of the four most important women in my life. Happy that Beau wasn't here because I would never have been able to admit this in front of any man. "No one would ever want someone like me." I finally, *finally*, said the part that had been rolling around in my head for almost two dozen years out loud.

"Justin, what in the hell are you talking about?" Stacey's voice was older-sister exasperated. "Have you secretly killed someone and buried the body in the basement?"

"What I've buried for longer than I ever should have is that I'm one of the victims of Monsignor Quinn."

"What are you talking about?" Stacey asked. "That stuff on the news about how the priest from St. Ignatius molested kids has something to do with you?"

"This isn't how I wanted to tell you. Actually, I never wanted to tell you. But Lori Pope, the Cuyahoga County prosecutor, is putting together a case. She wants me to be a part of it. I think I'm going to say yes. I knew Casey wouldn't want to be with a guy like me. Because I'm damaged goods. I have been since 1985 when I went down to Guatemala."

My mother's hands slowly crept up to her ears. Betrayal of my mother's faith in the church didn't even begin to describe the feelings inside of me. Even if she hadn't said it outright, I'd always known my mother didn't want to hear the truth, to *know* the truth.

"Monsignor Quinn was a credit to the church, to the school," my own mother insisted, defending the priest in spite of the facts I was laying before her. "He raised enough money to renovate the music room. The school bought all new instruments for the kids to take home." She spoke like fundraising was the equivalent of saving souls.

"*Mom.*"

"He helped all those poor Catholic families in Guatemala," she continued, as if I hadn't spoken in protest.

"That's not what he did in Guatemala, Mom."

"But he did. The pictures were in the bulletins. He helped build that orphanage. Had that whole vocational training center for those poor unfortunate boys without mothers or fathers. What are you saying about Monsignor Quinn?"

"He went there because those kids don't fight back."

"Justin!"

"Me too, Mom. I was a kid who didn't fight back. I didn't know what to do. When Father Quinn came to me at night...I let him do what he wanted. Saying no to him was like saying no to God." I returned all the Catholic guilt to sender. "Mama, you always said never say no to God."

TWO
BLAKE HARDIN TATUM
DECEMBER 15, 2008

I was at the long trestle table surrounded by two tall stacks of papers. Some that should be tossed out, and another pile that should be shredded. A third mess of pages was full of leads on various investigations I'd finally have the time to pursue. I dropped the page I'd been perusing when my longtime boyfriend came into the narrow dining room that served more as an office than eating area.

"You should have taken the buyout," Woody said, as if he'd seen a tarot deck I hadn't.

I was tired and disheartened and very sad that I'd gotten a master's in a dying industry, but I wasn't about to let Woodrow Dawson blame the demise of print newspapers all on me.

"How was I to know that I'd be one of the thirty-eight who were cut?" I asked, working hard to keep exasperation from my voice.

"It wasn't thirty-eight, Blake. Twenty took buyouts. It was down to eighteen."

"Then it makes even more sense."

"Then, what? You'd roll the dice? Take your chances? Where was your precious Northeast Ohio Newspaper Guild in all this gambling? What's the point of having a union, paying all those dues, if at the end of the day the *Plain Dealer* put you out with a few bucks in your pocket and zero health insurance?"

I'd resisted the first jab but couldn't help rising to the bait of the second. Woody, who'd never been in any kind of union, didn't have a problem expressing his uninformed opinions on the topic of collective bargaining. I sat up straighter, hooked my thumbs into the beltloops of my jeans. Looked him in the eye so he knew how serious I was, how much I didn't need to have this conversation right now.

"You know Dad was a Teamster. Shop steward too. I trust that they fought for us the best they could." I wasn't sure I still believed in unions as blindly as I once did, but I wasn't going to give Woody a single bit of ammunition. He tended to keep an arsenal.

"Damn paper's making a profit, but not a big enough one." Woody shook his head in disgust. "It's all growth and profits nowadays. Very unsustainable. Hypercapitalism is going to do us all in."

"I didn't want to talk to you about the layoff." This discussion needed to head in a completely different direction. I'd texted him a few hours ago that we needed to talk. He'd taken his sweet time in coming home to me.

"Layoff," he scoffed.

"Fine. Do you need me to say I was fired? I'm not so up my own ass that I'm not ready to admit that there's no going back. That's actually what I wanted to talk to you about. I'm going to have to switch it up."

"What does that mean?"

I paused for a long moment, trying to think of how I wanted to frame it. This second earthshaking thing we were going to have to manage in as many weeks.

"I need to move." Baldly was how I said it. Sugar-coating was going to take time I didn't have.

"Move? Where? You own this house."

"As you've just pointed out, the payout wasn't the best. Twenty thousand. A week's pay for every year."

"That's a bit of cash." Woody was notorious for spending the same dollar ten times, then wondering why he was nine dollars in debt.

"But it's fully taxed. I'm getting the money in the next two weeks, before the end of the year. My accountant said this severance will push me into the next tax bracket. At the end of the day, with the two city's taxes, the state tax, and federal, I'll end up with fifteen."

"You didn't answer my question, though. Where are we going to move?"

He didn't notice that his pronoun was different than mine.

"To the rental."

"The one on Larchmere?"

The sneer on his face and the tone of his voice made Larchmere sound like my building was middle of Cedar and East Fifty-fifth, an area recently proclaimed the murder capital of Cleveland.

"Yes, the one on Larchmere." I shuffled through some papers until I came upon the lease for the property. Gave the document an official shake. "It actually works out. I called the tenant to give them a heads-up. The law allows an owner to move back into their property. Fortunately they were in the middle of buying a house out of foreclosure and it's worked out. So they'll leave early. Put that two months of rent money they would have owed towards renovations or whatever."

"What about this place?" His neck swiveled around, his eyes taking in the single-family house we'd been calling home for a few years. "You love living in CHALK."

Our little acronym neighborhood consisted of five streets: Cormere, Haddam, Ardoon, Larchmere, and Kemper. Most homes were nearly a century old and required the kind of constant care property that age needed. "Money pit" may have been a more apt description. The Larchmere apartment was not in this neighborhood despite the shared street name. It was on the wrong side of East 121st Street.

"This house is too big for us," I said instead of focusing on the cost only. "You know that. I can rent it out for at least as much as the mortgage and taxes, if not more. With this covered and the rental money from the downstairs apartment at Larchmere, I won't go homeless." Or hungry.

"What about my studio? Remember how that was half the reason we bought this house?"

I noticed he was very careful to leave out the second reason. When I didn't answer, he continued.

"Isn't there an attic at that Larchmere place? It's not perfect, I'll admit, with only those tiny garret windows, but maybe I could use that as my studio."

Woody sat on the bench on the other side of the table, his legs spread wide. His right leg started jiggling. Without waiting for anything from me, he spoke again.

"Aren't you going to get another job? I mean, what about the *Sun* newspapers or *Akron Beacon* or *Journal* or whatever it's called?"

It was on the tip of my tongue to explain that the suburban newspaper chain was under the same ownership as the *Plain Dealer*, but if he hadn't listened the first hundred times, nothing said he was going to hear it this time. Since I was done with newspapers, at least in their current form, I chose a different answer.

"Print news is a race to the bottom," I said. "It would be like getting into film photography at this late date." I shook my head, trying to think of a way to make him understand that I was taking a break from being sole breadwinner. "What I'm going to do for the first time ever is take some time to figure out what I want."

"You sound like some white woman with a rich husband," he scoffed.

"What I am, Woody, is a forty-six-year-old black woman." With no husband, black, white, or purple, of any means went unsaid. "No one's rushing to hire older women, much less black women for the salary I had. The healthy salary the union negotiated for me. So my plan is to do freelance work. There's some online publications paying for contributors now, breaking away from the *Huffington Post* model. The rest of the time I want to use for an idea of something I want to try."

"Try what—at your age?"

"I'm not married." I paused, letting that one sit there between us for an uncomfortably long moment. "I don't have kids. So, I still think I can try new things without consequences, Woody." That first sentence was a jab, a stab directly at him. We'd been together off and on for nearly a decade. At the beginning I thought he'd be a whole husband and a great father.

The fact that he was an...artist was a bonus because as unconventional as it was, he could have been home with our theoretical kids all day while I chased down leads. But he was never prepared for any of those steps. It was always later...after the next show. After the next gallery took him on. After we bought this house and he had a full studio space...an *atelier*...where he could really concentrate on his work. When my period stopped earlier this year, I didn't even tell him the whole ship had sailed, taking the last of my eggs with it.

"You know I'm not ready for all that," he said. I think

the often repeated refrain came out of his mouth without connecting to his brain.

I shook my head. I wasn't even asking for anything from him anymore, but he was already backing away verbally, with one foot practically out the door. Suddenly, inexplicably angry, I decided to shove him through it.

"Then I think you'll need to move in to your own place."

"What?" His eyes went as wide as a nineteenth-century minstrel.

"Remember when you were invited to that collective in the Flats? Maybe you should take them up on it. And with downsizing, I'm going to need that other bedroom for my office, now that I'm working from home."

"A whole office to just type a few words?"

"Type a few words? This is a hustle, Woody. I'll need to turn in thousands of words a month. I'm only going to get paid for what I write. We're both moving into a new 'eat what you kill' phase."

"I haven't—"

"Figured out your artistic vision or signed with a prestigious gallery...yet?" I threw up my hands in a half-salute of victory. "I know. But what better time than now?"

Woody looked almost wild-eyed for a moment, but pulled himself back from the brink so fast I almost thought I'd imagined it.

Backtracking, he said, "I know that I've been slow to come around, but I want a future with you. You have to know that. This is just a big sacrifice while I'm on the cusp of breaking through to the next level. Surely we can stay in the house another six months. The money would pay for that. I could chip in for utilities more. I know it's a lot heating a place this size."

"Chip in how?"

"My mom would lend us something." That came out low enough for plausible deniability.

"I can't be indebted to your mother. I think you should take her up on the offer to move back home." Whenever I pushed, her wide-open revolving door came up. She'd made no secret that she'd never wanted to be my mother-in-law.

"What about us?" Woody's voice was almost a plea. Almost, but not quite.

"I think we need to go in different directions," I said. It was a sentence I probably should have uttered years ago. Only now did I finally have the guts. The idea of trying to build up my new freelance business all the while being his full-time cheerleader just felt exhausting.

"So you're throwing out the baby with the bathwater," he said without guile. I didn't point out there was no baby to speak of. Sometimes I thought I was all done with baby hormones. Every so often, being childless was a little jab to the softest part of me.

"It's time to change it up," I announced.

"But what are *you* going to do?"

For someone who'd always been more interested in my paycheck than how it got there, I was both annoyed and warmed by the question.

"After all these years, you deserve the honesty," I conceded. "I want to do a new project." I held up the iPhone that I'd started taking everywhere for work. "There's this podcast thing I've heard of. I want to do one in conjunction with a blog I'm going to start."

"A blog? A podcast? About what? What do you know about? I've only heard experts and radio guys doing it. Maybe one hack comedian."

Ignoring the jab, I continued. "My last three years with the paper were in crime investigation features. I want to follow up on some of those stories."

"Don't they belong to the paper?"

"Public information is just that. They already bought and paid for my labor. I take my skills and knowledge with me."

"What are you going to investigate?"

"Corruption in Cleveland." I shrugged. I didn't say that's why I was sifting through all this stuff, looking to answer that exact question. "Cold cases, maybe. There are plenty of both. I'm not quite sure."

"Good luck to you, I guess." I never thought the end would come with so little ceremony. Woody merely saluted as he backed out of the door. "I'm outta here. I'll pick up my stuff after Christmas."

And just like that, ten years went up and away like a puff of smoke. I wanted to be more sad, but I was mostly hurt at how cavalierly he'd walked out the door when the gravy'd stopped rolling off the train.

They say you have to murder your darlings. I guess the murders had begun.

A lightbulb went on.

I snapped my fingers because I may not have a nice house to live in, or marriage or kids, or a secure job. But all of a sudden, I had the title and focus for my blog and podcast: *The Murders Began.*

THREE
NICOLE THERIOT LONG
DECEMBER 25, 2008

Everything had changed and nothing had changed. I stood in the same place I'd been almost seventeen years ago to the day. The kitchen was filled with bright white cabinets and black granite countertops. The multi-hued gray glass-tile backsplash was awash in soft lighting. Magazine-worthy it was. Knowing my mother, it had probably been featured in *Louisiana Life* if not *Southern Living*.

I could still see the old kitchen underneath. Where two of the biggest secrets affecting my life had been spilled. One with blood that had stained the floors. As I took it all in, I had to wonder what Aubrey made of the whole thing. What it was like cooking in a kitchen kitted out like a restaurant.

"I'm not sure we'll be able to get a place for you at the club..." My mother, Margaret Long, trailed off as she waved her hand toward the landline phone that still graced the hallway table as if it were decades earlier and a gloved maid would be there to answer it anytime someone deigned to call from the world outside.

"We've had the same table for years," I explained, as if she didn't already know this. As if anything could have changed in all the years I'd been gone. Metairie and its most exclusive country club were not sowing the seeds of revolution. "It seats eight, ten if they squeeze in. Why wouldn't there be a space for me? Especially with Michelle and her brood in Texas."

"You didn't tell us you were coming home until your flight landed this morning at the airport."

The implication was that they'd raised me better than to show up unannounced on anyone's doorstep. Though they truly had instilled better manners, I'd been hoping for a bit of grace from my family. Looked like I was out of luck.

"Not that we aren't glad to see you, Nicky Mouse," my father butted in, doing what he always did: smoothing away the rough edges of whatever his wife had said to me, her *adopted* daughter.

I'd heard that refrain once before. The last time I'd been here. Really here with nowhere else to go. It was different now with having my own place to where I could retreat. As I looked between my parents, I was starting to regret my last-minute airplane ticket purchase.

Cleveland was truly Midwestern in a way that was starting to chafe with my single, career-focused life.

Without a family, I was well and truly alone. Which I could mostly handle except around Christmas.

The prosecutor's office holiday party had come and gone a week earlier. It hadn't been any fun sober. Being the boss made it even more awkward. And Lori Pope was starting to creep me out. I'd made the rounds, eaten three different kinds of meatballs, had two glasses of ginger ale, then had gone home early to my cold and empty condo.

Even with the comfort of bourbon and awful cable holiday movies, as I'd watched the city shut down this week, everyone snuggling in with their family and staying far away from the sleeting rain, loneliness had hit me like a box of rocks.

I had no real friends. I didn't have any family in Ohio. So I'd made the impulse decision to pay top dollar for a last-minute ticket, pack an overnight bag, and fly home to Louisiana. Daddy had picked me up at the New Orleans airport after my plane's late morning arrival.

Maybe Thomas Wolfe was right, that we can't go home again. Already here, I put a smile on my face and decided to make the best of it.

"Let me call Saunders, he'll fix it right up," I said.

Before my mother could object, I walked to the landline and dialed a number I hadn't realized I'd remembered by heart. The only difference between twenty years ago and now was that I had to cycle through some kind of inanimate menu before I got the maître d' on the line. Like I expected, he was able to accommodate my addition to the table. The Theriot side of the family had been founding members of the club. The white side, that was.

"He's happy to see me," I announced after hanging up the receiver. "Let me get my shoes and we'll go. I'll even drive, if you like; that way Daddy can enjoy his bourbon and you can have the club's famous brandy milk punch. They're heavy on the pour with that and eggnog this time of year."

Before they could make any more objections, I slipped into my ballet flats, picked up the keys to my father's latest Cadillac, and with them in the back seat, chauffeured my parents to the club.

All three of us hadn't been seated more than five minutes before the meet and greets started. On the short drive over, my parents warned me that I'd probably be the center of attention. Everything old was new again, I supposed.

My parents' friends came up by the ones and twos, proclaiming that I hadn't aged a day since they'd last seen me back in the early nineties after I'd graduated from college. Others that had heard I'd moved up north were perplexed by the choice of Cleveland over Boston, D.C., or New York. One of the boldest, or maybe rudest, of my mother's friends appeared like a specter between the entrée and salad course baldly asking about my marriage and children prospects.

I put my fork down and truthfully said that on the cusp of forty neither was looking likely, but pointed out my sister, Michelle, had made three grandchildren for my family to dote over, and given the world population was steadily ticking close to seven billion, that should be enough.

Delighted the dessert course had come, and the nosy folks had gone, I lifted my spoon ready to drown into the sensory delight of the club's specialty, banana sorbet. I'd never seen it anywhere else in the world. Most of my happiest childhood memories here at the club could be summoned with a single spoonful. I was ready for that trip down memory lane, when I felt the hairs rise on the back of my neck as someone came up behind me. My parents were mingling, so it was only me and some of Daddy's work friends left at the table. Doing what I could to keep my composure, I turned when I heard the first words from his mouth in seventeen years.

"As I live and breathe, if it isn't Nicole Long. Long time no see." The voice I'd hoped to never hear again—in person—was full of mirth at his bad pun. Whenever I heard or saw him on TV, I changed the channel or muted the sound. I couldn't do that here.

My spoon clattered from the table to the floor. A waiter was there to retrieve the soiled one and hand me a new one before I could sputter a greeting. My stomach turned. I wanted to get up and run away. I could feel my muscles twitch, but they didn't work because the only thing I could move was my jaw.

"Seth...Seth Collins. What on earth are you doing here?" It was impolite, but what I truthfully wanted to know because I'd fully never expected to see this man again, except maybe in his grave with me tap-dancing upon it pouring whiskey into the Louisiana soil. But he wasn't dead. My tap shoes were gathering dust in Mama and Daddy's attic.

"The same as you," he replied, his tone jovial. "Enjoying a beautiful Christmas meal and good old Southern hospitality."

"Why aren't you at the church?" I asked. It wasn't as if, in an anxiety-ridden missed night of sleep, I hadn't considered the possibility that I could run into him when I got home. I'd weighed the odds, though, and thought them in my favor.

Pastors of megachurches should be in them on Christmas Day. He was the kind of person who liked the largest crowd possible, and the holiest day would probably produce those numbers. Country clubs with their purposely limited groups had seemed like the least likely scenario. Yet, here we were.

I quickly summoned the waiter and with a flick of my fingers had a double bourbon neat at my fingertips. I downed the drink as if it were water, then stashed the evidence on a passing tray. All this before Seth produced an answer.

He'd taken his time before he spoke, looking me up and down in the smarmy way he'd always had. I wanted to run away and shower, but I held my ground. The alcohol had steadied me. I needed to assess the threat.

"We're trying out a new pastor. Giving him a little breathing room."

"Oh."

My father must have caught the exchange out of the corner of his eye because he stopped glad-handing and was back at our table in a flash, but obviously not soon enough.

"Seth…" Daddy's voice faltered, a rare occurrence. The man who had protected me for much of my life was on the back foot. I had to swallow hard to keep the bourbon and banana sorbet down.

"I was just saying hello to your beautiful daughter," Collins said. "I was about to ask her how she liked my spot at the table. I was glad that the Beaudrys were able to accommodate a little old pastor like me at the last minute."

I'd only seen my father's face turn red in anger, but I was pretty sure that wasn't the reason his neck was turning as crimson as a boiled crawfish. I didn't want to believe what I was hearing was true, but one look into my father's eyes and I knew I'd been betrayed.

"I think I see Georgianne Vogt over by the champagne fountain. She was a big donor to the parish before the… um…scandals," my father said grasping at straws. A little smile played around Collins's lips. The kind he'd always worn when he was on the brink of more money or more power. "I hear she's thinking of joining a nice nondenominational church," Daddy finished.

Both men turned toward Vogt as if Martin Luther were single-handedly leading her through the Reformation.

"I never miss an opportunity to bring wayward sheep

to the flock. With the glory of God we continue to grow our church. Nicole, you should ask your dad about what's going on at New Day. He's been so instrumental in our continued growth even though we're heathens. Catch you all later."

"Daddy, how could you? How...how can you even talk to that man after..."

"Nicky Mouse," my dad hissed while grabbing my wrist at the same time. It was the quiet way he'd disciplined me in public as a wayward child. "This is something to discuss at home. If you can't calm down, then we're going to have to leave."

"I'm not thirteen, Daddy. You can't just proclaim I have to leave." Even in my protest I was quiet. To anyone remaining at the table, it looked like we were sharing secrets. Pleasing the men around me was so ingrained, I didn't even scream about my rapist and my father becoming fast friends.

"I'm the member, Nicole, so I do get to say when we leave. And that time is now."

Daddy may have had a few drinks, but he was no fool. He took my purse and stalked from the room. Since the car keys were in there as well as all of my credit cards and my phone, I really had little choice but to follow. Plus Seth Collins's appearance had stolen my appetite for reminiscence and dessert.

A light rain meant the front porch of the club's dining room was empty. Without Mother, I wasn't ready to slip the claim ticket to the valet. Plus I needed a couple of minutes for the double shot of bourbon to wear off. I didn't want to chance a DUI. Suddenly, I could barely breathe. My nose tickled. In a second, I was going to be full-on ugly crying. I had to talk to him before I lost what little control I had left.

"How could you?" My whisper was already tinged with tears. "I mean, Daddy, how could you still...I don't know...consort with that man? You know what he did. You were ready to take him out behind a barn and kill him dead. Now...now you're giving money to him?"

For money was the only reason Collins would be consorting with my dad. It was the reason Collins hadn't gone to jail. Daddy had bailed out the church, and if New Day had imploded back then, so would my family's finances. That passage from the book of Timothy came to me: "For the love of money is a root of all kinds of evil."

"You still have a photographic memory." The silly compliment stalled my tears. He'd always overestimated the power of my brain.

"Just for Bible verses, Daddy."

My father's eyes met mine, and for a second, I glimpsed something like empathy.

"Not to him, Nicky. I'm still entangled with New Day." He didn't elaborate.

"What the ever-loving fuck?" Irrationally, I'd hoped my supposition was wrong.

"Nicky, there's personal and there's business."

"What business do you still have with New Day?"

"You've been out of the South too damned long. Business has been done in pews for hundreds of years. Well, the Catholic pews are empty, but the fracking guys are all at New Day on Sunday. So I go where the money is. I mean, the Catholics have money, but it's all locked up in some vault in the Vatican."

"Money?" I whined. I'd always known that my father worshipped at the altar of the Almighty Dollar, but I'd hoped his family—his daughter—came before that by now. "But what about me?" I cried as I gave in and took the handkerchief he handed me. Dabbed at my eyes. Blew my nose.

"That was the past." With those words, he effectively swatted me away like I was a pesky June bug.

"The past?"

"It was seventeen years ago. Your nieces and nephew are all in college. We have the internet. A black man just won the presidency of the United States. The whole world has moved on."

"What is America's obsession with moving on?" I had to ask the big question, because the small question of why he'd "moved on" from the rape of his daughter was too hard to voice. "It's sometimes like we have no past." I may have swallowed enough bourbon every night to forget the past for the eight hours I needed to sleep, but I expected my father to remember. To hold the grudge to his deathbed.

"We have to. It's the only way things work here. Otherwise we turn into those crazy men who are fighting the Civil War all over again every weekend."

Just then my mother joined us. She handed my father and me our coats. By then I'd composed myself. My mother did not take kindly to public displays of emotion.

"Nicole, did you come all the way here to cause a scene?"

"No, ma'am. I was just...surprised that you'd book a table with Seth Collins."

Walking ahead, Mother moved toward the valet stand. Unlike Daddy, she'd come to the family with manners, if not a lot of money. She cut her eyes in our direction, letting us know that neither Theriots nor Longs aired their laundry, dirty or otherwise, in public.

"I'm sure your father explained to you the importance of separating the business and personal." Her voice was low, her words generic.

"It's just that..."

"Nicole, you never wanted for anything—"

Except love, I wanted to interrupt, but I held my tongue like I had nearly my whole life down here in Louisiana.

"You had private school, any lessons you wanted. The newest clothes," Mother hissed. "The best gadgets. College up north. A car. Spending money. Sometimes things you want come at a cost."

"And that cost is my dignity."

"If you hadn't surprised us with a visit, you'd never have known," she concluded. The case was closed as far as she was concerned. More of the "if Nicole doesn't know, it won't hurt her" style of parenting they'd perfected. I had to wonder if there were more secrets. As if finding out Mother wasn't my birth mother and Seth Collins was still a family friend weren't enough.

We'd made it to the valet by then. I handed over the ticket. Daddy's late-model sedan materialized moments later. Before I could get into the driver's seat, Daddy grabbed my hand. His eyes met mine and he was the most sincere I'd seen him since I landed.

"You know this better than I, but I'm sure there's something in the Bible about forgiveness."

They would never let me forget I'd majored in religion at Mount Holyoke instead of business and marketing at Texas A & M.

"You've never read the damned Bible, Daddy. If so, you'd be quoting Leviticus instead of talking about forgetting."

"Leviticus?"

"If anyone causes injury to his neighbor, as he has done, so shall it be done to him, fracture for fracture, eye for eye, tooth for tooth; as he has caused an injury to another, so shall it be done to him," I quoted.

I let the valet open the driver's side door and slipped into the vehicle. Maybe Seth Collins wasn't going to get his on earth. I sure hoped he would get his in the hell the pastor believed in. For me, I needed to get back to Cleveland. It was time to put my beef with Lori Pope aside and hop on board with her prosecution of the pedophile priest at St. Ignatius. Someone needed to be punished, and I had the power to do it.

FOUR
JUSTIN
JANUARY 6, 2009

hope it's not too weird here in enemy territory."

Lori Pope and Nicole Long tittered at the former's joke. I tried to plaster an awkward smile on my face in the face of my...well...usual...adversary.

"We're all here in the pursuit of justice," I responded. At least that was why *I* was here. They were only here for the convictions and headlines and nothing more. Since our interests aligned for once, I just shifted in my seat and tried to put myself in the frame of mind to talk about something I'd tried hard to forget.

"I hope you don't mind," Long said while she fiddled with some buttons on a small digital recorder.

I did mind, but nodded anyway. Knowing everything I said would be saved for time immemorial nearly put me in a shame spiral. Pulled myself from the brink of that and fidgeted in my chair.

I looked at Long, who was on my right in the uninspired conference room with its brown walls and gray carpet. Pope was farther down, asserting her authority by holding down the head of the table.

"This case is a top priority for my office," Pope intoned. "It's why *I'm* here conducting the interviews."

"Okay," I said to say something. Everyone knew that Pope was the consummate politician. She only came out when the media's cameras did. Not that I faulted her. Her predecessor was the same as would be her successor. Nature of the elected official.

The top prosecutor gave a curt nod, then gestured toward Long. The assistant prosecutor on my right lifted the cover of a leather portfolio and extracted several sheets of paper which she passed to her boss, her bum lifting slightly from the padded fabric chair. When she landed back in her seat, I couldn't help but get just the slightest whiff of alcohol. Despite my attempt to suppress any reaction, I could feel my brows rise toward my rapidly receding hairline.

Pope nodded and Long pressed some buttons on the recorder. The small LED numbers started counting up in milliseconds, then seconds.

"It's January sixth, 2009, at ten fifteen in the morning. Present are myself, Assistant Prosecuting Attorney, Deputy Director of the Major Crimes unit Nicole Long, the Cuyahoga County Prosecuting Attorney Lorraine Pope, and the witness Justin McPhee. Mr. McPhee, can you state your full name for the record."

"Justin Patrick McPhee."

"When and where were you born?"

"Here in Cleveland, August sixth, 1969."

"If you could please answer the questions in the order asked."

I nodded my compliance, then answered a slew of questions about my family, where I'd grown up and gone to elementary and middle school. Though I was intimately familiar with the method Long was using, asking a lot of innocuous questions to make me comfortable, I had to admit it was working. When the next question came from Pope, though I expected it, it was a bit of a shock.

"How did you meet Monsignor Gregory Quinn?"

"He taught Spanish," I said. Took a deep breath. I had to keep myself in check. We were still on the easy questions. "We had to take a language all four years."

"Why did you choose Spanish?"

"My sister was learning it. Seemed easier than French with all its silent letters."

Long gave a small smile at that. She'd probably taken French. Seemed like the type to make things in her life as difficult as possible.

"What was the first year you went to Guatemala?"

"I went sophomore year. 1985."

"Why not freshman year?" Pope scribbled some notes. "Was there a program then?"

"It was a spring break trip, but for some reason I didn't know about it until January. I really wanted to go. Almost everyone who wanted to go did. But my parents...my...uh... family couldn't afford it." For the first time in a long time I had a lot of sympathy for my clients, for witnesses. I was telling the truth, but a half-truth, or possibly a lie of omission.

My father had died that fall. Taken his own life. Spring break trips and extracurriculars had fallen off the family radar. That winter Mama, Stacey, Krystyna, and I were doing all we could to cling to the lifeboat of a semblance of normalcy. We'd barely made it.

"But you were able to afford it in subsequent years?" Pope asked. While I took some personal comfort in the fact that she wasn't probing too deeply, a niggle of doubt about the likelihood of conviction was seeping in like water through a pinhole.

"Yes."

"What was different?"

I swallowed. I knew this was going to be hard, but I had to be the better person. The better lawyer. Fill in the gaps. Give Monsignor Quinn's motive on a platter. But that was going to require talking about what happened. My throat worked hard. What I hadn't considered were all the other hard things this was going to bring up.

"My father died twenty-five years ago in the weeks between Thanksgiving and Christmas. The funeral and burial used up all the family's savings."

"What about life insurance? Didn't he have any?" Pope had to probe hard because no defense attorney worth their salt would leave any of these questions unanswered. Surprises were the bane of a good trial attorney.

"He had life insurance. Plenty of it. One policy through

work. Another he'd bought. A third my mom had bought after my little sister was born. Not a single one of them paid out."

"Why not?"

I had to swallow the burning resentment in my throat to answer Pope's next question.

"Because the cause of death was ruled a suicide."

Long's swift intake of breath was barely audible, but it was there. I hated that gasp. It was the reason I never mentioned my dad, and if I did, not his death, and if I did, not how he died. His last act had been a mortal sin.

The other bitter pill I had to swallow was that my mother had gotten a boatload of bad advice from Father O'Malley. When Daddy had died, she'd gone to our local parish priest for counsel, advice. He's the one who'd told her that we couldn't collect because of Daddy's method of death. If insurance companies followed the Baltimore Catechism, that made sense. Something about it, though, had always rang a little hollow. At fourteen, my lay opinions didn't have much sway.

It was the first issue I took on in that first semester of law school, during our class on research methods. Turns out that we shouldn't have taken legal advice from clergy. Not only did I learn that most suicide exclusion clauses are only in effect for the first year or two of a policy, I also learned that the money would have escheated to the state five years later. Unclaimed funds could only be claimed for so long. By the time I'd worked out Stacey, Krystyna, and I hadn't needed to live hand-to-mouth while Mama had struggled to pay the mortgage, it was too late to reverse what the damage Father Ryan O'Malley had done.

"How did you afford the trip the next year?" Pope interrupted my walk down regret lane.

"I did work for the neighbors. Raked leaves and did chores around the house for them."

"That was sufficient?"

"No, not even close. When my mom realized that I didn't have enough money saved up for the trip, she went to the school and asked for help. Monsignor was able to get the school to kick in some scholarship money for the flight. My mother was very grateful. She said I needed to do whatever I could on the trip to show my appreciation."

After another hour of questions, Pope called a break. I went downstairs for an overpriced coffee, turning down Long's offer of something brown in a Styrofoam cup. I wasn't a fan of chain store beverages, but I needed to get out of that office. If it hadn't been pouring down rain, I may have made a break for my car and taken myself home where my dog Morro's only requests would be kibble, a walk, and some strokes along his fur. He wouldn't demand all my secrets be laid bare. I took the coffee with my name scrawled on the cup from the barista and slowly made my way back upstairs, letting many lawyers and litigants make their way first before I took my turn on the small elevators.

So far all the questions had been surface preliminary ones. I knew once I went back into that room, I could no longer avoid the thing I hadn't ever wanted to think about, talk about...relive...again. I couldn't see a path, though, to justice that didn't include a confession of all the monsignor's sins. So twenty minutes later, I was back in the uncomfortable swivel chair between Long and her boss. Long pressed the button on the recorder. Looked like Pope was still asking the questions.

"We need to focus on what happened on your trip to Guatemala in 1985. How old were you that spring?" was her first question.

"I was fifteen."

"Do you know the date, approximately?"

I would never forget it. Easter had been ruined for me that year and forever after, just like Thanksgiving had been when my father had passed.

"It was the beginning of April. We were there for two weeks, one before and one after Easter Sunday."

"What were your accommodations?"

"The church had built a school down there. I think some of the students from smaller towns or without transportation boarded. Those kids were away for the holiday, so we stayed in their dormitory."

"What was the sleeping configuration?"

"Each room had two or four beds. I was in one with two beds."

"Was there another student in there with you?"

"We were an uneven number, so I was in there alone." I didn't add that I wasn't popular among the altar boy acolytes. My crowd was a little rowdier. This trip had been for my mother, really. To make her feel like she was doing something for us kids. Giving us opportunities like other wealthier kids got. Her inferiority complex could be crippling for our whole family.

"Who were the adults you interacted with?"

"Monsignor Quinn ran the trip from stateside. Father Morales ran the school in Guatemala. And Sister Angela Parker was the go-between." I could hear my staccato speech. The answers were the equivalent of name, rank, serial number. It was what I had to do to maintain composure.

"Sister Angela?"

"She worked both with the school in Bárcena and St. Ignatius."

Pope turned from me, glared at Long. The younger prosecutor's shrug wasn't as imperceptible as she was trying to make it. Her shoulder move was as comically big as a bad child actor on a Saturday morning sitcom.

If I'd had to guess, I'd put my money on whatever alcohol she'd had with her coffee was affecting her fine motor skills. Drunks always overlooked those kinds of tells. And if anything were true in this room today, it was that Nicole Long was still a drunk. The carefully placed rumors of her so-called rehabilitation and sobriety was the worst public relations spin the prosecutor's office had ever done. I hope they did a better job on this case, because going up against an institution like the Catholic church was no joke.

"What was Sister Angela's job at the school?" Pope inquired.

"Nun? She didn't teach or anything. She had an office. Her title was facilitator. I never knew what that was. But as a student I wasn't in much of a position to ask, and to be honest, I didn't really care."

"We'll circle back to the nun later. What can you tell me about Monsignor Quinn?"

I lifted and dropped my shoulders; *my* shrug was honest and *sober*.

"He taught Spanish. He must have been at the school a while because he had the reputation of not being a hard grader. He used the same tests every year, so if you were in a pinch, you could find a copy and memorize the answers for an easy grade."

"Was he friendly toward students?"

"Maybe? It's hard to say. He only did Mass occasion-ally, I think, so it's not like he had a stable of altar boys at his beck and call." Not like all those other cases people were talking about. "It was a bigger parish, and the teachers came from different parishes all over the country, so I didn't pay any particular attention to him..." *before Guatemala* zinged through my brain, though I didn't say that part aloud.

"So you couldn't say that he had students he favored?"

"Well, yes, he did favor a couple, but I only really saw it in Guatemala. He was pretty neutral in school."

"Can you give me the names of the boys he liked?"

"Other than me?" I asked. For decades, there had been an unspoken code of silence. And even here, now, under the scrutiny of a prosecutor who was here to break that silence, I had a hard time speaking.

Pope nodded.

For a long moment, my brain froze. Not a single clear thought came through. This happened nearly every time I thought about the past. My mind just stumbled from eighth grade to college. The in-between was like a fog I never tried to see through.

I closed my eyes. Took a deep breath. Waited for the images to come. They would if I sat still long enough. I didn't often stay still.

"Jesse Cain. Brandon Rivera. Byron Mitchell," spilled out. "Mitchell was Irish Protestant, but his mom thought the Jesuit tradition would make him a good man." I stopped talking when I realized I was giving too much information. I should have claimed a faulty memory. No one would disbelieve me. Trauma was supposed to alter memory. That's what I'd learned in some continuing education class about witness testimony.

Long scratched out notes more carefully than before, and I felt immediate regret. Someone with a badge was going to knock on their doors. Dredge up stuff they probably didn't want to remember.

"Don't mention me if you talk to them." I directed that straight toward Long.

"Noted," Long answered.

"So, it was the three of them and you?" Pope probed.

"Yep."

"What did being Quinn's favorite look like?"

The fog descended one more time. I'm not sure how long it took to fight my way through, but when I blinked and looked at Pope and Long, both were waiting patiently with pens poised.

"He often had snacks in his office. Not like Cheetos or Doritos, but real Guatemalan stuff. He called it street food. Tamalitos de chipilín, or even paches. When he wanted us to stay later, he'd bring in hilachas or pepián."

"Can you elaborate?" Pope asked.

I huffed like the teenager I'd been back then.

"Sometimes he'd bring the Guatemalan version of tamales, other times some kind of stew. We were teenage boys. You have to understand that the four of us had single moms, either with three or four kids, and our moms were working all the time to support us.

"None of us had dads at home. A home-cooked meal was nice. His food, if he in fact made it, was good, hearty... filling. He always promised not to talk about God or religion when we came to the reconciliation room at the church. It was a chill environment. We could just relax and be ourselves."

All these years later, I now knew what his welcoming friendliness was called in pedophile parlance—grooming.

"If you didn't talk about religion, then what *did* you talk about?"

"I guess it's what we'd call a 'safe space' nowadays. Back then he let us talk about what was going on at home, video games, even sometimes let us play them. He had an Atari 2600 and a big color TV. We even discussed girls, and sex. It was so taboo for the church in the eighties. A free for all, really."

"Did he bring up girls and sex, or did you?" Long asked.

"I can't remember." But after I said that, I did remember. Quinn had done that thing I hated from adults. That joshing pretend friendliness. He'd punched one or another of us in the shoulder. Asked if we had crushes on girls. Whether we sinned by spilling our seed. He'd said that last with a wink and a nudge that said we didn't need to go to confession for that.

"Do you speak Spanish?"

"Not anymore," I ground out. I'd heard my accent when I'd talked about the food. It was that of a native. I'd pushed the language from my head the minute I'd landed in Cleveland from our senior trip to South America. Univision and Telemundo were blocked on my TV. Spanish brought back too many bad memories.

"Do you want some water?" Long offered. I wanted to ask for whatever she was having, because a stiff drink wouldn't have gone unappreciated.

"No, let's just get this over with."

"Nearly all victims find this difficult," Long sympathized.

I didn't want their sympathy. I wanted my freedom from this conference room turned prison.

"Do you have a question?" I asked, shifting my gaze between them.

A flash of something more sinister than annoyance

flitted over Pope's face. In the next moment her expression was as serene as a Zen master and I wondered if I'd imagined it. I didn't have time for all this analysis. We weren't adversaries on this one. Put Pope and all the rest out of my mind. I'd learned the fine art of compartmentalization while in Guatemala.

"When did Monsignor Gregory Quinn first touch you in an inappropriate way?"

Boom went the dynamite. The fog was a little clearer here.

"The first day we arrived in Bárcena."

"The first day?"

"He showed each of us to our rooms. When he got to mine, he was friendlier than he'd ever been. More... touchy-feely. First it was a hand on my shoulder as he guided me toward the bed I was to take. Then we both sat down on the bed. There was a chair, but he didn't take it. He said he just wanted to outline expectations. I needed to be well behaved. Even during our leisure hours we were representing the school, all that jazz. But he touched my leg. I shifted away and he didn't do it again, but I didn't yell or say anything or ask him to leave. So he probably knew then I was an easy target."

Long turned. Her eyes pierced me.

"I'm sure a thousand people will say this to you in the next however long we're on this case," she said, "but it wasn't your fault. You do no one justice by taking the blame in public or private. Please remember that, okay?" Long's voice was unusually sympathetic. She was normally so ballsy and strident, this side of her threw me for a loop. Maybe her courtroom demeanor had always been theater.

"That's all he did the first night?" Pope asked. The top prosecutor didn't ooze one iota of feeling. I didn't think Pope was anything more than her abrasive front.

"Yes. He had to see to the other kids, get them settled. I unpacked, then went to bed. It was the first time I'd flown on a plane and the adrenaline had worn off."

Pope asked me more about the volunteer work and language classes. The change of topic was deliberate. It was a one-two punch. The next was coming. I almost counted down out loud because the prosecutor was as transparent as plastic wrap.

"What night did he come back?"

"It was a Thursday."

"What time?"

"I don't know. Late. We had lights out at nine, so after that."

"What happened after curfew?" Pope had finally gotten to it. Asked the one question I didn't want to answer.

FIVE
NICOLE
JANUARY 10, 2009

"M a'am?" I waited as the beat cop in uniform questioned the woman in front of me. I tried not to tap my foot in frustration as she dug through her oversized shoulder bag. Even with my Canada Goose parka all buttoned up to my neck, freezing rain had somehow found a way down my back. That's what I got for leaving the bulky, visibility-limiting hood at home.

"I have my press pass right here," the reporter said as she finally fished out the laminated card on a lanyard.

"Plain Dealer?" It was already dark and the officer was squinting at the card. Probably decided not to use his flashlight as he'd have to have taken off his gloves to push the Maglite's button.

"You're Blake Hardin Tatum?"

The woman nodded. The uniform looked at her card one more time before flipping it back to her. She had to reach into the air to catch it. She didn't miss. It was just this side of rude, but nothing the woman could complain about.

"You have ID?"

The woman, Tatum, tilted her head in confusion.

"To prove that it's you," the officer said.

More cold water snaked its way toward my waist. I zipped and snapped my coat tighter even though it would make me too damned hot.

Another deep dive yielded a long red leather wallet. Tatum took off her gloves, then plucked the small plastic square of her driver's license out. The officer looked between it and her for a few long seconds. Gave it back, finally convinced she belonged there.

"Huh? Thought you guys had all these layoffs and cutbacks, but you send two people to a murder scene. Go figure." The officer shrugged and half-lifted the crime scene tape.

Apparently not slighted by the overly long identification process, Tatum scuttled under the plastic like she was doing the limbo. I shook my head. Maybe I was getting it all wrong. I'd thought the cop had been just this shy of rude with the reporter because she was black...like me in genes if not color.

"You could have been a little nicer," I said, trying to play it as an offhand comment. Too many cops had a hairpin trigger.

"Why? You know how they are."

"They?"

The cold, damp hairs on my neck stood at attention.

I'd heard that I needed to stand up for my fellow black women, but I'd never really done it. It had been hard to make the switch from a majority mindset to the minority.

"Reporters. Come in. Stomp around. Get it wrong half the time."

I wasn't sure I bought his explanation, but decided to let it pass, this time.

"Long. County prosecutor," I announced, flashing my own ID card on a lanyard.

No fuss, no muss. He raised the tape well above my head.

"The detectives are waiting for you."

"Thanks. Can you point me in the right direction?"

The officer threw a thumb over his shoulder. I would not come back to him for anything more. He was the type who liked to phone it in. There were far too many of this kind in both the police department and the prosecutor's office. As far as I was concerned, they could all be shed and leave us, the true believers, behind. We were the only ones who did any work anyway.

I stepped carefully around chalk and tape and continued down the alley that a street sign said was Courtland Court until I saw a couple of detectives leaning over something or someone.

"Assistant county prosecutor Nicole Long. Why the callout?" I asked.

While in a perfect world, it was preferable for a prosecutor to be at a crime scene and shepherd a case from the very beginning to the end, it wasn't the normal course of business. We got cases when the cops had done the leg work of an investigation and were ready to have us write up an indictment. Or even later when the case needed to settle or go to trial. There weren't enough of us to go around watching an investigation from start to finish like it was a TV crime show. True justice like that would grind the system to a halt in short order.

"This is Loren Logan, new detective," Neil Walsh said to me by way of greeting.

Walsh. The detective had to be well over sixty. When the rumors swirled about his being pushed out due to mandatory retirement rules, I was surprised to see that somehow he'd kept his job on the force, but he'd been shifted from narcotics to homicide.

He was a good detective in that he usually zeroed in on a suspect. Walsh did not hem and haw or dilly dally during an investigation. Not so good in that he liked to use shortcuts to get to a quick arrest. He also spent more time in the Zone Car cop bar than I spent trying to stay sober.

Openly, I took in Logan. His appearance was as different from Walsh as night and day. Walsh was tall, thin, dark hair and eyes. Logan appeared to be shorter, stockier. Too-long-for-his-job blond hair and blue eyes. Where Walsh was in a sport coat and overcoat, Logan had a yellow oilskin over what looked like a hoodie. I wondered how he'd gotten that special dispensation.

"Why am I here?" My automatic Southern politeness wasn't present just now. It was cold, and wet, and I wasn't in the mood to meet new people. I wanted to go home, have a hot toddy, and call it a night. Every health care article touted how warm honey and lemon were great for digestion and building immunity.

"Called you here because the vic had your card in her wallet," Walsh explained.

"My card?" The only people who had my card were victims and witnesses I thought were squirrely. The kind who didn't really want to testify and were apt to disappear on me. The minute one of those got pulled over, and the squirrely witnesses always did, they used my card. I was always the lesser of two evils.

Logan held up a clear, sealed evidence bag between his thumb and forefinger. My name, title, and phone number stared back at me. Some movement caught in my peripheral vision and I looked over to see a technician straightening the tarp over a small mound about five and a half feet long. Presumably, the victim. I turned back to the two-man detective team.

"Jesus. Do I want to look?"

"You don't," Logan said. "The photos will be enough. It's pretty brutal. She was pushed out of her window. An air-conditioning unit followed."

"Which killed her—the fall or the air conditioner?"

"Autopsy will tell us that," Walsh said.

"The victim's name?"

"Sister Angela Parker," the detective answered.

"Shit." I wondered how that would impact our case against the monsignor.

"Wasn't suicide?" I asked. The bodies didn't usually start piling up this fast. I'd only just started poking.

Pope'd had an unusual merciful moment. We'd let Justin go when it was clear he wasn't ready to relive the trauma of that first trip to South America. Then I'd had our investigator locate Cain, Rivera, and Mitchell, drop my card at their work and homes. None had left the county after graduation.

Next I'd had the investigator find Parker, let the nun know that I needed to talk to her, drop my card. I'd wanted to let them all know I was poking around, but not exactly why. I found giving people a chance to stew made them much more forthcoming when I finally showed up. Every word that they spilled relieved their anxiety and usually bolstered my case.

"You knew her, then? The card was legit?"

"Different investigation. She was a key witness." I didn't know that to be true, exactly, but I waved that last before Walsh like a red cape before a Spanish bull.

"Nun, huh?" Logan's blue eyes pierced me as if he could see right through me. "Probably the best witness ever," he continued. "Like having the Pope on the stand. Who boy. Sorry to hear that. Kill your case?"

"Not in the least. But you're right. A nun was a no-brainer. I couldn't wait to see some effing defense attorney try to cross-examine her on the stand. Alas, it's not to be. Thanks for the callout. Couple more questions?"

"Yeah. Got time for a couple," Walsh said. "Waiting for the wagon."

"Where did this defenestration take place?"

Walsh turned toward Logan. "She likes the big words, this one. And Bible verses. Good thing you went to college."

Logan's smile was fleeting. He pointed to the right. "Small convent over there. Has ten rooms. Only six are occupied. Nuns are becoming as obscure as newspaper reporters."

"Funny. There are two of them here tonight," I said.

"Anyway, all the sisters come home before eight. Not sure if there's a curfew or some such, but they're locked up tight in the convent before eight oh five. Doer must have been waiting and she knew them, let them in. Or they were waiting. There wasn't any argument anyone heard or signs of struggle. Just her screaming as she went down. Everyone on both sides of the alley ran to their windows."

"Which means the killer probably walked out of the front door." I closed my eyes briefly. Turned them up to the sky. Felt a drop, like a cold tear, run down my cheek.

"Cameras?" I asked when I opened my eyes and looked between Logan and Walsh.

"Church only has them around the sacristy. Keeps an eye on golden chalices and the like. Not the people."

I bit back a comment on churches and riches. Didn't need to alienate two likely Catholics.

"You'll canvass the houses?" I gestured toward the residential side of the alley where a bunch of newly built homes stood, dark and quiet now that the initial excitement was over.

"Of course," Logan said.

"Do you have a list?" Walsh asked me.

"Of what?"

"Suspects. Maybe someone thought the nun was too believable. Wanted to make sure she wasn't on the stand."

"You know I'm not here to do your job. I'll see what I can do. Come by my office."

"Will do." Got a two-finger salute from the senior detective. "We'll walk the scene again. Everything will be washed away in the rain and sleet."

"That's too bad."

"God wasn't doing much to protect one of his own," Logan added.

When I screwed up my face, Logan answered my unasked question. "He's washing away sins. Maybe he doesn't want us to know who did it. Maybe there's some justification for what happened." That was my cue to leave him to his supernatural speculation, and I took it.

Walsh didn't say anything, but the other guy, Logan gave me a half-jaunty salute. I walked away toward the far end of the alley to get a quick lay of the land. There was nothing like seeing everything in three dimensions. I might even have a look at the body if I could work up the courage.

Other than my grandmother at her wake, I'd never seen a dead body. My job was nothing like television where prosecutors seemed to roll up to murder scenes and autopsies like they were getting muffins and coffee on their way into the office.

I took a few steps and looked up to the remaining window shards in the wooden frame now crisscrossed with yellow crime scene tape and covered in fingerprint dust. My eyes made their way up to the roof of the squat two-story building, then past the window again and back down to the ground. Though Sister Parker's form was covered in a dark-colored tarp, I could see a trickle of blood making its way from her body down the pitched gulley where water runoff from the church buildings and houses inevitably ended up in the drain in the middle. I tried not to think too hard about what the sanitation worker who cleaned out this particular catch basin might find.

After a lungful of air came in through my nose, I held it, then gingerly, so as not to disturb a single thing, lowered myself into a half-squat. Lifting up the tarp, I tried not to gasp. Failed. Wished I had braced myself.

"Told you not to look," Logan said.

I stood. Shrugged.

"When in Rome."

"I didn't go to as fancy a school as you probably did," Logan said, "but even I know the Roman empire didn't make it."

"Touché."

BLAKE

JANUARY 11, 2009

The alley was a beehive of activity. As if I were an empty battery hooked up to a charger, energy flowed through me. Ideas ping-ponged around my head. The first lines of the article—scratch that—blog post I'd write about this possible murder itched at my fingertips.

I'd missed this.

It had only been a few weeks, but sitting in my tenant's old apartment by myself, setting up my blog, learning the ins and outs of WordPress and the finer points of HTML while prowling through scraps of paper and old Post-it notes looking for ideas was a lonely bit of business.

Cops, techs, nosy folks with nothing better to do, these were my people. I had to find a way back in to the world of crime investigation. It was only a matter of time before someone caught me using a press pass that I was no longer entitled to carry. Until then, I would stay at this callout at least.

Murder wasn't a rarity in Cleveland, but this many cops and forensic technicians were. My Spidey senses were tingling. There was something here. I could feel it. Might as well start at the top. I collapsed my umbrella, then walked over to the two detectives who were clearly in charge.

"I'm Blake Hardin Tatum." Fingered the press pass hanging around my neck. Kept me from lying out loud. "Can I ask you a few questions?"

I nearly slipped in a puddle when I started after I saw who had been squatting near the body. The woman coming to her full height was the infamous Nicole Long. She'd been promoted a year ago. Probably the longest stint that she'd been in any job in the prosecutor's office, if all the rumors were true. I squinted a little in the mist, wondering if she were inebriated. Rumor was that there was a fifty percent chance she wouldn't be sober at work, even after county-funded rehab. I personally felt there were people far more deserving, but I wasn't in charge of her particular collective bargaining agreement.

"Step back, ma'am," the older of the two detectives said. "This is a crime scene." I knew I'd seen him before, but couldn't place him. Craggy, florid faces, and salt-and-pepper buzz cuts ran together in my memory.

"I don't think I misstepped. This is not my first rodeo." I wasn't some rookie who could be shooed away.

I looked between the three. Long stepped away. When neither detective spoke, I poked at the bear a little.

"Prosecutor's out. Must be an important matter."

"There are two of you here," the younger cop said. "So you must think so as well. Is it because she's a nun? It's usually like pulling teeth to get one of you out to a scene. I didn't think crime reporters did much more than listen to the scanner and write two-liners about drug and john arrests."

It only took me a split second to assess the mood, change tack, and try to lend a positive and helping vibe.

The older detective was from an era where the police brass thought reporters a nuisance. Asking too many questions. Tainting the jury pool. Younger ones thought we could give cops credibility, urge reluctant witnesses to come forward.

I thrust out my gloved hand, reintroduced myself to the younger cop.

"Loren Logan at your service." After his hand left mine, he threw a thumb in the general direction of the other plain-clothes cop. "Neil Walsh. Used to be in narcotics. Instead of retiring, he's now murder police. Not how I'd spend my last years on the force. To each his own, I guess."

Walsh's expression told me they'd had this discussion dozens of times. He gave me the slightest nod, then went back to surveying the scene. I didn't make the mistake of putting out a hand for him.

A few years ago, Chief Kelley McCormick had come on board. He was one of the new community policing breed.

The police chief believed more witnesses and more victims would come forward if we published more crime stories. On the one hand, we reporters were grateful for greater access the initiative brought.

On the other hand, the editors often killed crime stories the moment we got emails from the chamber of commerce and complaints from the African American community that we were too negative about a city trying to burnish its image, and that repeated mug shots of black men perpetuated an unfair stereotype.

I think the chief and the boosters both had a point. So we'd walked the third rail. Now that I wasn't at the *Plain Dealer* anymore, I thought I'd lean in to the crime stories. No matter what side people fell on the idea of crime reporting, they were avid consumers.

"In the new year, they want us out more," I interjected. "Meeting with the stakeholders. The community. Working with the police and not against you guys." None of that was a lie. It was the straight party line from the paper which came down from on high after our editor in chief and publisher had made a new detente with McCormick right after New Year's.

"Same here," Logan said, nodding in sympathy.

"So, a nun?" I pressed, now that we had a rapport and I could see that I might get some answers.

"Came out the window of the convent."

I tried very hard to hide my surprise. This was leagues from the normal crimes of passion, domestic violence, or gangbanger disputes.

"Accident?" I certainly hoped it was anything but. Accidents were a one-day story. Murders could occupy a good dozen.

"Subject of a current investigation. You know how it goes. But how many nuns fall out of windows?"

Long wandered away. I was half-worried that I'd lose the chance to question her, but more than half-relieved I wouldn't come under her scrutiny. She was way more likely to have heard about staffing changes at the paper than rank-and-file cops.

"Catholic church in the news a lot lately," I said conversationally. Idle chitchat often got me more information than straight interrogation.

"Pedophile priests finally getting prosecuted."

It was Logan's "finally" that told me he, at least, was on the right side of history. There were lots of Catholic cops who thought the church should be left to police itself. They were probably the kind that thought departments could investigate their own wrongdoing. Neither could be further from the truth. Sunshine was the best disinfectant.

"How are those cases going?" I asked Logan. It was the story of the moment in the city, but one I was going to leave to the reporters with budgets. I was looking for a wedge, an angle that would get eyeballs to my page.

"Not murder, so not my department."

"Did you work on them at all? I mean, you're new to homicide as far as I can tell."

"True enough." Logan stood. Snapped off his gloves. Shoved the latex into the pockets of his oilcloth jacket. The signature Barbour plaid lining raised more questions about Logan. Clothes from the classic UK retailer weren't in most civil servants' budgets. "Just got assigned around Halloween," he added.

"Hell of a time to join the squad."

"Easy last year." His lopsided half-smile was genuine. "Warm-ish night. Clear. Kids got their candy. No razor blades or arsenic."

"Thought those were urban myths." I'd written that story at least a dozen times in my career.

"Obviously. But gotta keep an eye out for those who want to make a myth reality."

"Crazy world. But at least the crazy is out in the open now."

"Not hiding like the priests did."

"Usual victims are criminals, female victims of their male partners. But clergy? Nuns?"

"Hasn't happened that I've ever heard of, beyond bystanders or something."

"So what's going on here? How do you think you'll proceed?"

"Off the record?"

I threw up my arms, showing Logan my gloved hands empty of pen, pencil, paper, or any kind of recorder.

"Nuns' pots don't get stirred often. But over in sex crimes, there are some rumors that one or two of the priests have run through the convent like it's their personal brothel."

"Jesus Christ," I blurted out. "Sometimes I'm still

surprised by the depths of human depravity." Though I knew I shouldn't be.

"*He's* innocent."

We both laughed at the silly joke. He was right. The son of God wasn't on trial here, though the Catholic church was in many respects.

"I'm sorry. I only thought about the kids while we were reporting on the priest abuse. But predators are always looking for prey. It's best not to forget that." If children were scared into silence, I could only imagine the nuns were as well. Their very livelihood depended on the church's largesse.

"For sure."

"Who are you looking at?" I pushed.

"Can't share that," he blocked.

"Fair enough." I shrugged, ready to chase down Long. Prepare a blog post that was sure to grab some eyeballs. I'd billed my blog as the place to come for crime stories not hampered by milquetoast editorial boards or artificial publishing deadlines.

"Your name again?" Logan squinted at me.

"Blake Hardin Tatum."

"You have a card, Ms. Hardin Tatum?"

Shit.

I hadn't thought about that. The first thing I'd always done was to give a source a card. Reporting was a two-way, scratch-my-back-and-I'll-scratch-yours street. Had to improvise. I scrawled my name on a page from my notepad, tore it out. Logan stuffed it in the other glove-free pocket. I hoped he didn't lose it.

"That's my cell. Best to reach me there," I said. At least that excuse I'd practiced. It had worked so far. Everyone liked the idea of direct access to a reporter. No switchboard or nosy receptionists to wade through.

"You'll be the first, as long as it's reciprocal."

I pulled my brand-new cell from my pocket. This one wasn't tied to the paper, of course. "What's your number?"

Logan gave it to me freely. Was he too new to know better?

"Let me let you get back," I said, not wanting to press my good fortune.

"I hope it's who we think, because otherwise, this one will truly be a mystery," Logan blurted in a flurry of speech. I glanced around. We were alone, Walsh also having wandered somewhere else. "I mean," he continued, "how many nuns get murdered? Seems like the least likely person ever to get hurt. Who in the hell holds a grudge against a woman of God?"

I had to nod in agreement. It *was* curious. Who indeed?

SEVEN
NICOLE
JANUARY 12, 2009

n ninety-nine percent of cases, the victims came to me like all-you-can-eat conveyer belt sushi. I'd pluck a file, meet the victim. They were always eager to tell me their story seeking justice at best or retribution for the rest.

Today the script was flipped. I was seeking out those allegedly molested by Monsignor Quinn. Male sex abuse victims were the most reluctant to talk, much less seek out prosecution. They silently punished themselves, stuck for years, sometimes decades in a prison of their own making.

My only job today was to give Byron Mitchell the keys to the jail door, let him know that the book of John had it right: that truth would set him free. I'd decided that a surprise visit would be best. Not give any of these potential victims time to think too hard. I'd picked Mitchell because something about McPhee's brief description made him seem like the easiest to crack.

Plus Byron Mitchell lived in one of the brand-new downtown apartments in one of the city's historic buildings. Only a fifteen-minute walk. If I didn't have to drive, then a little fortification beforehand wouldn't get me pulled over for drunk driving, but it would make this very awkward conversation go a lot easier, at least on my end.

I looked up at the white terra-cotta façade of the nine-story edifice that had once housed a luxury department store nearly a century ago. The last time I'd been in the building on the corner of Euclid and Ninth, it had been filled with the offices of small firms and solo lawyers. Now, like all the downtown renovations, it was another block of cookie-cutter apartments. Gray walls, beige floors, granite, tiles, and stainless steel. With my county prosecutor lanyard and badge, I had no problem with a random tenant letting me in the elevator, then asking what floor I needed as they swiped a keycard against the black box under the call numbers.

I stepped out on the fifth floor, then consulted the sticky note I pulled from my parka's pocket. Five oh six was the door I needed to knock on. Like I was on a cop show hiding from a suspect, I flattened myself in the space between the elevator and stairs. Found a half-bottle in my other pocket, twisted off the top with the remaining red wax on it, let the golden liquid slip down my throat. Let it warm me. Put that bottle back, drank some water from a different bottle, then ended with a curiously strong mint.

Ready, I pushed myself from the wall and proceeded down the corridor, then knocked hard on the designated door. A man in an unbuttoned pale green oxford over a snow-white T answered the door. From the open belt on his slacks and stocking feet, it was clear he wasn't expecting guests.

"Byron Mitchell?" I asked. Had to. The number of people who let other people stay in their places was much higher than I'd ever thought before I had this job. In my world, everyone rested their head at their legal address.

"Can I help you?" He looked right and left down the hall as if I were lost. But I knew I was exactly in the right place.

"I sincerely hope so. My name is Nicole Long," I started. I gave him a rundown of my credentials, showed him ID. "Can I come in?"

He stepped back out of politeness, but I could see that he immediately regretted the move. It was easier to close a door on an unwanted guest than to get them out.

"Is someone I know in trouble? Am I in trouble? Do I need a lawyer?"

I shook my head with vigor. Too many damned cop shows had people skittish.

"No, nothing like that at all," I reassured. "Can I sit?" I didn't wait for an invitation. Took a seat on a gray sectional straight from Ikea.

"Do you want some water or something?" Mitchell backpedaled toward the open-plan kitchen. He fiddled with the fridge door, a cabinet holding glasses. "Other than that, I only have beer. Not really set up for unexpected guests."

"I'll take the water, thanks."

I didn't need more water. Certainly didn't want to have to use his bathroom while I was here. But Mitchell looked like he needed to settle himself. I'm sure in his gut he knew why I'd invaded his apartment. Even if he didn't avidly read or follow the news, it was nearly impossible to ignore Lori Pope's constant drumbeat of how she was going to save Cleveland's Catholic children from the evil hands of pedophile clergy. With a change in statute of limitations, stories from older victims of Mitchell's vintage popped up here and there in back page newspaper articles or short nightly news packages.

When he put the blue plastic bottle on the table, I picked it up, untwisted the cap, took a sip. Out of things to do, Mitchell finally sat. Far across from me in an uncomfortable side chair that had ex-girlfriend written all over it. I leaned forward, hands on my knees.

"Again, I'm Nicole Long. As you may know, our office is investigating child abuse that occurred at St. Ignatius or was perpetrated by those affiliated with the school or the church."

Mitchell reared back in his chair as if I'd lashed out.

"How did you get my name?" He croaked out the question.

His inquiry wasn't an outright denial. I took that as him not being completely closed off. It was only a sliver of an opening, but I'd take it.

"It's a large-scale investigation going back decades.

You came up on a list of the monsignor's—for lack of a better term—favorites from the mid to late-eighties."

"Favorite?" Mitchell's voice had gone from croak to whisper.

"It's what one person said."

"Who?" He looked wild-eyed, as if a pedophile priest were going to jump from the shadows.

I swallowed hard because I very much wanted to share McPhee's name. Somehow pull all the victims together to support each other. But neither social work nor psychology were part of my job's description. I'd have to toe the party line.

"I need to protect everyone's anonymity here."

"Okay. I get it." When he nodded, I knew he was ready to talk. His subconscious had outed him. He was quiet for a long moment while the last of his internal debate played out. "What do you want to know?"

I didn't have time to sugarcoat anymore. Pope had tasked me with getting as many victims and witnesses as possible lined up. Her plan was to blitz the church. Get a quick plea. Open the door to civil damages. Label herself a hero come reelection.

"What was your relationship with Monsignor Quinn?"

"He molested me," Mitchell answered, his response as plain as my question. "From the time I was fourteen when I was a freshman at St. Ignatius, until I graduated in eighty-eight."

I sunk back into the couch cushions. I'd never met

anyone as upfront and honest as Byron Mitchell. My backup plan had included a list of soft-pedaled questions, with the hope that I would get a disclosure if a blitzkrieg had gone sideways. Maybe I *could* learn something from Pope.

"I'm sorry." My next words were the most honest I'd spoken in a while. "I guess I didn't expect such blatant honesty." Even all these years after my own assault, shame kept me mostly silent.

"What's left?" Mitchell's question was rhetorical. His entire upper body slumped as if his spine had been removed. "I can't keep the secrets and shame of the church. That's theirs to reckon with. So what do you need to know?"

"Everything. Everything you want to tell me."

Mitchell took a deep breath. The first part of his story mirrored Justin McPhee's. Absent father, though Mitchell's didn't die, just moved back to Belfast. I'm guessing the feeling of abandonment is the same, maybe worse because Mitchell's dad made a daily choice not to be with his son. His mom struggled. Quinn invited a vulnerable Mitchell into the so-called inner circle.

"He fed us teenage boys with hollow legs. Bought us the kinds of video games and consoles our moms couldn't. He had a Sega *and* a Nintendo in his office. We could play without anyone yelling about doing homework."

My sister, Michelle, and I had every console and all the games we'd ever asked for. Not every family did. I had to wonder where a priest who'd taken a vow of poverty had come up with the money for very expensive toys.

"Nothing happened here in Cleveland?" I pivoted from grooming to violation.

"No. I always speculated about that. It was weird. Although I've always wondered if maybe it wasn't illegal in Guatemala or something."

I'd read about how some countries were quite complacent especially around child trafficking and crimes against children. I remember a college friend coming home from a tour through South and Central America and commenting on how many of the hotels had signs prohibiting bringing unrelated children to guest rooms.

"So how did all this happen?" I made my face a mask of empathy. Though to be honest I was very worried that we might not have jurisdiction over Quinn. You'd never know it from the news, but some of the pedophile priests were clever. Maybe the ones who were less popular with the archdiocese or Vatican and worried they might be sacrificed.

"Somehow, Monsignor arranged a scholarship and got plane tickets and flew me down with the other kids. He put us in this dorm, and I got my own room, which of course seemed like a huge score. That first night, he came to make sure I was settled in. He leaned over like he was going to tuck me in. Then he talked about how I was the youngest kid on the trip and he'd stay with me until I fell asleep. I'm not embarrassed to say this now, but back then my mom still put me to sleep every night. I could totally see her mentioning it to him in passing. She was kind of anxious about anything happening to me and was probably a little overprotective.

"So I allowed Quinn to lie on the bed beside me because it felt kind of normal, even though he wasn't a parent." Mitchell closed his eyes and shook his head. Looked like he was questioning every decision he'd made there. I knew that move because I'd done the same more times than I could count. "I must have fallen asleep," Mitchell continued, "because I woke up with his hand on my..." He trailed off. What little confidence and bravado he'd mustered to share his story with me had left him.

"On my penis," whooshed out. "I kept my eyes closed, squeezed tight because I figured maybe if he thought I wasn't into it, he'd leave. But he didn't...leave. He kept jerking me until I came. Then he wiped his hand on my sheets. He leaned down and kissed me, on my mouth, then he left. I turned over and the sticky sheet was on my shoulder. It was gross, but I just couldn't get up and go somewhere else. I just couldn't move. Get up. Get out of there. Get new sheets, I don't know. I thought it was my fault. I thought I must be gay and giving off some signals. I'll spare you the whole blame game, because now I think it was part of a bigger conspiracy."

"How do you mean?" I asked before my brain went wild. I'd seen more than one rational-seeming witness prove themselves not to be when the crazy thoughts they had couldn't be contained. Before I got him fitted for a tinfoil hat, I leaned forward waiting for an answer.

"What I mean is that Monsignor Quinn wasn't acting alone."

I waited for alphabet soup to come out: FBI, CIA, maybe even a little Lyndon Johnson or Fidel Castro. Pulled my mind from 1963 Dallas and back to modern-day Cleveland. Maybe he wasn't crazy. Maybe.

"So who were Quinn's coconspirators?"

"Gerry Morales and Sister Parker."

If I'd had antennae, they would have stood at attention.

"Gerry?"

"Father Geraldo Morales. He ran the school down there. But him and Quinn had been at some parish together. Maybe Boston? New York? That part I don't remember. But if I were a guessing man, I'd say they figured out something they had in common."

Before the internet, it had probably been hard for like-minded pedophiles to find each other. A bond like that would be difficult to break, maybe last forever. Especially if they'd colluded to assault minor children.

The prisoner's dilemma didn't apply to these people. There was no dilemma. They took their shared secrets to the grave.

"Where is Father Morales now?"

Mitchell seemed to have way more information than McPhee did. Probably farther along in his healing process. McPhee was stuck so deep in denial, it was a miracle he'd agreed to testify. Usually men like him hid from us. Pope had worked some kind of magic there.

"In South America, I think. He did a stint in Africa, then he came back."

"Do you keep track of his movements?" Healing was one thing, vigilantism another.

"Not exactly. I just worry about the wreckage he leaves. I'm sure you know of the church's...*policy* of moving problem priests around. Morales must have been a bigger problem. Quinn was never moved."

That was something to consider. If Quinn and Morales had kept all their criminal behavior outside of not only Cuyahoga County but the United States, prosecution would be harder. We'd be leaning heavily on conspiracy. That was not the easiest conviction to get with a jury.

"And Sister Parker?"

"The plaque on her door had the word facilitator. That was the most accurate job description I've ever heard."

"What was her role?"

"In the school? I don't know the details of her job description or anything, but she was really the go-between for Monsignor Quinn. She got the food he gave us. I think she bought the beanbag chairs and picked out the video games."

"What makes you think that?"

"She said it. To me, at least, she pulled me aside and told me that I should be very sure to express my gratitude to Quinn for all the things she provided."

"Do you have any idea why she did that?"

"Truth?"

"Nothing but."

"I think she had a...thing with Quinn."

I shook my head. It was like a very sick soap opera.

"Every adult in this picture took a vow of celibacy," I protested, albeit a bit weakly.

"The statistics don't bear that out. At least fifty percent admit to not adhering to their vows. That's self-reported. Probably a lot higher."

Maybe I wasn't the only one who couldn't keep a promise to abstain. At least I was only hurting myself.

"Did everyone know what Parker did?"

"Eventually. I'm not sure how they couldn't. She's the one who arranged the scholarships." That last word was in air quotes. "She came to Bárcena. Assigned the rooms. Checked on us in the morning...offering anything we might need."

"Like?"

"Topical creams for pain, suppositories, that kind of thing."

"Oh...*oh*. Sorry."

Mitchell pushed past my awkwardness.

"She had keys for everything. Like a huge janitor-type ring folded in her habit. She was the only one who wore a habit, by the way. Anyway, she could get in everywhere. The school. The church. The rectory. The school in Bárcena. The dorm there. It was like she was moving pawns around on a chessboard."

"Did the other kids understand her role as well as you?"

"They had to. She was an easy target, I think. Maybe

because she was a woman? But there was no shortage of murder fantasies where she was the star."

"Like what?"

"Justin McPhee used to talk about pushing her out of a window. Ooof. I didn't mean to name any names."

I worked very, very hard to keep my eyebrows down on my face and nowhere near my hairline. I was thinking that one crime had just turned into another.

"Don't worry. Your secret is safe with me."

EIGHT
JUSTIN
JANUARY 13, 2009

Nicole Long and I were in the prosecutor's top-floor conference room. One I'd never been in while I'd worked to defend men and women charged with crimes. This time, however, it was only the two of us. I'd expected the top prosecutor to be there as she'd said publicly and privately that she was nearly single-handedly spearheading Cleveland's Catholic abuse allegations.

"No Pope?" I glanced meaningfully at the seat at the head of the table neither of us was occupying. We'd chosen swivel chairs across from each other. Hers at the back of the room, mine closer to the exit.

"There's probably a news conference calling her name," Long said.

I wouldn't touch that one with a ten-foot pole.

"So it'll be just you and me. It's been a long time since that's happened," I said.

"Did you quit criminal?" she asked.

Though I was kind of sure the answer was yes, I hadn't made any definitive decision. I didn't think now, with all this Quinn stuff occupying my headspace, was a good time to decide. But for the sake of any future clients, I gave Long a sort of half-answer.

"Just taking a hiatus."

"You guys did get that big payday," Long said. She was referring to the large settlement Casey Cort and I had gotten in the Strohmeyer case where the brewery made no admission that they'd contaminated the drinking water of the Brighthill community.

"Gives me a bit of breathing room," I acknowledged. "Time to create the exact kind of practice I want."

"Breathing room can be nice."

I wondered if Long was obliquely referring to her unsuccessful time in rehab. Didn't seem like something I wanted to address. That list was getting long.

"So what's next?" I asked, getting us back to the reason I was here.

Long shifted from personal to professional. She schooled her face into something a stern elementary school teacher would be proud of. Then she took the flat of her hand and squared the papers in front of her. Finally, she flipped open the leather portfolio front and clicked her ballpoint pen into position.

"Let's finish the conversation from last week. I know it was hard, so I hope you've had time to collect your thoughts during this little break."

"I'm ready," I said, all the while hoping she didn't notice that I was white-knuckling my grip on the chair's armrests.

"Let me be candid with you," Long started. "We've talked to some other victims—"

"You didn't use my name—"

"No, of course not. As I was saying, we've had a chance to speak with some other victims and a curious fact has come to light."

"What's that?"

"It appears that Monsignor Quinn was very careful to keep all of his activities confined to areas outside of the United States."

"Oh...oh...then jurisdiction—"

"Becomes an issue. As a lawyer who has done defense work, I knew you'd understand immediately the problem that presents."

"So what are you going for?" I asked more eager to help than before. Too many Catholic priests were slithering away from taking responsibility and being punished. I didn't want that to happen with Quinn. Not if I could do anything to stop it.

"Fact gathering." Long wrote something on her pad.

"Okay."

"I trust your observations more than the average person because you'll be able to view them through the lens of the law. Maybe not on purpose. But our training never goes out the window, does it? With that in mind, can we continue?"

"The new lens over the old information?"

"Hindsight *is* twenty-twenty."

I nodded. Understood what she was getting at. Hoped I could provide what she needed. I wasn't as confident in my analytical ability as she was.

"Okay," she started. "Let's talk about Monsignor Quinn first. Last week you identified other boys that Quinn may have molested. Because they were among his favorites, you said you think they may have been among his victims. Are there any more boys—now men, I guess— you think may have been...hurt as well?"

I had to appreciate that even after years of doing a job prosecuting people who hurt other people, she hesitated over descriptions of violence.

For a long moment, ones that were coming far too often these days, I cast my mind back to the memories I'd buried far deep.

"Here are my guesses on a few others," I started before I let other names of boys long become men roll off my lips. She carefully cataloged the list of names.

"Thank you for this. Can we turn our attention now to Father..." She flicked through some pages on her pad, checking her notes. "Geraldo Morales?"

"He let us...asked us to call him Gerry."

"Gerry, then. Was he ever here in Cleveland?"

Father Morales was a fixture of Bárcena...of Guatemala in my mind. Given the issues that were arising around prosecution, though, I really wanted to give everything I had to this.

"Maybe." I paused even longer, plumbing the depths I'd purposely let lie still and stagnant for years. "You know what? He was here once. Maybe even more than once." I was sure of the first statement. Not so much the second. It was people pleasing at its finest. Had to hope she didn't call me on it.

"Tell me."

"It was 1987. March. The only reason we knew, I knew he was in town was because he'd gotten stuck."

"How so?" Long looked genuinely perplexed.

"Right." I closed my eyes for a second, thinking about how it would be for an outsider. "You aren't from here. You'd have been down south, I suppose. They say you're from Louisiana. Anyway, there was a huge storm. Blizzard of eighty-seven. Lasted a couple of days. Dumped like twenty inches everywhere in the snowbelt. Hopkins was closed."

"Schools closed?"

"Of course. But Mom and a lot of people still had to go to work. No snow days for them. Sister Parker called, I guess. Told my mom or sisters that the church, basically Quinn, was having a kind of field day. I figured I wouldn't be alone. And hanging with the guys would be better than fighting for the TV remote with my sisters."

"Sister Parker? Hmmm. You went?"

"Trudged through the snow. Can truly say I walked to school uphill both ways through a blinding snowstorm."

Long's chuckle was quiet, but I heard it. At least there was a tiny bit of levity to break the tension.

"And Morales?"

"He was there. Opened the door to the rectory. It took me a second to recognize him."

"I thought you knew him well."

"In Guatemala. He was very much out of context here." I hated when I didn't recognize people, like a librarian at the grocery store or the store clerk at the library. Often they said hello and I felt like a snob for not knowing who they were, especially when they referred to me as that downtown Cleveland lawyer.

"What did he say to you, if anything?"

"Not much. Just that he'd be glad to see me...us in a few weeks for spring break. He came close like he wanted a hug or something. I excused myself to go to the bathroom. They did that, Quinn and Morales, invaded spaces."

"Did other kids come?"

"All in all there were six of us, I think. It felt like an all-male version of *The Breakfast Club*. We talked a lot about the snow. Morales was talking about how he really needed to get back to his school so he could manage the kids there, get them home for Easter, then prepare for our arrival in a few weeks.

"When Brock...Daniel Brock arrived, Morales got pretty agitated. Kept pacing in and out of the room. We...I could hear him talking on the phone to an airline, the airport, Guatemala. I'm not sure, but he was very much concerned with getting out of the city."

"You said he was nervous when Daniel Brock came in.

What did you make of that then? What do you make of it now?"

"That Brock hadn't expected Morales to still be there. That Brock's secret would be exposed. I mean we know *now* what they did was wrong. We probably knew it then. But they made it out like *we* were wrong. Like we had somehow lured them in to doing stuff with us."

"Common pattern. I think it eases their guilt because they're sociopathic. They know on the surface or deep down that what they're doing is very wrong. You mentioned Sister Parker a few minutes ago. How involved was she with Quinn?"

"I don't know."

"What was her job at the school?"

"Not sure."

"Did she go to Guatemala with you?"

My mind went completely blank. I'd been about to say no. Say that Sister Parker had never been down there. After Long asked the question, though, I knew my original answer. My kneejerk answer would have been a lie. Something...someone else I'd blocked out. After a long pause, I answered.

"Yes."

"Have you been reading the papers?"

"Not at all," I said. It was the kind of question a defense attorney would ask to see if a victim had been improperly influenced. "I've ignored it all," I assured Long. "Cancelled my subscription to the *Plain Dealer*. Haven't turned on the TV."

"What have you been doing to fill your time?" It was an odd question, but I shrugged it off. If she'd been a doctor, no one would have accused her of having a great bedside manner. Maybe she thought the alcohol helped. Maybe it *did* and this was the best she could do.

"Just doing some work at the office. Maintaining some ongoing cases. Walking my dog."

"What about Saturday night?" I hoped this awkwardness didn't mean she was veering into date territory. We were both single. She wasn't my type. Too pulled together on the outside with severely cut suits and tight skirts on the one hand and an internal mess, what with her not-cured addiction on the other. I'd once heard a rumor that she'd danced on a bar. That dichotomy was too messy, even for someone like me. Casey Cort was the exact kind of mess that meshed with mine. These days, though, I was spending all my weekend nights alone.

"The one just past?" I asked.

"Yep."

"I wasn't at that meeting, if that's what you're asking," I clarified. Maybe one of Quinn's other boys had told her about the proposed get-together. Some of the other victims wanted to sit in a circle and sing kumbaya or some such.

"Meeting?"

"I'm just going to assume that you saw Byron Mitchell last week. He reached out to a bunch of us. Even Daniel Brock. Took a back room at that new Mexican place in Ohio City."

"Near you, then," Long said like I'd arranged the location for my convenience.

"On the other side of I-71."

"What was the plan?"

"I don't know. When you read about this happening in other places like Boston or Chicago, it's like some victims put together a support group or whatever to talk... commiserate. I don't know. Not my kind of scene."

"So you didn't go?"

"Not a fan of Mexican food." Or sharing my feelings about a past I wished were dead and cremated.

"That the reason?"

"I worried a bit about the collusion of witnesses," I lied.

When a case goes to trial, every judge separates witnesses. They can't see the others' testimony until they testify themselves. But if I'd gone to the gathering, I'm pretty sure any defense attorney worth their salt would have pulled apart our stories. There were already a lot of assumptions of false or implanted memories in sex abuse cases. This gathering could have been the icing on an acquittal cake. It was a good enough excuse and the one I'd given Mitchell when he'd called. I guess he hadn't heeded my unsolicited legal advice.

"Have you gone to the school in the last year? To Saint Stephen's?"

"No," I said, "except for maybe driving by, I guess." Did she think I toured Catholic churches for funsies? They were like mushrooms after a rain. I ignored every single one. I'd told my mom I was lapsed, but the truth was that I disavowed the church and everything it stood for. Contrary to popular belief in my family, Kenyon hadn't made me an atheist, Monsignor Quinn had.

"West Fifty-seventh Street? Have you been near there lately?" Her questions were coming fast now. Wariness came over me like a shroud. I'd been lulled by our professional relationship. By collegial camaraderie. Suddenly it was as if I'd been awakened.

"Did something happen?" I pressed my right hand on the table. Leaned forward. Tried to glimpse at her notes. Long pulled her pad closer to where her torso met the edge of the conference room table.

"Where were you between six and eight p.m.?"

"Home," I answered without thinking.

"Can anyone vouch for that?"

"Why is that starting to feel like an interrogation?"

Long took a long sip of who-knows-what kind of liquid. Put down her insulated plastic-topped cup slowly.

"Maybe it is."

"What's going on?" She hadn't given me a *Miranda* warning, so I was probably in the clear on whatever I'd said so far. None of it could be used against me in a court of law.

I hoped the St. Ignatius crowd hadn't gotten drunk and done something stupid. There was probably nothing more dangerous than a pack of inebriated men.

"Sister Angela Parker was murdered on Saturday night."

She could have knocked me over with a feather. Of all the things I'd imagined would come out of her mouth, this had not been one of them.

"Killed?"

"Dead."

"Who's your top suspect?" Guilt gnawed at me for putting this prosecutor in touch with victims. No good was coming of dredging up all this stuff from the past.

"Given what's come to light, I'm looking at every victim of Monsignor Quinn."

"I think I need a lawyer." I knew I wasn't guilty, but innocent men went to jail more often than anyone would like to admit.

Long stood. Pulled down the curled pages on her pad. Closed her portfolio. She was treating me like a suspect who'd invoked.

"I hear you have Casey Cort on speed dial," she said as she walked from the room with no goodbye, no offer to walk me out. It was true that I did have Casey on speed dial. I didn't know if I was brave enough to make the call.

NINE

BLAKE

JANUARY 16, 2009

Even though I wasn't thrilled to be carrying a monthly car note, without the income to support it, I was grateful for the 2007 splurge I'd made on my Jeep Wrangler. It had kept me from slipping and sliding too much on the roads between my apartment and this house on Liberty Road in Solon. The Lake Erie snow-belt effect meant the farther east I went, the more treacherous the drive.

Solon was one of the oldest of the outer-ring suburbs of Cleveland. Ruthlessly zoned and planned in the forties, like many of the northeast Ohio cities, the house I pulled up to had kept its original acreage, if the barren, snow-covered landscape was any indication.

I checked my printout one more time. This run-down home had been the place listed on the birth certificate of Mary Elizabeth Parker, who later became Sister Angela. Tax records indicated the home had never been sold. Since

Mary Elizabeth had two brothers—one older, one younger —I made an educated guess that one of them would be living in the inherited property, maybe with one of her parents even, though that was a longer shot. I could have taken a deeper dive by going into census records, but it was Friday and government workers, both federal and state, tended to leave early. I was taking a chance by coming out here, but wanted answers more than I wanted to observe proper formalities.

Every Catholic priest was recorded every year in the Catholic Directory. That annual was one of the points of data that made it easy to follow priests who were moved from parish to parish. Made it easier for reporters from the Pulitzer Prize–winning *Boston Globe* team to trace the trail of destruction abusive clergy left in their wake.

There was no such directory for nuns.

Women were erased from history in so many ways, big and small. The Catholic church was no different, though their erasure of the women who selflessly served them was probably more egregious.

Sisters took a "name in religion," then essentially disappeared off the face of the earth. For hundreds of years, they'd swathed themselves in identical habits, then tirelessly worked as teachers and church servants with little pay and gratitude in the form of glory from God.

Fortunately, I'd had a decade-plus of training that made finding the true identity of Sister Angela Parker only a two-full-day endeavor. Without the internet, it may have taken a week. Blessing and a curse the net was.

Despite the below-freezing temperatures, I didn't want to lose any momentum on the case. I'd already made my first blog post on the Parker murder, and I had way more hits and comments than I'd anticipated.

True crime readers were a voracious bunch, and a mention on some amateur investigator forum had taken me from fifty hits to five thousand in a week. My email inbox was full of one question: When would I post an update?

I was here to get that for them. But before posting, I needed to add a subscription-only page, tip jar, or even worse—ads. America loved a free internet, but Society Bank liked my mortgage payments to be in cash. So while truth and justice were important, so was monetizing my work.

I knocked on the front door. No answer. When one of the neighbors from across the street came out onto the porch and then down to the mailbox, giving me a slow once-over, I pulled my press badge lanyard from my messenger bag and looped it around my neck. I'd waited until six in the evening to get on the road, giving whomever lived here plenty of time to get off work and get home. I glanced in the long driveway again. There was an automobile-sized lump down toward the garage, but it was covered in snow, so hadn't been used in the last few days, if not years.

While I was contemplating my next move, a giant Ford SUV pulled into a tramped-down area of snow at the front of the drive just off the small two-lane road. A man about ten years older than me, mostly gray, with a growing potbelly, got out. Gave me a stare.

"Blake Tatum," spilled nervously from my lips. "*Plain Dealer* reporter."

"What are you doing out here? Lost?" The way he said lost was full of the implication that bad things only happened within Cleveland city limits.

"Are you Peter Parker?" I strained to say that with a straight face. I could only imagine the ribbing he'd experienced in all his years. Though to his mother's credit, the superhero had come much later than his birth.

"That's me." He didn't crack a smile. "How can I help you...ma'am?"

"I'm here about your sister. Sister Angela." I kept my eyes on his face below his wool peaked cap. He didn't seem sad or shocked. Instead, he walked up the icy stairs, pulled open the storm door, then fitted a key in the lock. He paused before pushing in.

"Do you mean Mary Elizabeth?"

I'd come up the steps behind him. A stiff wind blew, freezing the tears in my eyes.

"It's practically zero out here. Would you mind if I come in?"

He didn't hold the door open for me, but didn't shut it in my face, either.

"I guess. Badge says you're a reporter? Mary Elizabeth is a nun. That's the opposite of reporting."

He'd said *is*. How had it taken the police longer to find Parker than I had? Next of kin notification was always top of the priority list. First, because it wasn't cool for family members to read about their loved one's death in the paper. We never printed a victim's name before the notification had been made. Not hemmed in by strict journalistic standards, I'd put Sister Parker's name on the blog. Peter Parker wasn't a reader.

Second, because they were top suspects or witnesses right after a lover. A vow of celibacy meant lover was crossed off first thing in this case. Maybe that fact had delayed the cops. I followed him in but didn't move too far past the threshold.

Parker flipped a couple of switches and all the lamps in the room glowed. My eyes darted around the room at the flowered wallpaper above original dark wood waist-high wainscot. I wanted to scream out: *The 1940s called and wanted this house back.*

It was rare to see a place that hadn't been renovated at least once in the seventies or eighties if not recently. I had to wonder if this guy was stuck in a time capsule. Hadn't heard of stainless steel and granite, obviously. Wasn't a devotee of HGTV like my parents.

Parker took off his coat. Hung it on a wood hook by the door. Pulled off his boots and put them right under the outerwear pegs. I didn't comment on the water damage he'd done to the floors. Wasn't in the position to tell him that boots never came inside. He turned to me. Finally looked me straight in the eye.

"Is this about that scandal you all have been reporting on? All those priests?"

"Honestly, I thought the police would already have been here—"

I was cut off from sharing the bad news by a knock on the door. Parker looked at me as if I should know who it was. I shrugged and stepped aside. He went back toward the front door.

"Can I help you?" Parker asked of the visitor, who I assumed was the nosy neighbor coming to make sure I hadn't killed anyone dead.

I turned to have a look. It was Loren Logan.

"Detective Logan." He pulled out his badge. Parker didn't look as closely at the detective's shield as he had at my press pass. "Cleveland Police. Can I speak with you?"

"Ain't had no one but the neighbors and Bible-thumpers come by in ten years and now all of a sudden, it's a party."

Logan took that as an invitation and came on through. I lifted my right arm, encased in a puffy sleeve and hand in a glove, and gave a little wave.

"Didn't expect to see you here, Tatum." Cool as a cucumber, he was. Probably made an awesome detective.

"Thought you'd have already been here," I said, cutting my eyes toward Parker in what I hoped was a subtle sign.

An almost imperceptible nod told me Logan wasn't stupid. He turned toward Parker.

"I think you need to sit down."

Grateful neither cop nor brother had thought to throw me out, I tried to make myself as small and unobtrusive as possible by wedging myself in a corner. Flicked on my recorder and waited.

Parker ignored both of us and left the room. Noises indicated he was taking off his more clothing layers. Next was the sound of liquid hitting liquid. A toilet flushing. No running water sounds before he opened and closed his fridge. Came back with a twelve-ounce Strohmeyer, flicked at the pop top, and took a long drink. He then situated himself on an ugly-ass La-Z-Boy and looked at Logan. That was the detective's cue, I suppose.

"I'm sorry to tell you this, but your sister died on Saturday night."

Logan and I watched in silence as Parker finished the can of beer. His right hand nearly crushed the can before he put it down oh-so-gently on a side table.

"Died? Took you nearly a week to come here?"

"It took some time to find you, her next of kin. St. Stephen's wasn't her home convent, where she was made a nun."

"No, that was Our Lady of Sorrows in Massachusetts."

Logan pulled a notebook and pen from his pocket, scribbled down a note. Glad I had my recorder in hand, I didn't bring any attention to myself by doing the same.

"Church records aren't the most comprehensive for nuns," I interjected. Wanted to make myself part of the conversation.

"You going after Quinn?" Parker's eyes were on Logan. "*He* knew I was the next of kin."

"Who?" Logan asked, though surely he knew the answer. I just watched and waited.

"Monsignor Gregory Quinn." Parker stated the obvious. "The St. Ignatius priest, though maybe not for long."

"Why do you think we should talk to him?" Logan's question was open-ended. He'd have made a great reporter.

"Aren't you already investigating him?" Parker's question was fair. There wasn't a newscast that went by without mention of Cleveland's Catholic abuse scandal. The only thing that had dominated the news like that was the sex trafficking case from a few years back.

"Different special investigation team—"

"Because he was her...I don't have a word for it," Parker interrupted Logan. He wanted to talk, point a finger in blame, more than he wanted to listen. "Mary Elizabeth had sex with him. She didn't want to, but he pressured her. I told her a long time ago she should tell on him. My sister insisted it wouldn't make any difference. I thought he'd be disciplined, sent somewhere to get a handle on his problems. But seeing how no one was punished for abusing children, maybe she was right."

Logan had an excellent poker face. He didn't give a single thing away. But he couldn't have expected that sudden turn. Or maybe he did. Maybe homicide detectives were hit with curveballs all the time.

"Pressured her, how?" Logan asked. I had the same question. "He couldn't exactly get her fired or blackmail her."

Parker slapped his palm on the side table cluttered with remotes and magazines and now the beer can. Everything rattled and shifted, but nothing toppled. An anti-gravity miracle. Then Mary Elizabeth's brother put his head in his hands. It was the first time Parker had expressed any emotion beyond annoyance at being interrupted in his nightly routine of releasing liquid and replenishing it.

"He owns two-thirds of this house. If Mary Elizabeth didn't do what he wanted, he'd have put me out on my ass."

"The deed shows your parents as owners," I interjected. Shouldn't have, but couldn't help myself. If I was good at one thing, it was research.

"That's right. If you go down to the county, my deceased parents are listed as owners of record."

I hadn't gone to law school, but being a crime reporter gave me a little bit of insight into the laws and legal procedure. I'd come across this kind of thing one other time years ago after a murder of one of the inheritors of a large estate.

An attorney had told me that a deed didn't have to be recorded to be valid. If it were recorded, then the rightful owners could use the court system to enforce their rights, but as long as taxes were paid, there wasn't anyone in the county's fiscal office who would go out of their way to validate ownership.

"So how is a priest a two-thirds owner?" Logan asked.

"What about the vow of poverty?" I asked nearly simultaneously.

Parker lifted his head, his eyes swiveling between us. Finally, he said, "Maybe it's you two who need to sit down."

Sitting always made me less intimidating, so I took the invitation immediately on a plaid couch that looked like a seventies sitcom reject. Logan took off his coat and followed suit, but his seat of choice was an Edith Bunker–style armchair. Logan's big frame made the wood chair seem very small.

"Are either of you Catholic?"

I shook my head. Didn't go into my African Methodist Episcopal background.

"Raised agnostic," Logan offered. I worked to keep my eyebrows down. I could have sworn Logan was an Irish name. But maybe I was conflating the fact that heavily Catholic Boston's airport had that name. Police were allowed to lie to suspects. I wondered if that extended to witnesses. Wasn't my show to direct, so I tamped down my curiosity. Watched and waited.

"Our parents were devout Catholics," Parker said. Whoo boy, he was starting at the beginning. As quietly as possible, I slipped my arms from my parka. He didn't have much heat on, but a zero-degree-rated coat was too much for inside most places. After Wisconsin, I was afraid to be that cold again. Parker continued, "Mom went to Mass on Sundays *and* Wednesdays. My brother, John, and I were altar boys at St. Rita's. All three of us took holy communion."

"Your dad?" Logan asked.

"Worked. Came home. Read the paper."

"Didn't go to church?"

"He wasn't Catholic. Left all that up to my mom."

"How did you feel about that? Rebel?"

"Rebel? We're not Gen Z or even Gen X. Disobedience wasn't on the menu. Besides, the church was the air we breathed."

"Your sister?"

"Do you know that phrase, you give one to the church? There's this idea that if you have a bunch of kids, you can give a son to the priesthood or a daughter to the convent. My mom started on John, but he wasn't having any of that."

"Where's he now?" Logan was in a rhythm now.

"California. Moved out at the first chance. Did aerospace. Retired. Lives in Southern California. Can't remember the name of the town, but not Los Angeles. El or La something."

"So your sister was the sacrifice?"

"She went willingly. Kind of felt left out when we were doing the altar-boy thing. There wasn't some kind of equivalent for girls. This was before the days of youth groups. Boys could become acolytes, lectors, all that. Girls just went to church. So when Mom mentioned the convent, I think Mary Elizabeth finally felt like she had a place in the church. She didn't even go to college or anything. Mom found her a spot in Massachusetts that would take someone as young as her and that was that."

"When did she come back to Ohio?"

"Maybe after about ten years? There are some steps to becoming a nun. I don't know. Devotion, studying, a certain number of prayers on your knees or something. She was in New England. Then somewhere in South America."

"Guatemala, maybe?"

"Yeah, that was it. I mean, it's not like I had the kind of money and time for international trips. And of course she was poor and didn't come home, here often. I took care of Mom and Dad. She did come back for Dad's funeral. She was at the convent on the westside when Mom died."

"How was the inheritance split? I mean, the house from your parents to you guys."

"Whatever Dad had went to Mom. Then Mom had a will that gave each of us a third, but I could live here and could veto their right to sell."

"Did you want to stay?"

"I did. But neither of them wanted me to go or anything. John has a wife, kids, grandkids. He's not coming back to Ohio. Mary Elizabeth was a nun. Comes with a place to live, this time at the convent next to St. Stephen's. So there wasn't any kind of fight or anything."

"That all sounds like ordinary family decisions," Logan said. "I don't understand how Monsignor Quinn comes into the picture. It's not like priests all over the world are inheriting property. They'd have to give it to the church anyway, wouldn't they?"

"So here's the catch. Not all Catholic priests have to take a vow of poverty. Just some sects. Probably a majority of them, if I had to guess. But diocesan priests don't." Parker had stumbled over the unfamiliar word, but didn't pause. "Mary Elizabeth said they're all to live modestly, but they don't have to be poor."

I hadn't known that. Took it in. Would have to add it to not only the blog, but to the pile of research I had to do on Catholic dictates and policies. The Vatican seemed to have loopholes someone could drive a tractor trailer through. It was like they legislated outward, but not internally.

"Rules for thee, but not for me," I heard myself say.

Parker met my eyes for the first time, nodded.

"Anyway, there's a second deed that has all three of us listed as joint tenants."

"What does that mean?" I asked, once again a little lost. Logan didn't pipe in, so either he didn't know or he was just letting Parker talk.

"If any of us die, the other two get their property equally, going from third to half and possibly to whole for the last one of us living."

That made sense to me. Kept the property division fair and in the family.

"I'm not sure my parents thought ahead, exactly, because if one person transfers, it breaks the joint tenancy."

"So if, say, your sister transferred, then what happens to you and your brother?"

"We each have our third, but Monsignor Quinn has her third."

"You said he had two-thirds...?"

"I'm not sure of the details at all, but she and Quinn flew out and convinced my brother to transfer to her, which meant he got it."

"Is this guy some Svengali?" I had to ask. Keeping quiet was proving very difficult. "How did he go from...you know ministering to parishioners to owning two-thirds of a house in Solon?"

"I wish I could tell you. All Mary Elizabeth said was that he was planning for when they both left the faith. If they leave before retirement, they don't get taken care of or a pension or however it's handled."

That made a lot more sense now. Many a woman had been swayed by a man who made big promises he never intended to fulfill. I'd certainly fallen for Woody's promises that he'd marry me and contribute to our finances as soon as...pick your excuse. I'd held on for years. Probably would *still* be holding on if I hadn't lost my job. Quinn's excuse was far more compelling. Could inspire far more loyalty. He was a man of God, after all.

"Why would he kill her, though?"

"I talked to a lawyer. Quinn could force me out. Sell the property to get the cash. Worth a lot more now than when my parents bought It in the 1940s. I can't afford to buy him out. All I have...had was this. I have a pension, but I'll need that when I retire."

Logan laid out what had happened. Sister Parker going out of a window. The fact that the Cleveland Police hadn't ruled out suicide, but were investigating her death as suspicious for now.

"To be frank, Mr. Parker, there aren't many people who have it out for nuns. We'll look into this thing with Quinn to be sure, but unless there's more, we may just rule it a suicide. You've said, she was breaking her vows. Her lover is in hot water for maybe being a child abuser. Without a future, maybe it was all too much to handle."

"Mary Elizabeth wasn't that kind of girl. Before you give up, have a look into what happened in Guatemala. After the first trip down there, she was never the same."

"Why don't you call her Sister Angela?"

"Because Quinn picked that name for her. It was never who she was."

TEN
NICOLE

Tequila? Absolutely.

Mexican food? Not so much.

It hadn't taken the investigative skills of Sherlock Holmes to find the gathering spot for Quinn's victims. Even with the growing popularity of Mexican food in the U.S., the restaurants were few and far between in northeastern Ohio.

There were only two in this Ohio City neighborhood, and the other didn't seat parties larger than six. I was sure that this restaurant on a mixed-use block of Fulton Road was the place. I parked across the street in front of a turn-of-the-last-century home where there was a car-sized, snow-free space.

After I made my way into the spot, I ignored the "wait to be seated" sign and helped myself to a back corner table, then glanced at my watch. It was seven fifteen. The newly formed Quinn victim support group was to meet here at seven thirty. I had no doubt they'd show up.

Before a defendant was charged, victims were usually full of righteous indignation. After an indictment came down, they were happy to hand off most or all of the responsibility to me. In fact, I encouraged it. Kept down vigilantism. And as a side benefit, I also hoped it helped healing. Despite how lawmakers and elected prosecutors framed it for voters, a conviction wasn't enough to take away the sting of that original crime.

Following the bartender's recommendation, I took a shot of some overpriced designer small-batch fermented cactus juice, then asked for a virgin margarita to wash away the smell of alcohol.

By seven forty-five, Byron Mitchell was there as well as Daniel Brock. I recognized some that I'd paid visits to, and others from their pictures in Lori Pope's growing file. From the thirteen guys who'd pushed two tables together, there were only two or three I couldn't pinpoint.

The way I saw it, I had two crimes to investigate. The men at the back table were victims of one and possible perpetrators of the other. I know Lori Pope would have tossed Sister Parker to the wind, probably encouraging Logan and the medical examiner to rule it an accident or suicide, so we could concentrate on bringing down the big game.

Bringing down the Catholic church was much better for a reelection campaign. Don't get me wrong: I really wanted to take down Quinn too. With the perpetrator of my own long-ago assault still walking free, happily eating at my parents' holiday table, I needed a win. Something in my gut, though, was urging me to find Sister Parker's killer. If I were a betting woman, I'd say that the two were inextricably linked somehow. Smoke, fire, and all that.

I let my brain noodle on my instant dilemma while I nursed my too-sweet drink. Whoever thought virgin drinks were a good idea should be shot. That's an offender I wouldn't prosecute. After I polished off the margarita, I worried the napkin, then got out a pen to write on the only dry spot left.

I viciously circled Parker's name on the napkin until it was in ink-blue and white shreds on the table. Pushing aside the chips and salsa I hadn't touched, I got to my full height in snow boots with heels and strode over to the victims' table laden with salsa, guacamole, chips, and taquitos. With a loaded table, it was a good time to ambush. No man I'd ever met walked away from food voluntarily, especially after braving winter weather to get it.

From the number of raised eyebrows kissing newly receding hairlines, the men I'd already met were very surprised to see me. When their expressions registered with the others, all conversation stopped. It was an oasis of quiet in an otherwise raucous establishment.

When no invitation materialized, I chose a spot and angled a chair in. Raised my hand for the server, and ordered a Perrier with a twist of lime. Put my sobriety right on the table, so to speak.

"Anyone want another round? It's on me," I offered.

Most of their Modelos and Coronas were still more full than empty. I got no takers.

"I guess I should introduce myself." I shook the hands of the people I could reach from my seat, gave a nod to the rest. "I'm Nicole Long. The head of major crimes and an assistant county prosecutor for Cuyahoga County. I'm one of the attorneys investigating the abuse allegations directed at the Cleveland diocese's clergy." I waited a beat. My drink came. I took a sip. Not a word from any of them. Polite former altar boys or cowed victims, I couldn't decide. "I've met a couple of you," I continued. "Can you all introduce yourselves?" I asked, not really giving them an out.

Catholic schoolboys were too polite to push back against me, so in quick succession starting with the guy at my left, they told me their names and when they'd graduated from St. Ignatius.

By my count there were thirteen men here. My lucky number today.

"Sorry to barge in," I apologized. Though I wasn't at all sorry. "Normally I wouldn't ambush you like this, but something serious has come up that I'm hoping you can shed some light upon."

When no one spoke...again, I took up the mantle of conversation.

"I'm sure you've read in the paper or seen on the TV news that Sister Angela Parker died."

"Was she murdered?" one man, who'd introduced himself as Cesar Dennis, asked.

"There aren't a lot of nuns who fall from convent windows by accident. Right now the police are looking at the death as suspicious."

"Do you think one of us has done it?" Dennis probed.

"I'm sure one of the detectives will interview you if they think you have a connection. Check out your alibis." I shook my head, though the action didn't match my words on purpose. "I'm not a cop nor an investigator. I'm here because I think you may be able to shed some light on Parker."

A guy I hadn't met before tonight must have taken pity on me because he put down a soft taco he'd been gnawing at and broke the icy silence that had taken hold of the men.

"Brandon Rivera," he repeated. "I was at a basketball game on the night Parker died. Cleveland State beat University of Wisconsin-Milwaukee, fifty-four–forty-nine. The weather did a number on the drive home. Glad for the win, though."

"I'm not here checking alibis," I assured.

"I know. Just wanted to put that out there."

I looked at Rivera, then at the rest of the group. He was the only person of color at the table besides me. I could imagine he only wanted to get out in front of any possible implication of guilt. Our justice system was certainly infamous for pointing the finger at the wrong person for the wrong reasons.

"Did you know Parker?" I asked. Since he'd volunteered, I wanted to take advantage to get my questions answered.

"If you were part of the Bárcena group, it was impossible not to know her," Rivera said.

"It's been mentioned that she was a facilitator. What did that mean for you?"

Rivera looked at me, then tried to catch the gaze of a couple of the other men. They looked down at their food and beer, anywhere but at him or me.

"I'm younger than everyone here. By the time I came along, I think Quinn, Morales, and Parker had it all down to a science."

"A science?" I guess every endeavor needed a project manager.

"They didn't wait for me to get to Guatemala."

"So something happened to you here?" I tried to keep my voice somber, the excitement out. This was probably going to be a big break in the Quinn case if not the Parker matter.

"Quinn maybe lived at the rectory, I don't know. But he had a building too. I'm not sure how he managed it, but he had a little place on Lorain Avenue not too far from here, actually." When Rivera paused, I could see him mentally mapping out this near westside part of Cleveland. "On the bottom, it was a real estate office. Upstairs was an apartment. The residence entrance was from an alley in the back. Parker asked me one day if I was interested in getting new shoes and sneakers. Mine were a hand-me-down mess from my cousins, and the guys were making fun of me."

One of the men at the far end of the table hung his head in shameful posture of a former bully. I took that moment to peek at what Rivera was wearing tonight. Frye chukkas that probably cost at least three hundred if not more. Wasn't a poor kid looking for a handout anymore.

"So we drove to a shoe store somewhere near the West Side Market," Rivera continued the story. "She let me pick whatever I wanted. I was so happy at that moment. That I finally had shoes that would make me look more like everyone else and not be another thing that made me different. Sister Parker told the sales clerk to throw away the shoes I'd worn there. I got to wear Reebok high-tops on the way out."

"Freestyle?" For a brief moment I joined him on that walk down memory lane to bridge the gap between prosecutor and victim.

"Those were so out. These were the Pumps." His nod was vigorous. "Blue, black, white, and gray."

"Oh, I'm old. I had pastel pink Freestyles. My sister had powder blue."

"The eighties," another man chimed in. We all laughed. Each of us probably had a memory in our heads of some of the more ridiculous fashions of that era. I let everyone have a few minutes to eat and drink and engage in a little nostalgia talk.

When there was a lull in the conversation, I prompted, "You were saying about going to a place on Lorain."

"Sister Parker was driving Monsignor Quinn's car," Rivera continued telling the story.

"What kind of car was it?"

"An Audi 5000."

"Did you wonder about that at the time?" I had to ask. My father had always driven a Mercedes, but back then his German car was a standout from the other oil and gas guys in their F-150s and Cadillacs. German luxury hadn't yet become as ubiquitous as now. That had to be especially true in northeast Ohio.

"I supposed it was expensive. There weren't any of those rolling around the city, especially the part where I lived. But I figured maybe a parishioner had handed it down or something. People donated all kinds of stuff to the church."

That was fair enough. It was a lot to ask teenage boys to be analytical, especially in the face of an out-of-the-ordinary outing to get the latest kicks.

"What happened next?"

"We stopped at the building. I think I probably asked why we were here. I don't remember what she said or even if it was a good reason or excuse. But at that age I didn't think I could get up and walk away or leave. My mom told me that I should be grateful to be at a school like St. Ignatius. That the diocese had done us a huge favor with scholarships and help with paying for the uniform and everything. If they asked me to sweep or clean or help with Mass, then I was to do what I was told."

"To obey?" I asked.

"To submit," he agreed.

"We went down the alley to a door. Parker used a key to open it. There were stairs right behind it. She urged me to go first. At the top was an apartment. Wood floors. Kind of an old building, but everything was fixed up. Like a new kitchen with a microwave and everything. A big Sony Trinitron with a VCR and tapes and games.

"He even had a full-size Ms. Pac Man arcade game. Sister Parker asked me if I wanted anything. It was a snack heaven. The cabinets were chockfull of Little Debbies and Hostess cakes. Eventually I picked some homemade brownies and milk. She said the brownies had something special in them. It explained the taste."

"What do you think was in there?" I asked. Drugging kids was next-level depravity.

"As an adult? Pot brownies for sure. I hadn't eaten anything since I'd left my mom's house, so I gobbled down two."

"Two?" I asked, trying to gauge the effect something like that would have had on him.

"Eighties-teen-boy size"—he demonstrated with squared-off fingers of about four inches by the same—"not the little two-by-two squares you see at one of those overpriced bakeries nowadays."

"Did they get you high?" Everyone knew the problem with edibles was the varying concentration of THC.

Rivera nodded.

"When I was at Princeton, we called it couch lock. I sat

down on this brown corduroy sofa. Sister Parker put in a movie. It was like I was underwater or something."

"What was it?" I asked. Juries loved details. Helped give them a sense of time and place. Made the victim and the situation seem less alien. "The movie?"

"*Back to the Future*. Still can't watch that movie or any of its sequels to this day."

"Did Quinn eventually come?" I tried to keep my wince small at my very unfortunate choice of words. Everyone pretended not to notice.

"He'd been there the entire time," Rivera said.

"What?" I was thoroughly confused.

"The living area was kind of open plan. Popular now, but was kind of different back then. Off the kitchen/living room area, there were a couple of closed doors. Eventually Sister Parker gets up and opens one of them. From my place on the sofa, I hear her asking someone what they need..." Rivera trailed off.

My imagination went wild. Seth Collins had used alcohol to subdue me. But he hadn't worn a condom or anything. I had to wonder if Quinn was cunning like that... thinking ahead about limiting his culpability even though DNA wasn't a thing back then. The completion of the human genome project was a good decade-plus into the future.

Laughter erupted from one table at the front. Someone was singing happy birthday at another. In stark contrast, our corner was a black hole of misery.

"What was needed?" I eventually asked.

"K-Y." I hadn't heard anyone refer to the personal lubricant in at least a decade. Back when it had been the punch line of every late-night comedian.

"I'm so sorry." I was so very sorry because I knew once Quinn had summoned Parker, nothing good was going to happen for Rivera after that. The victim confirmed my thoughts with his next words.

"So he comes out. Put his arm around me. Talked about the Reeboks and Michael J. Fox and how much fun it was to be with him. How much my mother would appreciate all the special attention I got. He was talking and talking and all the time I felt like I couldn't really lift my arms or legs.

"Parker helped him take off my new shoes and my pants. Eventually he jerked me off. Then he...well, you can guess what happened next if he needed lube."

A server came close, but turned abruptly on her heel when Rivera's words filtered by. She was happy to leave plates of half-eaten congealed food on the table.

Food that hadn't looked appetizing to begin with was making me downright queasy. If I could, I'd have asked for another tequila to calm my stomach. The faster I got answers, the sooner I could take myself home and chase away my own demons with a nice bedtime shot of bourbon. I pressed on with my questions.

"Where was Parker during all of this?"

"She just sat on a chair and watched. When I said it hurt, she didn't even move or blink or do anything. She just stayed right there. All the love and warm feelings from the shoe shopping evaporated. I never trusted her after that. I threw out the Reeboks the minute I got home. Buried them deep in the outside trash bin. Stole my cousin's holey Nikes."

I tried to blink away the memory of my own assault. I'd done the same with the bloody shoes I'd worn home on Thanksgiving after. Too bad trauma didn't stay buried like a shoe in a landfill.

ELEVEN
JUSTIN
JANUARY 18, 2009

"You brought Simon," I observed as Casey maneuvered her buggy up the narrow stairs. I wished I'd heard her coming, but I did the best I could lifting the carriage up the remaining wooden steps. Though my apartment had been completely renovated with all the modern conveniences, it was one of the oldest buildings in the neighborhood. The hundred twenty-year-old steps were made for smaller people with a lot fewer things.

"It's Sunday," she said once she was in and the door was closed behind us.

I didn't know what that meant. Sunday had been the day we'd somehow informally agreed upon for our weekly...romps. One that had led to the creation of the tiny person in the too-big baby buggy. She'd had to have been referring to something else. I chose not to probe like I wanted.

Casey patted Morro in greeting. My dog was ignoring his training and had his paws on her parka. Once his need for acknowledgment was satisfied, she pulled off her jacket and hung it by the door, the motions familiar for both of us.

"He's asleep. Even after bumping upstairs?" I asked, eyeing the stroller.

She lifted an eyebrow. "Simon could sleep through the apocalypse. He's not an ER physician or firefighter. He doesn't need to sleep light because he's on call. That's my job now, actually."

I desperately wanted to steer the conversation from how and with whom she was spending her nights.

"Where are you living these days? You finally get that Shaker house that you've always wanted? Or did you lug this down all four flights?"

"Yes and yes. A house came up a week or so ago. Well out of season, but a good bargain. Just around the corner from Shaker Square in CHALK. Too good to pass up. I'll move when it stops snowing. Has a master bedroom, a room for Simon, a library on the first floor I can use for a real home office. You know there are a lot of lawyers who work from home. See clients at rented conference rooms, coffee shops."

"So you'd let go of your office at fifty-five Public Square?"

The idea that she wouldn't be working next door, even if it was Public Square and next door was a good five-minute walk, was a little kick in the gut. I closed my eyes briefly, trying to shake the feeling of missing someone who was right in front of me. Casey moving her house or office was really the least of my problems.

"Maybe. Just making some decisions." Instinctively, Casey reached out her hand and gently rolled the buggy back and forth. Simon was all zipped up in his navy-blue thing. I could only see a single tiny fist curled up above his little head. "A child does really change how a person prioritizes. In ways I didn't imagine or think of." She waved her hand dismissively. "But that's too much about me."

"I asked." It was deeply ironic how much I'd wanted to pull away from her before, and now I couldn't get enough of her. As long as Simon was a factor, I'm not sure how I'd ever untangle myself from her, physically, psychically, or otherwise.

"I guess you did."

Casey peeked into the navy-blue fabric. Satisfied with what she saw, she left him, walked to my open-plan kitchen, helped herself to a glass of cranberry juice from the fridge, and took her usual stool at the kitchen counter. I took my usual stool at the end, leaving the one between us empty. On those other Sundays, I used to sit next to her. Didn't feel like I had the right, now.

"What's the emergency, Justin? It's coming down outside. I don't want to get stuck."

With me were the unspoken words. She didn't want to get stuck with me. Who would?

"Do you remember when we talked in September?"

Casey got off the stool she always occupied when she

was at my place. I had no idea what she was doing, where she was going. I waited it out. Morro nosed her hand, and she pet the dog's head, smoothed along his shoulder and withers. He preened under the attention. Then she moved toward me, not quite invading my space, but close enough to touch...kiss. I cleared my throat. She put a hand on my shoulder.

"Yes, Justin. We talked about me possibly being your victim advocate. If that's what you need now. Of course, I'll do it. You know that." Her hand moved to squeeze my shoulder reassuringly. "I'm still only taking a handful of cases, but if you'll have me despite my...um"—she gestured toward Simon—"time limitations, then I'm more than happy to do this for you. No charge, of course." She squeezed again. I tried not to feel the pity coming through her fingers. "Is there something coming up? Some kind of questioning, press conference? I need to know how and what to prepare."

She grabbed my right hand in her left one. Squeezed it. I liked that she wanted to take care of me. Loved the feel of my hand in hers. But I wanted to run away as well. This isn't the context in which I wanted her to be there for me. Not something that invoked shock and disgust. Not to mention the real danger I was facing now.

"It's more complicated than that."

Casey scrunched up her face in question, but didn't let go of my hand.

"I'm confused. But that doesn't matter, right now. Tell me, are we going to need more than ten minutes?"

"How long can you stay?"

"I have to go to my car," Casey said, then strode out without her coat. A few minutes later, she was back. Her sweater and hair were dusted with snowflakes that were melting into tiny beads of water. In her hand she had a bulky black nylon bag.

"Are you going to record this?"

"Record?" A moment passed as confusion flitted across Casey's face. She lifted what was in her hand. "You mean this? It's a baby bag. I need to...well...feed Simon now." She cast an eye around the room. Then her eyes met mine. "Can I use your office? Shouldn't take more than fifteen minutes. Twenty tops."

"Of course. Why don't I run the dog out."

"Good idea," she said before lifting the sleeping baby from the stroller and disappearing again, this time behind the second bedroom door. Simon was so much bigger than even a few months ago. I pulled the laces of my boots extra tight rather than let my mind go off to wondering how much of Simon's little life I was missing.

When Morro and I got back, Casey was zipping up some kind of tiny green footie pajamas on Simon while he lay on the couch with drooping eyes. I dried off the dog and stood awkwardly. I wanted to be past this discomfort, but that seemed like a very far-off future.

"I think you're going to want to sit down for this."

"I'm already sitting." She waved her hand over herself and her son. "What's going on, Justin?"

I lifted a cotton blanket dotted with blue elephants. I

fingered it and wondered if Casey realized that it looked like a huge gauze bandage. I tucked it in the corner of the couch, then took a seat. Looking at Casey and Simon was hard. Thinking about what I was going to ask of her was harder.

"I think I may be a murder suspect," I blurted when I could keep it in no longer.

"Think? Murder?" Simon stirred, seemingly annoyed with his mother's loud voice. She smoothed a hand against his sparse hair, little curls already popping up. When he stopped fussing, she continued in a softer, quieter voice. "What in the hell? Justin. What happened?"

"Have you been reading the papers?"

"No time. There's a stack by the door. They've been coming in one week only to go back out to the recycling the next. But this isn't about how busy it is being a new mom. Just talk to me."

"Sister Angela Parker was possibly or probably murdered last week."

Casey lifted her phone from her pocket. Held it out past the baby. Fingered the tiny screen.

"Do you mind?"

I shook my head. Rubbed my sock-covered foot along Morro's flank as he dozed on the floor, his back pressed up against the couch we were occupying. Edified by what she'd read, Casey shoved her phone back into her sweater's kangaroo pocket.

"Have you been questioned? Interrogated? Arrested? Indicted?"

"You know how I told you I was willing to help out Pope and by extension Nicole Long as a...victim of Monsignor Gregory Quinn?"

Casey nodded. Squinted.

"Well, I was on the second round of questioning with Long on Tuesday—"

"This past?" she asked. This is what I liked about her, when she really dedicated her intellect to something, it was full on.

"Yeah. It started like before, but a little more nitty-gritty. Nicole said that they were having some jurisdiction issues and also needed some deep background. I jumped at the chance to help. Easier to talk about that, you know..." I trailed off. Swallowed. "At some point I twigged on to the fact that she was questioning me."

"Did she give you a *Miranda* warning?"

"No."

"So how did you end things?"

"She said she considered anyone who'd been a victim of Quinn a suspect. I told her I think I needed a lawyer... that I needed you."

She lifted a sleeping Simon, put him back into his rolling bed. She laid a hand on his chest when he stirred. Casey didn't move until he settled.

"Defense lawyers fall on both sides of the idea of asking this question, but this is you and me, Justin. Did you push that nun out of the window?"

"Absolutely not."

She fiddled with the phone in her pocket but didn't

pull it out. Apparently, she'd memorized the facts that she needed.

"So where were you on Saturday, January tenth?"

Rethinking my whole life and pining for you wasn't a really good answer, though it was the absolute truth.

"I have the worst alibi ever." I shrugged hopelessly. "I was here. Alone. Just me and the dog."

"Given the popularity of cell phones and high-speed internet, that isn't as awful an answer as it used to be. Did you call anyone? Your parents? Your sisters?"

Her use of "parents" made me wince inwardly. I always referred to them plural, though I only had one. She knew so little about me, and it was all my fault. Keeping one secret had made me keep so many others.

"I'll get my phone records," I promised.

"What about online stuff? Play multiplayer games? Post on Facebook?"

"Facebook?" We weren't friends on the social media platform. "You're on there?"

"Everyone wants baby photos. I hate it, but it makes my parents and their parishioner friends happy."

I resisted the urge to get up and go to my computer to peruse her profile, check her relationship status.

"Again, I'll check," I promised.

Casey's phone rang, the distinct iPhone ringtone filling the room. I wonder when she'd traded in her Blackberry.

"Did you rub it on his lip?" she asked the person on the other end of the line. "I don't know, maybe half hour.

Depends on the snow." She paused to listen. "No, I haven't. Not really. Hold on." She walked toward my front windows and flicked at the blinds. "Closing the roads? Okay. Let me see what I can do. I'll keep you posted."

"Need to leave?" I asked once I was sure I'd swallowed the longing that almost crept into my voice.

"Not yet, Justin. I have Simon and I'm his food. He's set. What we need to do here is formulate a plan, because you and I both know the finger of justice always points at someone rightly or wrongly. We need to be prepared if it happens to land on you."

TWELVE
NICOLE
JANUARY 19, 2009

"Thanks so much for coming in for some last-minute prep before you appear before the grand jury. We're expected upstairs in about an hour at eleven," I said to Brandon Rivera as I retrieved him from reception.

"A grand jury," he muttered. "Feels like some surreal TV universe."

I tended to agree with him in some ways. There were so many times I'd presented cases to the grand jury or appeared in court, and I was amazed that making arguments in open court was my actual job. Not what I'd imagined as a kid.

"I like your shoes, by the way," I said to Rivera as I guided him to the small conference room we used for witness prep. He was in another expensive pair of boots. He was head to toe a model of low-key expensive design, from his white cashmere turtleneck to his neatly pressed designer jeans.

"I want to nail the bastard to the wall. It's too bad crucifixion isn't a thing anymore."

Rivera was surprisingly forthright. So many victims wore their shame like a cloak and swallowed down their anger. He was the opposite. Though I did wonder if him being a man made a difference.

Sadly, the vast majority of victims I encountered were women.

"We're going to try very hard. Your testimony could break the case wide open."

"Why me, though?" Rivera asked. "You were at that restaurant the other night with all of us. There are dozens of victims, and at least ten or so willing to step forward."

"Have a seat," I said as I urged Rivera into one of the four chairs in the small conference room. In order to keep up our rapport, instead of sitting across from him as I did with most victims and witnesses, I sat next to him. Gently, I laid my portfolio on the table, scooted my lidded coffee cup as far away from him as possible.

"What's the story? There must be a story. I fully expected Quinn to be in court right after the news broke," he said.

"Unlike hundreds of other Catholic priests across the U.S., and across the world, Quinn was very crafty. Except for you, our investigation has turned up no abuse that occurred in Cuyahoga County, or even Ohio for that matter. Yes, the grooming occurred here, but that is not a crime."

Rivera was quiet for a long moment. So long that I almost grew hopeful. Maybe he knew of a victim, of a stone left unturned that could lead us to another Ohio abuse victim, bolster what was admittedly a borderline case.

"It was genius. I can see it now. Father Morales abused kids in Ohio. Sometimes he brought boys with him to Cleveland. Monsignor Quinn took us to Guatemala." Rivera shook his head. "I'm only an art teacher. Didn't go to a fancy law school like you did, but isn't there a way to prosecute them for the crimes they committed where they did them?"

"Extradition is what you're thinking of. The short answer is yes. The U.S. and Guatemala signed an extradition treaty way back in 1903. The practicalities of that are a little more difficult to execute."

"Why?"

"The Catholic church is a worthy opponent. They have money, time, and resources that our office does not. Our analysis concluded that they'd tie us up for years. In the meantime, they could move Morales and Quinn to Vatican City where they're untouchable. They'd get to live out their last days in peace and comfort with great Italian food. Quinn is not a young man. Our best bet for getting the justice you want and the others deserve is to strike now, while the iron is hot. Any other strategy risks no punishment at all."

I knew I'd used a lot of words to say we didn't have that kind of fight in us. Sure our office had more resources than our foes ninety-nine percent of the time. For that other one percent, freedom and justice could be bought. Just ask O.J. Simpson, Matthew Broderick, or R. Kelly.

"It all rests on me, then," Rivera said as his shoulders slumped under the weight of it.

"Not *everything*. We are not putting that pressure on you. Only the prosecution of your case relies on your cooperation. You're here today. That's the first step."

"Okay. What do we need to do?"

"In Ohio, we can have a grand jury decide to put forward felony charges or have a judge decide at a preliminary hearing."

"But we're doing the grand jury, right?"

"Yes, I used to be on grand jury duty, so I'm familiar with the process. You'll appear before nine Cuyahoga County voters. The prosecutor will ask you questions, and all you have to do is answer them. The grand jurors themselves can ask questions of you about the facts or of me about the law. We'll leave and they'll vote whether to indict."

"Does it have to be unanimous?"

"No, it's nothing like a trial. It's not adversarial. Only prosecution witnesses testify. Only seven out of nine have to vote for indictment."

"What happens if I know them?"

"Know them? The grand jurors? That's never happened."

"It's just that I'm an art teacher at an all-boys school. I'm not tooting my own horn, but I've been very popular there. Plus I also teach drawing and painting for Shaker and Cleveland Heights Rec."

"The proceedings are supposed to be a secret. In my experience, our jurors really don't discuss cases or deliberation. The indictment won't mention you by name, of course, but will be public," I said once I realized what he was truly getting at...everyone knowing he's a rape victim. "Newspapers mostly have a policy of not publishing the names of sexual abuse victims. If Quinn takes a plea, then you should remain mostly anonymous unless you choose to speak out. If there's a trial, that's a one-step-at-a-time kind of thing. We could close the gallery. There are ways to protect your identity. It's not perfect or bulletproof, but—"

"It's just I think one of my students mentioned being on the grand jury," Rivera interrupted before I could finish my spiel on what we did to protect victims.

"They'd have to recuse themselves is all. Don't worry. There are five alternatives just for this reason. The justice system isn't perfect, but we do what we can to keep the process sacrosanct."

When my phone beeped, I touched his arm lightly.

"It's time."

In five minutes, we were out in the hall before the grand jury room. Stone and wood and large wall-mounted letters lent gravity to the process.

The jurors, their badges conspicuously displayed, and

likely full of county-provided donuts and coffee, filed past. Two different men in their twenties made eye contact with Rivera. Once they were past, he gripped my arm hard and jerked me into a corner.

The contact was unexpected, and it took everything in me not to throw his hand off and engage in any of the self-defense moves I'd learned in a series of classes over the last years.

"Is there any way to talk to you off the record?" he whispered.

"I'm a prosecutor, not a reporter," I said. I was starting to wonder if I'd imbibed too much this morning because nothing about his behavior once we'd left the conference room made any sense. Witness panic usually didn't take this form.

"Are you required to prosecute anything that may violate the law?"

"Not anything. Not everything. We have broad discretion to prosecute cases that will do the most good, bring the most justice." I gave my stock answer, the same I'd give at a party. A neutral response that normally upset no one. He didn't look reassured.

"The two men who looked at me?" Rivera radiated nervous energy as his neck swiveled and his eyes darted. "I've had relationships with them."

"You're gay?" I asked, finally happy to have landed on what he was trying to say. "Consensual relationships, of course. There's no reason that has to come up—"

"They were students of mine." Rivera's voice had gone emotionless, flat. All my hairs started to rise.

"How old were they at the time?"

"I don't think I can answer any of these questions without a lawyer."

"Wait here." I held up my hand like I was playing the part of a defense attorney. I really didn't need to know more. Even though I had all that prosecutorial discretion I'd prattled on about, I really didn't want to move so much as a toe into mandated reporter territory. I should have seen this coming. A victim had become a predator.

I ran to the room and pulled the on-duty prosecutor aside. Let him know that my witness was going to bail and that there'd be no testimony, at least not today.

THIRTEEN
BLAKE
JANUARY 20, 2009

wanted to holler and cry and whoop. I only let myself do the last one of those as the thirty-inch TV displayed the first black president take the oath of office from my seat on a cheap hotel bedspread.

When my grandparents had migrated from Alabama in the thirties, not a single one of them imagined this, I suspect. Seeing a first lady and first daughters who looked like they could be in my own family, standing on the United States capitol portico, watching her husband and their father take the oath of office was blowing my mind and pushing tears from my eyes.

Despite all the feelings coursing through me and an urge to sit and watch hours of news coverage, I snapped off the set. I had a meeting in thirty minutes and I didn't want to show up puffy-eyed and emotional. I'm sure I could catch a replay of the speech on YouTube later.

In my winter boots, I trudged through dirty Massachusetts snow to the Our Lady of Sorrows convent. Neil Simon's *Brighton Beach Memoirs* was clearly based on *another* Brighton.

As I walked toward the dark wood front door set under a vaulted stone arch, I tried not to shiver. It was a scene straight from a Gothic horror—they never ended well for the innocent-eyed woman knocking at the entrance, nor black characters. God knew I was both. Monsignor's crimes were infiltrating my daydreams and nightmares. Best not to let my imagination get away from me.

Despite the shiver that went through me—cold not fear—I lifted and lowered the knocker a few times with no response. Eventually, I located a small lighted bell nestled in the mortar between two bricks. Pressing it did not yield any better results than the knocker. Convinced someone must have heard something, I simply waited.

A woman in a long gray-blue habit finally answered. Her eyes were the same color as her robes. She was tall, thin, and pale, with many keys dangling from her waist chain. Without guilt for my ongoing deception, I pulled the lanyard holding my *Plain Dealer* press badge from my parka.

"I have a twelve-thirty appointment with Sister Mary Katherine Cortez."

The tall woman didn't say a word, but stepped back. I took it as an invitation and came through the door onto a cold-looking floor of large tiles. Robes sweeping the slate, she disappeared through a door under a highly decorative wood staircase that climbed steeply from the back of the hall. Weak light from stained glass windows filtered through the cross cutouts in the balusters. The nun came back, but made no move to speak. I stood patiently across from her for a good five minutes. Just when I was going to question this woman, who'd obviously taken a vow of silence, another woman in identical garb came in.

"Miss Tatum?" she asked. I nodded as I confirmed my name *and* marital status. "Come back to the lounge."

I followed this second woman who wasn't nearly as pale or as tall. The "lounge" was the size of a private college dining hall. All that was missing were heavy wooden tables and benches.

A large unlit fireplace, nearly as tall as me, framed the far end of the room. A couple of mission-style chairs and a matching couch were all the seating provided. Following Cortez's lead, I took a seat after I'd unzipped my parka and stowed it next to me.

"You didn't say much on your phone call, so I'm wondering how I...we can help you."

In my line of work, the less said when setting up an interview, the better. Either the person overprepared with self-serving statements or was ready to stonewall with excuses. When I gave little, their curiosity about speaking with a reporter usually got the best of them. Despite how it looked on TV, heavy-handed techniques were rarely necessary. Everyone was the hero of their own story, and I could be the one to share that with the world.

"Unfortunately"—I leaned forward to convey sincerity

—"I do have some sad news to share. I'm here to ask you about Sister Angela Parker, who received her orders here."

"Oh, yes, Sister Parker. She's a dear."

Present tense and Cortez's residence in a convent some six hundred miles from Cleveland eliminated her as a suspect, in my mind at least. With her innocence solidified, I delivered the bad news.

"I'm sorry to have to tell you this, but Sister Parker passed away nine days ago."

"Oh!" Grief washed over Cortez's face. "I'm sorry to hear it. Sister Angela was so well-loved during her time here."

"That's what I'd like to ask you about, if you don't mind."

Cortez clutched at the large wooden cross hanging over her habit nearly to her waist. There was a long pause before she gave me an answer.

"I suppose." The nun lifted rimless glasses and dabbed at her eyes with her fingers. When that didn't work, she extracted a handkerchief from a hidden pocket. The square of cloth soaked up the remainder of her tears. She replaced her glasses and looked at me, clear-eyed and stoic.

I took my mini-recorder from my bag and placed it on the dark-stained wood table between us. "Okay if I record?"

Cortez nodded her agreement. I'd been recording interviews for years. It was a great offensive against any libel or slander suit an interviewee even had the merest hint of a thought of lodging. Everyone who came across as less than heroic said they were misquoted. It was almost never true.

I'd been gathering interviews and editing them for the podcast that I still hadn't had the guts to release. I wasn't even sure it was legal to record people for one purported purpose, say, an interview for the major Ohio newspaper, then use it for another—a podcast with little credibility and an even smaller following. Either way, her agreement was on the record. I'd sort out the rest later. Cortez had probably never heard of a podcast. Most people hadn't. The blog was gaining popularity, though. I'd have to look into whether a blogger could get a press card.

"How do...did you know Sister Angela?" I started as I usually did with the broadest question possible.

"We were ordained together here in 1965."

"Have you spoken with her since?" I tried to imagine the social lives of nuns. Came up with nothing. "Do you send letters or make visits to other convents?"

Cortez squinted at me. Tilted her head. Answered.

"We're friends on Facebook."

"Facebook?" Could have knocked me over with a feather with that one. It was both unsurprising and completely unexpected at the same time.

"We're also in an online Yahoo group together of nuns who came out of this convent. We also use chat often."

I wasn't sure this gothic building had much in the way of heat or electricity. The fact that there was high-speed internet hiding somewhere blew my mind. I mean, evangelical churches were on the forefront of technology, but the Catholic church seemed stuck in the dark ages in more ways than one. I took a moment, readjusted my frame of mind, pulled a notebook and pen from my messenger bag to give me an anchor in these uncharted waters, then got back to it.

"When you talked, did Sister Parker ever say anything about being in some kind of danger?"

Sister Cortez looked up at the vaulted ceiling. Wiped a stray tear from her eye, then looked at me.

"Not in the way that you're thinking. Have you heard of the Apostolic Visitation?"

I shook my head, imagining some kind of descent from heaven. "What is that?"

"The Vatican has a Congregation for Institutes of Consecrated Life and Societies of Apostolic Life," she started. I was glad for the recorder because this was well outside of the kind of thing I encountered on a regular basis. My lack of understanding must have come across in the involuntary shake of my head. "In light of the priest sex abuse scandal, the Church is investigating nuns," Cortez simplified.

My motto was that a poker face was the best face for a reporter. Despite that, I could feel my eyebrows inching up to my hairline as she described the church's attempt to lay some blame for men's behavior at the feet of the women who served the church selflessly. Felt like the Vatican was looking in all the wrong places. Instead of searching for bogeymen in the sacristy, they were looking for dirty laundry in the convent. I knew some reporters at the

Boston Globe who could and had pointed the church's bishops in the right direction.

"When was the last time you talked...or chatted online?"

Cortez's face got serious. It was the expression I saw most often when someone realized they could be truly helpful on a quest for the truth.

"Maybe before Thanksgiving or right after. Churches are very busy during the holidays, so it's quiet online at the end of the year. Maybe I should have checked in on her."

"Did you do that often? Check in?" I asked before she could talk herself into a shame and guilt spiral. I'd seen that one too many times. A kind of form of survivor's guilt it was.

"All the time. Nuns have been isolated, cut off from each other for centuries. This...social media thing has been a...dare I say it...Godsend. So in the group, we usually talk every day about devotion and the church, of course, but it's also a way to have community, especially as ours is dwindling by the day."

Before I'd come to this convent, I'd found research that talked about the great decline of women entering convents being such that there wouldn't be any more in the U.S. in the next thirty years unless there was some kind of recruitment miracle.

"Can I speak plainly?" I asked. Cortez was more of a realist than I'd expected. Kid-glove handling wasn't required.

"Sure. Go ahead."

"Sister Parker was found dead outside the convent where she lived in Cleveland. Unfortunately, she fell to her death from the window of her room." I paused for not only the gasp that came from Sister Cortez's mouth, but to give her a moment to absorb the information I was sharing. Death was one thing. Murder another.

"Was that what you meant by danger? Was she pushed?"

"That's the hundred-thousand-dollar question." Though Cortez had already turned me on to another line of investigation. Maybe Angela had found something or revealed something about a priest and he'd killed her to cover it up. Made the suspect list much more manageable.

"You're not a cop, so what's your interest?" When I'd said plain, I'd meant forthright. Cortez had obviously seen that as a two-way street. I countered the blunt question she'd put to me with another question.

"Are you aware of the investigation into Quinn by cops and prosecutors in Cleveland who are looking to file criminal charges?"

"It did come up in our chat."

"What was Sister Parker's general—I'm not sure of the right word—mood about the investigation?"

"There's no easy way to say this exactly." Cortez hesitated.

"We're plain speaking here," I reminded her.

"While the focus in the St. Ignatius investigation has been on the boys, what's gone overlooked is what's happening to nuns. I'm not saying that the abuse of children isn't a heinous thing. The extension of the statute of limitations allowing prosecution is a good idea that will deal with priests who otherwise would have gone unpunished. But what feels hidden just underneath is how sisters are faring."

"What's happening to nuns?" I asked, though after talking to Peter Parker I had a pretty good idea of the answer to the question I'd posed.

"The priests...they were abusing us too. Maybe not the same priests in all cases. All pedophiles may be predators, but not all predators are pedophiles. Some of them prey on any vulnerable population. And women who take a vow of chastity, but more to the point vows of poverty and obedience, are sitting ducks."

I was both surprised and not...*again*. While nuns were cloistered from most of society in many ways, they couldn't escape the world, the patriarchy, or the ills of either. When I hadn't spoken, struck dumb for the second time in a day, Cortez leaned forward, dropped her voice.

"Is there any chance of anyone being prosecuted for the crimes against *us*?" I could see her weighing what she was going to disclose.

"Depends on the facts. It's not something the police are looking into, but I am. And if there's anything that forces police and prosecutors to act, it's publicity. I'm not sure whether they're taking Parker's case seriously or whether it'll get buried in favor of the case that is on the front page. There's too much that's gone on for the child abuse to get swept under the rug."

"Not to sound like an evangelical, but I think you're a blessing from the Lord."

I'd take the compliment. Many others thought most journalists were the devil incarnate. With the invention of twenty-four-hour news, I was inclined to agree.

"What do I need to know about Sister Parker?" I asked, pen poised.

"I think we got along well because she was from Ohio. I was from Michigan. I know that it's an hour flight for most people. But once we got here, we didn't go back and forth. It's a ten-hour drive and we didn't have any money or a car. We were each other's bulwark against homesickness."

"Is convent life lonely?" I'd kind of thought of it like a college dorm. But with the silence of the woman who answered the door, it was more like a monastery.

"It's an adjustment from civilian life with friends of your choosing and a family to a cloistered life of devotion."

I noticed she didn't answer directly, but left it.

"Did you ever know Gregory Quinn? He started out in the Boston area not far from here."

"Unfortunately."

"Oh." I had to wonder if I was losing my edge. As a longtime crime reporter, I almost always assumed the worst of people or guessed at their motives. The Catholic church was outside my wheelhouse. Black was white and up was down. Or maybe I'd mistaken good for evil.

"There are some people that you meet," Cortez was saying, "that you know you'll never forget. In the beginning, I thought that was a good thing. Turns out I was right about the first and wrong about the second."

"Why were you wrong?"

"He's a predator."

"Of boys...children."

"No. Of everyone. We're all prey."

I let that sit for many long moments. The problem with my job is that it revealed that the world had so many monsters. Churches were no exception.

"Did he...hurt you?" I braced myself. A man with no compunction for hurting children may be far more cruel to adult women.

"My family, they came to the U.S. from Cuba. For many years before we got out, my parents had to regularly fight for what we needed—for survival. They taught us kids here those skills. For so long I thought it was stupid, learning how to defend ourselves, how to be self-sufficient in this land that was safe and had plenty.

"When Quinn was in his training at seminary, he was assigned to hold Mass for us. He was very friendly. Even charming, I'd say. Stayed for dinner on the days he was here. One night, he was very nice to me. It was like the sun was shining on me. He must have followed me upstairs. I didn't hear him come up behind me. He walked like a ninja. I was taking off my robes when he came in. My first instinct was to cover myself, to run. He was smooth-talking from the moment he shut the door behind him. He's very charismatic."

"Jeffrey Dahmer was said to be charismatic." It was the most often used adjective when people wrote about the brutal serial killer.

"Something like. Antelopes don't chase prey looking for the weakest of the herd for dinner. Humans aren't herbivores. Humans are no different than the world's fiercest carnivores. We have to use brute force if the prey isn't willing. In absence of that, we have to charm, cajole, persuade.

"Quinn tried that second approach. Talked about how difficult it was to honor the vow of celibacy. But if something happened between us, two celibates, then it would be okay because no one outside the church would be hurt. He got very close. Physically close. Too damned close. I acted before I thought. Shot out my arm and grabbed him by the throat a second before my knee went up. Just like my father had taught me all those years before."

"Did he leave willingly after that?" I asked. These kinds of stories went one of two ways. The attacker saw red and turned to the brute force she mentioned, or they went in search of easier prey.

"Once he was able to stand up straight, he left *me* alone. Never talked to me or bothered me again."

Easier prey, then. My sigh of relief was short-lived.

"But others weren't as lucky." My next question was wrapped in a statement.

"His desires went unsatisfied, that night at least."

Cortez stood. Walked toward the cold hearth, rested her hands on the large mantel. Praying without the kneeling. "But he was like a beast that couldn't be satisfied. Sister Angela told me years later that he visited her on one of his days here. She became his regular Wednesday night companion."

"Do you have any sense on whether the relationship was consensual?"

While her face said no, Cortez's shrug was more ambivalent. "Maybe it was consensual in the way that anyone with Stockholm syndrome consents."

"What gave you the impression that she'd gone from victim to sympathizer?" People were very critical of Patty Hearst, but they often forgot that the fourth F of the acute stress response was to fawn. Seemed to me like a good way to survive when playing dead wouldn't do.

"I had some suspicions," Cortez started. "She was changing, but trying to hide it. So I went to her on a night when Greg Quinn wasn't around." I noticed but didn't comment on her lack of honorific use. "It didn't take much to get her to open up. We were already close, and I think she really wanted to tell someone. He'd not only convinced her that he loved her, she believed somehow that they were this tragic love story. If only they could live a civilian life."

"Why couldn't they? It's not like they were cheating on their spouses or had kids to consider." I almost censored myself, but I didn't as we were speaking *plainly* after all. "It's not like the Catholic church is a cult. They do let people leave. There are tons of ex and lapsed Catholics all over the world, and it's not as if they're shunned by the rest of society."

"It's not that. Of course they could have left, though they'd probably have been counseled against it by the bishop because no one would have replaced them. Lifetime devotion is hard to come by these days."

"Then why?" I believed in not blaming the victim, but I did have to wonder why Sister Parker hadn't gotten out. It wasn't as if the nun were in need of a constant crop of new kids to abuse.

"Nuns and priests don't really have transferable skills. Gets worse as we all get older. We're not contributing to a pension, or a 401(k), or even social security."

All of that gave even someone as jaded as me pause.

"She's not much different than any other abused woman," I mused out loud. "Isolated. In love." Those last two words I said with air quotes. "And no clear path to get out because of lack of connection to family and financial constraints."

"It's an unholy mess." Cortez allowed a small smile at her choice of words.

"She followed him to Ohio?" I knew I was playing devil's advocate. Rightly or wrongly, people always asked the same question: *Why didn't she leave?* When a woman followed her abuser, especially when she didn't have kids, the questions were all the more pointed.

"He made it easy. Found her a place in the convent there. Set her up with the job at St. Ignatius."

"Teaching?"

"Administration. Us nuns hardly teach anymore. Most diocese schools have handed that over to the certified professionals."

"I know that you're here in Boston and haven't talked to her since last year, but do you have any idea who'd have had a reason to push her out a window?"

"I think Quinn is on the hook for that one."

I'd expected more hemming and hawing. For some reason, her quick rush to judgment left me with doubts.

"Why? He was getting everything he wanted. Her. Kids." I almost mentioned the real estate he'd slipped out from under the Parker family's collective noses. But I didn't want to influence her answers if she didn't know about it. Sister Parker had years of compartmentalizing her life. I didn't yet know who knew what.

"She was going to testify if asked," Cortez stated.

"Wasn't she worried about being implicated?" I asked. "Was she seeking immunity?"

"She didn't have any idea of the extent of the stuff with the boys. Quinn had mentioned slipping once under the influence of alcohol. Sister Angela talked about this other priest, Morales, being a bad guy. But all that stuff in the papers was completely new to her. For all those years she'd thought she was his only vice."

Monsignor Gregory Quinn went right to the top of my suspect list as he'd been on Cortez's. My only decision was how much to share with Loren Logan. It was looking like an information trade was in order.

FOURTEEN
NICOLE
FEBRUARY 2, 2009

t had been many moons since I'd been downstairs in Cleveland city's municipal court. The lower court was appropriately on the bottom floors.

Some states had unified their court system, but Ohio still split out different functions to different courts, even if most were in the same building or complex.

While common pleas handled felonies and took up the top ten floors, the municipal court adjudicating mostly misdemeanors got the first three.

I was in courtroom 3-D where preliminary hearings were held. When I'd filed criminal charges against Monsignor Gregory Quinn, I'd fully expected to receive a written waiver of this hearing from his lawyer and move right on to his swift guilty plea to a felony sex abuse charge. That shortcut would have solved two big problems: Rivera being outed and Quinn getting acquitted.

Bringing this single charge was a stretch on my part. In my defense, though, I'd figured the defendant would be so embarrassed that he'd waive this hearing, plea out, and be grateful there was only a single charge rather than the dozens I could have theoretically lobbed against him. Catholics weren't exactly known for their Quaker-like peacefulness, but I hadn't expected a disgraced priest to fight.

Without a plea from Quinn, I was at a loss on how to turn my single chance at conviction into a sure win. Pope wouldn't accept anything less than that.

Promptly at eight thirty, the municipal court bailiff started calling cases. It was the usual string of nonviolent drug offenses, OVIs, and domestic violence. I flipped through my file in last-minute preparation for my time in front of the judge. Coffee had not chased the fog from my morning brain.

"Ohio versus Gregory Quinn!"

The bailiff's cry was my cue to make my way to the prosecutor's table. I put my intimidatingly large, boxy trial bag on the top. It was mostly empty, but no one else had to know that. The box's sturdy leather sides and top hid the contents or lack thereof.

"Nicole Long, assistant county prosecutor for the state," I said once I'd steadied myself.

"Gordon Yarbrough for Monsignor Gregory Quinn." I knew the use of the defendant's title was no accident. Nearly a third of the city's population was Catholic. Even with non-believers and lapsed, there was a certain reverence for the church that had not lessened even with the abuse scandals piling up like Mass cards at a funeral.

The judge, perhaps sensing the import of the case, scooted her chair forward and leaned toward us.

"Mr. Quinn—"

"He's monsignor or father, Your Honor," Yarbrough insisted. Ballsy move correcting a judge right out of the gate. Without a pause, Judge Marguerite Bowers Graves resumed speaking as if the defense attorney had never uttered a word.

"*Mister* Quinn, you are here for a preliminary hearing. You have been charged with gross sexual imposition and sexual abuse of a minor." Judge Graves read the relevant statutory provisions while the gallery grew quiet.

There were a few reporters in the back, but the rest of the audience was filled with the usual assortment of defendants, their families, and lawyers. Without turning around, I knew without a shadow of a doubt that the crime beat journalists hadn't any expectation of today's spectacle but were riveted nonetheless. Clevelanders still read the paper...in print, and being the first to print with a story was still important.

"Mr. Yarbrough, is your client going to waive?"

Invisibly I crossed my fingers hoping for a miracle.

"No, Your Honor."

It wasn't to be. Our evidence was going to be put to the test. Rivera's honor as well. Municipal court flew well under the radar. I'd have liked to keep my amateur-level tactics in the local court behind the third floor's closed doors. With a defendant so notorious, though, keeping my little play a secret was a toss-up.

It was my best play.

It was my *only* play, really.

"Well, *Mister* Quinn, I have the obligation to explain your rights to you." Something about the third "Mister" unsettled me. Did the judge doth protest too much? Was she biased the other way? In most cases, we knew a judge's predilections. Some sentenced harshly when a defendant exercised their right to trial, crowding a judge's docket. Others were lenient on women or marijuana offenses. But knowing how any given judge, more than half of whom were Catholic, felt about priest abuse was a mystery.

I looked at Quinn, who'd remained silent in the face of the judge's inquiry. He was expressionless. When the judge didn't speak, he finally nodded in acknowledgement.

"Thank you, Mr. Quinn. I'm going to need you to speak aloud. Do you understand?"

Goosed by Yarbrough, I finally heard Quinn speak.

"Yes, Your Honor."

I'm not sure what I thought the voice of a pedophile —*a predator*—would sound like. But it was so very ordinary that I was disappointed. It was nothing like the hoarse, throaty rasp of a devil incarnate I expected or like the smarmy timbre of the man who'd harmed me.

I noticed that the monsignor had gotten the judge's

honorific correct, even if she'd refused to use his. Such was the power dynamic in every courtroom.

"This hearing is to determine whether or not the charges just read can stand. The prosecutor is required to present evidence to the court, which in this case is me, of the probability of your guilt. Do you understand, Mr. Quinn?"

"Yes, Your Honor."

Judge Graves lifted a laminated sheet from the bench.

"Further, the Ohio codes require I advise you of the following: First, that any testimony offered by a witness on your behalf, if unfavorable, can be used against you at trial. Second, you can make a statement, not under oath, for the purpose of explaining any facts in evidence. You can, however, refuse to make any statement, and that can be held against you during this hearing or at any subsequent trial on these charges. Any questions so far?"

"No, Your Honor."

Graves flipped the laminated paper to the other side like she'd ordered her mains and was about to check out a drinks menu.

"At the conclusion of this hearing, one of three things will happen: Either I will find there is sufficient evidence of a felony to bind you over to common pleas court, or that there's sufficient evidence of a misdemeanor and you'll be the subject of further proceedings in this court. Or I will find that there's insufficient evidence of any crime and you will be discharged from custody. Any questions?"

I was surprised when the defendant uttered one. It was very rare for the accused to speak up voluntarily.

"If you discharge me, does that mean I can't be tried again on these charges?"

"As your attorney should have advised you, double jeopardy does not attach with this hearing. Only if and when a jury panel is sworn. Knowing this, would you like to waive your right to this hearing?"

"No, Your Honor. I want to have full due process."

I had to marvel at the gall of Quinn. Defendants were always going on about the rights *they* deserved, though they'd been more than happy to deprive their victims of their right to be left unmolested.

"Do you understand your rights and obligations as I've explained them today?" Judge Graves asked Quinn.

"Yes, Your Honor."

"Then let's proceed. Ms. Long, please call your first witness."

I shuffled my papers a bit as if I were deciding which of a long list of finger-pointing, damning witnesses to call. This was the first time I'd ever gone to a prelim with only a single witness. Usually it was a cop or two. Maybe the witness to the crime.

Never the victim.

I always saved the victim for trial. In this case, though, the other only witness was dead. But I'd put out the bait and Quinn hadn't taken it. So I was here pushing a strategy I wasn't fully sure would work. But giving up would read to the press and abuse survivors like failure. Rock, meet hard place.

"Your Honor, I call Brandon Rivera to the stand."

There was the sound of scuffling behind me as Rivera made his way down the aisle. The bailiff helped him get situated in the chair and swore him in. After a deep sigh and a sip of fortification from my travel mug, I straightened my notes and got into it.

I had Rivera give a briefer retelling than he'd done in the Mexican restaurant. I didn't need to persuade a jury of guilt beyond a reasonable doubt. I only had to convince a single judge that it was more likely than not that Quinn had committed a crime. A lot easier burden.

After Rivera ended his testimony describing how he'd been sodomized by Quinn in the Lorain Avenue apartment, I stepped back. In a preliminary hearing, both the judge and the defense attorney could question the witness. I'd tried to prepare Rivera as best I could, but there was no doubt this was going to be hard for him, even if it was a necessary part of the adversarial process. My only hope was that Rivera's possible reputation hadn't preceded him. Mild-mannered art teacher was all I wanted anyone to know about him.

"Before you had the brownies at the apartment on Lorain Avenue, what had you eaten that day?" Yarbrough asked while he stood and buttoned his suit jacket.

"Nothing much, I think I'd had a Coke for breakfast. Maybe a couple of Chips Ahoy."

Not the breakfast of champions. No parent around to

make sure he had a balanced diet. Easy prey for the likes of Quinn.

"You testified that Sister Parker offered you a lot of different options when it came to snacks. Can you elaborate?"

"It was like going to a party store. There were those chocolate cakes with the spiral on top, Twinkies, coffee cake, and then Oatmeal Creme Pies and Pecan Spinwheels."

"And then what you have described as"—Yarbrough used air quotes here—"pot brownies?"

"Yes."

"Why didn't you go for the known quantity in flashy packaging? Hostess or Little Debbie? Why did you choose something as plain as a brownie?"

I wanted to object to Yarbrough skirting close to blaming the victim, but that wasn't against court procedure, just common dignity.

"I was thinking of my mom," Rivera answered.

"Excuse me?"

"If I came home and told her I'd eaten junk food, she'd have been mad. But if I told her that a nun had offered me something homemade, she'd have understood."

"Why is that?" Yarbrough's tone was unusually cordial. If I'd had hackles, they'd have risen.

"She had a rule about not turning down homemade food people offered. She said it was rude."

"Fair enough reason. It's always good to listen to your

mom. Sound advice for visits. What made you think these brownies were laced?"

"When I was there, it was like I was underwater. I couldn't move as fast or even think as clearly. Later experience gave me words for it. When I was at college at Princeton, pot brownies were really popular. The first time I had them there, it brought me right back to the time Sister Parker had given them to me."

"What was the effect on you, of eating these while you were at the Lorain apartment?"

"Couch lock. I mean, it was like I couldn't move. Or maybe more like I was all the way at the bottom of a swimming pool trying to push my way up to the surface."

"Let's go back to...Princeton was it?" Yarbrough questioned.

"Yes, in New Jersey."

"Ivy League school."

"One of eight. Not Harvard."

"Looked it up this morning," Yarbrough said, as if he were Joe Lunchbox. "Six hundred acres. Tuition at thirty-four thousand. That seem right?"

"It was cheaper when I was there, but the rest is right."

Unless his mother's financial situation had improved overnight, then he'd probably been on scholarship. In his bespoke suite and neatly cut Bill Clinton hair, he looked like the rich kids he'd learned to emulate.

I wished I were telepathic because I wasn't picking up what Yarbrough was putting down. I debated whether a sip from my mug would make it clearer or foggier. I elected to take one, hoping for the first.

"When you were high on the pot brownies at Princeton, what did you do?"

"How do you mean?" Rivera was confused as well.

"Literally what did you do? Stand up? Go for a run? Study for a test?"

Rivera shook his head sharply.

"Didn't do much at all. Couldn't really when my limbs were heavy and my mind was moving slow. I don't know. Mostly sat on the floor of the common room. Watched some movie that was much funnier when I was high."

"Do you remember the title of the movie?"

"Nope. A bad comedy, though. Someone had rented it on VHS."

"What else do you remember from that first night you were high in Princeton?"

"Not much," he admitted. It was just at that moment, I realized the tack Yarbrough was taking and my victim was about to bury himself as if he'd dug his own grave.

I jumped up.

"Objection, Your Honor!"

The judge turned toward me.

"Basis?"

"Relevance. While I appreciate this little walk down memory lane, we're talking about a sex crime committed in 1992 when Mr. Rivera was a vulnerable young boy. Not what he was doing while in college."

"I'll move on, Your Honor," Yarbrough said, nullifying my objection.

Judge Graves nodded toward Yarbrough, her accompanying hand motion communicating that the defense attorney needed to move on.

"Mr. Rivera, you don't remember much from the night in Princeton, but you claim to remember in stark detail all that happened in Cleveland some seventeen years ago, much farther in time from today."

"He's testifying, Your Honor," I protested, as if my words could pry the metaphorical shovel from Rivera's hands.

"I have a question of Mr. Rivera," Judge Graves interjected, ending what could have been a fight between Yarbrough and me. "I'd like to know how you can remember startling detail from when you were a fifteen-year-old child, who at the time was smaller in size and stature and hadn't eaten all day before consuming pot brownies, but can't remember a single thing from college, which was years later and by your own testimony you weren't nearly as high?"

I felt my mouth fall open. Closed it. The judge was picking up Yarbrough's baton. This couldn't have gone any worse. Like everyone else in the silent courtroom, I waited for the answer, hoping above hope it was good.

"I remember because it was the first time I was sexually assaulted by *Monsignor* Quinn."

Boom went the dynamite. Rivera had done what I couldn't: try to save my case.

I had to hope it was enough to refute Yarbrough's well-placed argument that someone high on drugs for the first time wouldn't have perfect recall of his assault.

Yarbrough chipped away at Rivera a little more but ultimately left him alone.

"Ms. Long, any further witnesses?"

Normally, I'd have a cop or two, maybe someone who'd been at the crime scene, but with a crime that was seventeen years ago, that wasn't an option this early in the game. It took time to find, nurture, and prepare witnesses. And one of those was dead. This preliminary hearing was going to be decided on he said, he said.

"No, Your Honor," I admitted.

Judge Graves looked at the notes or whatever it was she'd scratched on her legal pad. Pulled the leather portfolio closer to her. Took a beat or twenty before she spoke. The gallery that was normally a low hum of murmurs and ill-timed phone notifications was unusually silent.

"Mr. Quinn. I've had an opportunity to listen to the evidence put forward by the state in the testimony of Mr. Rivera. And while I do think it's possible something happened in that apartment on Lorain Avenue, I think the witness's admitted impairment does present a problem of proof without corroboration. For that reason only, I grant the defendant's motion to discharge for failure of proof.

"Ms. Long, when you shore up your case, you are more than welcome to bring charges again or move for indictment." The gavel fell. "It is so ordered."

FIFTEEN
NICOLE
FEBRUARY 3, 2009

"The *municipal* court discharged Monsignor Quinn yesterday," Lori Pope said. I worked hard to keep my face neutral because my boss seized on weakness like a lion in the African Serengeti. "What's your plan to save this case? Every other priest has moved voluntarily, *been* moved involuntarily, died, or resigned. But here we have a career pedophile, who by last count, has abused at least thirty-five different boys, walking the snowy streets of Cleveland with no consequences." Lori Pope said all of that without so much as a "hi, how are you?"

"Good morning, Nicole. How was your weekend, Nicole? Would you like a chance to get some coffee, Nicole?" I mimicked the greeting I should have received from my boss. It wasn't done to mock her but to relieve the extreme stress I'd been under for the last twenty-four hours. I'd been waiting for the other high-heeled shoe to drop all the way from her office on the eleventh floor from the moment I'd taken my defeated self up the elevator from Judge Graves' municipal courtroom to this office.

When Pope hadn't appeared or summoned me by lunch yesterday, I'd gone home and given myself a different kind of solace. Hangover only partially tamed by two hastily swallowed pain pills only twenty minutes ago, I didn't have the strength to handle the beating she was now prepared to deliver.

"We don't do small talk."

"I have a lot of cases on my plate. Why don't we set up a meeting later," I said. I figured with a few more pills in hand and maybe a nip of the hair of the dog, I'd be in better form in a few hours. "I can review the file and meet with you later today. There are a few pleas I could run by you then as well."

"I don't care if you plea every defendant on the common pleas docket to a misdemeanor. We don't need a meeting, Nicole."

"Okay." I braced for my scolding.

"Where are we on the Monsignor Gregory Quinn matter? You may remember that he's accused of molesting dozens of children from St. Ignatius. You didn't run this single Rivera charge by me or the fact that you decided to toss caution to the wind and try your luck with a muni judge instead of the grand jury.

"Obviously that worked out as well as anything could in a baby court like that. What happened to all of the other crimes against all of those other boys? Surely we're not just walking away from this case. We've promised those boys that we're going to do everything in our power to bring this guy to justice. Yet, we've got zero charges pending."

I didn't point out it was *her* promise at a press conference to the voters who could get her reelected. Not to the victims.

"Did you see my memo?" I often treated Pope like a toddler. If I waved a hand over in one direction, she'd look. If I threw glitter in another, she'd marvel at the sparkles. I only needed to decide today's distraction.

My head pounded.

I swallowed.

Waited.

"I couldn't quite believe what you wrote in it, so I'm here to let you explain to me in person how *I*"—she jabbed her finger on my desk—"*the* Cuyahoga County prosecutor don't have jurisdiction over Monsignor Quinn's many, many crimes."

I wanted to tell her to save the hyperbole for the next press conference, but I wasn't so brave nor stupid.

"He was a smart cookie. I only have evidence of a single crime against a child here in Cuyahoga County, Ohio. That was Rivera."

"If not here, where?" Pope asked, as if we were all prisoners of county borders.

"Guatemala."

"What?" she asked, her face all screwed up. Obviously

she hadn't read my memo. She'd never let on, but I would pay for her ignorance.

"You remember Justin McPhee talking about him going to Bárcena? That town where the school is? Well, that's where the bulk of the...assaults happened."

"Bulk. What happened here?"

"So far. I've interviewed seventy-five men who were possible victims. Many here in person. The rest by phone for those that scattered. There's only one story of a kid who was molested in an apartment on Lorain Avenue. That was Rivera."

"An apartment?"

"Jesuit priests don't take a vow of poverty. Monsignor Quinn owned this commercial building with an apartment above it. He took Rivera there."

"A whole building?"

"Small. Residential over a single commercial space."

I watched my boss take that in. Nothing about this case was going as expected. I could tell that Pope had hoped for a meeting with the bishop where she offered reduced charges for a perp walk. Some kind of contrition, maybe even a joint press conference with her and Bishop Kollie. Her in a suit. Him in robes. A big win for her. Boost to her reelection campaign. All with me doing the work to make that happen. Not a single thing had gone well enough for that scene to play out. Plus we had a nun dead in suspicious circumstances. So many side plots from the main play.

"This makes no sense, Nicole. Predators don't work

this way. You're saying he was able to save his desires and all his predilections until the one or two blissful weeks he was in South America?"

I kept my shudder at her use of the word blissful to myself. In her own way, she was a predator. She couldn't know I was prey.

"Plenty of people do it. It's what spurs the sex tourism industry, like Thailand or Colombia. These guys, they save up money and vacation time, then travel to Bangkok or Cartagena. Then come home and do it again the next year."

"You know what those guys always have? Magazines. Videos."

She looked at me expectantly.

"Well, we haven't gotten a search warrant," I said. Shrugged. "So maybe there's child porn."

"Why haven't the cops done a search?" Pope probed.

"We need a basis. Just having a reputation as a rapist doesn't automatically lead to one being in possession of child porn."

"So don't go after his office or whatever at the church or his rooms in the rectory. We're talking a regular old property," she insisted. As if judges were jumping up and down to upend a priest's constitutional rights. "Why can't you start there?"

"With what basis? A rape occurred there about twenty years ago? No judge is going to fall for that. Talk about disappearing evidence and spoilation."

"What are you doing? We have rape. We have a

suspect. We have the will of the people, the legislature, the courts to finally go after men who've escaped crimes for decades, and all you're doing is fishing in the shallow end of the pond."

She was right, though. I was making all sorts of mistakes. Maybe the whole forest was blocking the trees.

"There's still the murder of Sister Parker," I threw out like a lifeline. Didn't need to be long in these superficial waters.

The truth was Logan had a new murder on his plate, and without me goosing him, this crime along with Sister Parker's death was about to be put on the shelf pending a coroner report. Even then, without a suspect... I decided to throw suspicion off myself.

When Pope didn't bite, I threw up another roadblock because I wasn't ready to lose again so spectacularly in public. Everyone was going to think I wasn't sober, that I wasn't ready for major crimes. This job was all I had. There was nowhere else to go from here.

"After yesterday, we may look like we've got a vendetta," I tried again. I needed her to go. To have a moment to beat myself up, have a drink in commiseration, then get on with it: Quinn, Parker, the rest of my job putting Cleveland's worst behind bars. The last, at least, would give me some kind of vindication, solidify my reasons for being here.

"But we do. We're seeking vengeance on behalf of those who were victimized by this man."

"That's one way to look at it." My tone was neutral. I

was only waiting for her to decree what was to come next. After my screwup, I was happy to turn over the decision-making.

"That's the *only* way to look at it. Any cop worth their salt, or prosecutor, for that matter, would be able to get a warrant application for the Lorain Avenue property past a judge. I bet you not one of them on the bench wants to be on the wrong side of history on this."

"Maybe not. But this is a big case. Moving fast could be a problem." It had been a problem when I'd lobbed that first salvo without knowing all the possible pitfalls. Now cautiousness would guide my way. I couldn't lose again. My only hope was that Lori Pope didn't ask about ownership of the Lorain Avenue property. My failure to check county records would be glaring if brought to light. The property could well have been sold ten times since 1992.

"Moving slow looks like inaction." Pope actually wagged a beringed finger at me.

"There's careful and there's stupid," I countered. There's nothing Pope hated less than looking stupid.

"I think Sister Parker's murder is something we need to prosecute." I hoped my desperation didn't show with that statement. I had a feeling, but no facts behind it. But instead of hand-waving and glitter, this was throwing a firecracker over the fence.

"Sister who?" Pope had tunnel vision.

"Sister Angela Parker. Mary Elizabeth Parker is her legal name."

"Murder?"

"She was a nun who facilitated Quinn's crimes against the boys."

"What do you mean...facilitated? How was she not part of the original investigation?"

"It was something that evolved. This was an investigation into priests. Nuns weren't originally part of the equation. They never had been in any other case we've studied. We'd have gotten to her, eventually. But who would suspect a nun of delivering boys to a priest to molest? It doesn't fit with any of the patterns or cases we've known of so far."

"Sometimes I think your...experience clouds your judgment." Again, I made an effort not to flinch at her unkindness. She continued, "Do you remember your prosecution of Sledge Hammer?"

"Of course," I said while gritting my teeth. Who wouldn't remember losing twice against Casey Cort as I tried and failed to bring down the city's most notorious sex trafficking ring.

"Girls were delivered to him. That guy who worked for him was clean cut, seemed nice, not overly violent or brutal, but he was still procuring and providing underage girls for his boss."

"I get it." I didn't, actually, but pretended for the sake of this conversation. "Anyway, Parker was pushed out of a convent window—"

"What? How did you not tell me this before? When did it happen?"

"January tenth."

"That's twenty-two days ago, and you're just bringing this to me now?" I didn't correct her assumption. Once she left, I'd forward her the email I'd sent summarizing my thoughts on Parker and Quinn. My ass would be covered.

"The death has yet to be ruled a homicide."

"What's the holdup?"

"Logan. Loren Logan. Neil Walsh. Coroner's office. It's not on the fast track. Plus, the church isn't exactly open to us these days. They don't trust we're asking what we're asking."

I could practically see the gears turning in my boss's head. Pope was more politic than smart. It was a case of dueling priorities. Either we go after Quinn with only one victim, or find and prosecute the murder of a nun. I knew which I'd choose, but despite my deputy title and the new brass affixed to my office door, I wasn't calling the shots.

"It's too bad we can't prosecute him for grooming," Pope spitballed.

"If you're willing to turn it over to the feds, they can do that. Section twenty-four twenty-two of the federal criminal code will give a defendant ten to twenty for coercion that leads to foreign travel and illegal sexual contact."

I'd done the research one night when I'd had too much bourbon for a sober woman and had needed to know that there was a proper punishment out there for Quinn if we so chose. Someone needed to get what they'd deserved even if our office couldn't get the credit.

"What about Ohio's coercion law?" Pope asked. I knew that her glory-hogging would keep the case from the feds.

She was still mad about our losing out to them on the Judge Eamon Brody case and the big sex trafficking case. Bottom line is that the Department of Justice had powers we didn't.

"You could drive a tractor-trailer truck through section twenty-nine oh five. First, the child has to be under fourteen, which doesn't apply here. He always did the trips in the spring, and all the boys were fifteen by that second semester, if they were freshmen, which most weren't. Second, the perpetrator has to do it without parental consent. In every single case, there was a detailed, signed permission slip. The diocese wouldn't have let the kids go without it."

The Catholic church always protected themselves. It was an institution built on self-preservation.

My voice was all confidence even if I hadn't yet checked whether every *I* was dotted and *T* crossed on permission slips or checked birth certificates for a precocious child who may have skipped a grade. Managing my sobriety and chasing down every possible legal theory weren't compatible.

"Which puts this squarely in the hands of Guatemala and the likelihood of their prosecution or the United States Attorney's Office," Pope accurately concluded.

I only nodded. I left out the fact that it was the Department of Justice that had finally brought down Sledge Hammer's syndicate. They'd won where I'd lost—twice. Not that Pope would cede jurisdiction...yet. Not as long as she had something to gain. If the tide turned, though, she'd be glad-handing with the U.S. Attorney at the next press conference. For once, I think I needed something for my career more than she did for hers.

"I have a theory." I threw out my last distraction like candy.

"Go on." Pope rolled her hand and wrist.

"Sister Angela Parker was going to testify against Quinn. Dodds was this close"—I put my fingers together —"to getting her to talk." It was an exaggeration...maybe a bit of a fabrication, but one Pope wouldn't check. After that night in the Mexican restaurant, Dodds had made some headway in getting a second meeting with Sister Parker. During the first, the nun had towed the party line of non-culpability of every crucifix-wearing church member.

Because Parker was brainwashed or because the nun didn't see anything wrong with what she'd done, Dodds and I hadn't yet figured out. I took a deep breath as if I'd been deep in thought and said to Pope on an exhale, "I think we should check where he was that night because I think he should be the prime suspect. I still have my eye on Justin McPhee, but that may have been a false start."

"Another way to get to Quinn?" Pope was scratching her chin.

"Murder *is* a life sentence." Sexual assault wasn't. I could see the moment she took the bait in the flick of her eyes.

"You're head of major crimes. Make it happen."

SIXTEEN

BLAKE

The internet was finally living up to its hype. Several database providers gave me access to their information in the comfort of my own home and made it easier to find public records. As happens when government partners with private industry, the fees were high and starting to rack up. When I'd been at the newspaper, the cost of research had been invisible to us reporters.

Today, I was going old-school because in-person records searches were still free. No government contractor had yet figured out a way to put a price on that. Plus, with ten-plus inches of snow on the ground, the roads had been empty as was the basement of the clerk's office. Quinn's unannounced hearing had provided more leads, for which I was grateful because after my trips to Solon and Massachusetts, I'd run out of lines of inquiry.

It had only been a stroke of luck that had landed me in the municipal court on the day of Quinn's preliminary hearing. Turned out that one of the followers of my blog, *And Then the Murders Began*, worked the clerk's office at the lower court.

The deputy clerk had emailed me to double-check that the Quinn on the docket was the same Quinn in the papers. I'd called her right away, and when she read the charges to me, I'd hung up and had driven downtown as fast as I could on icy roads covered with a thin coating of fresh snow.

All the way west toward the courthouse, I flicked through the AM news stations looking for a special report on the notorious priest. None came from the staticky broadcasts. Sure that either I or the city court clerk had made some kind of error, I almost turned around.

There was no way an attention hog like Lori Pope would have filed charges and not have announced it from every rooftop. She'd have wanted the glory buffeted by a perfectly filmed perp walk. But another hour of white-knuckling it back home was more unappealing than staying the course.

Whether it was him or not, I was going to get a coffee and spend an hour or so thawing out in the courtroom. Maybe something would come on the docket and be juicy in its own right. Or maybe a case would spark something else I should add to my list to investigate and report on. One crime did not make a blog or a podcast for that matter.

I'd quit brainstorming when I'd seen Quinn and his fancy lawyer walk down the hall. Immediately, I'd tossed my unfinished coffee in the bin and had hustled my way to the courtroom.

After Nicole Long had tried and failed miserably to get the municipal judge to bind Quinn over to felony court, I knew why Pope had kept it quiet. There was something wrong with the case. There was no way a man rumored to have abused upwards of two dozen kids wouldn't have already been indicted by a grand jury.

There had to be a problem with the evidence or a procedural error had been made along the way. There was no way Long or Pope were going to tell me, even with my *Plain Dealer* badge dangling in front of them, what the true story was. So I'd gone home, posted about the failed hearing, then scoured my notes for clues.

The one thing that had struck me was the issue of real estate. First Quinn pulled Parker's family's property right from under their noses. Then he was buying at least one mixed-use building on the west side, if Rivera's testimony were true.

Either Quinn was part-time priest, part-time real estate mogul, or there was something more sinister going on. Rather than speculate, I decided to get my hands dirty with actual paper research. The county building was on Lakeside. As cold as that sounded with arctic winds coming straight from Canada across Lake Erie and cutting through my parka like an icicle, I made my way to the WPA-era granite edifice.

Dutifully, I walked past the classical Greek columns and magazine-worthy marble mezzanine, then took the elevator to the basement. The computers were ancient affairs that functioned like the later years of DOS or the last gasp of Windows 3.1. It was going to take a while.

I unzipped my coat, then my bag. Pulled out the small notebook I was using for this case. Then after commandeering the newest of the aging desktops, I typed in my best guess at the address that Rivera had described. During my drive over to that neighborhood, I'd clocked only four blocks that could fit the description in his testimony. I'd marked down the twenty-six buildings' addresses. I typed in one after another after another, quickly skimmed the ownership looking for Quinn, then moved to the next when I struck out. I did this twenty-two times while slowly disrobing, peeling away one layer at a time. The radiators were on full blast. On the twenty-third search, I typed, then skimmed, then nearly dropped every piece of clothing I was holding in my lap.

Laying the pile of fabric on another wood chair, I scrolled up and down the record, not once, not twice, but three times to make sure my mind wasn't playing tricks on me. Then I asked the admin working behind the counter to get the laser copy from the printer behind her. After a search through the detritus of my messenger bag, I found and extracted the magnifying glasses I saved for microfiche and looked at the warm sheet she handed over. The information was the same in black and white as it had been in green on black. 3232 Lorain Avenue did not belong to Monsignor Quinn. Not one bit. The current owner was one Mary Elizabeth Parker or, in the case of her death, her heirs or assigns.

SEVENTEEN
JUSTIN
FEBRUARY 6, 2009

"Thank you for coming in today," Nicole Long said. I was back in the same conference room I'd visited two times before in the last few weeks. But the people in the room and the feeling in the air were far different than the last time.

Casey Cort was on my right. Across the table were Long, a detective I'd been introduced to as Loren Logan, and another attorney whom I'd come up against nearly a decade ago when I'd worked in juvenile court, Valerie Dodds.

I just nodded in acknowledgement. Casey did the talking.

"We're only here as a courtesy," she started. "To clear my client's name. That said, Justin isn't answering a single question that would lead to evidence that could be used against him in common pleas court."

"We'd expect no less," Dodds responded.

"How did you know Monsignor Gregory Quinn?" It was Long's first question. Casey and I had worked out a system. Until she nodded, I wasn't to utter a single word. As a lawyer whose job was to speak up and defend, keeping quiet was hard. But I bit my tongue. After more than a decade of practice I held no illusions about justice.

"My client isn't going to answer that. I believe that you have already extensively interviewed him about his relationship to Quinn."

"What about Sister Angela Parker?" Long asked. "What can you tell us about your relationship with her?"

"Again, he's not answering."

"So are you going to just decline to answer every question?" Long was audibly exasperated, as if she'd expected one attorney represented by another to behave as carelessly as the average defendant.

"My client is not sending himself to jail." Casey shook her head forcefully. "Not while I'm sitting here."

"What is it going to take?" Long had finally asked the magic question. As Casey had predicted, Long needed me more than I needed them. There was nothing that could change what had happened to me. I wasn't so naïve as to think punishment of Quinn would wave my trauma away like a magic wand. But Pope's, Long's, and probably even Logan's and Dodds' careers were hanging in the balance.

"Transactional immunity," Casey stated rather than requested.

It was a big ask. Blanket immunity meant that I could

never be prosecuted for anything related to what I said here.

Valerie Dodds actually laughed out loud.

"I'm not sure what's so funny." Casey's tone was drop-dead serious. "I'm aware of your usual suspects. Your usual defendants. The attorneys that don't much care about their clients. This here"—she circled her index finger—"is not that. So, immunity or we get up and leave."

To put a fine point on it, we stood, gathered our stuff, and walked out of the conference room. Before we could get too far down the hall, Long, her high heels clicking rapidly, came up behind us.

"Why did you leave?" Long's voice was conciliatory, as if we were the best of friends chatting about the weather and not prosecutor and potential defendant.

"I didn't want to interrupt your laugh fest. You have our conditions."

Long looked down the hall toward the conference room and elevator.

"Let's talk."

She and Casey moved away in the opposite direction. They whispered loudly for a good five minutes. Eventually they quieted and shook hands. Nicole went to the elevators, jabbing at the call button. Casey came toward me. We moved as far from the conference room and any other stray prosecutors as possible.

"It worked, to a degree," Casey said.

"So use immunity."

This would only protect me from the use of today's

testimony against me. If the cops or prosecutors found independent evidence of any crime I'd committed, they could hang me out to dry.

"As long as you didn't kill anyone, then that should be sufficient."

"I promise that the father of your child is not a murderer."

Casey studiously ignored my last statement, but she didn't refute it. She lifted her coat from her arm and slipped it on her shoulders. "Let's get breakfast. By the time we get back, they should have a written agreement."

"Written?" I was surprised. Somehow I thought their handshake would be enough.

"Maybe Dodds and Long are aboveboard. I mean, we know Dodds and she's always been truthful. But I don't trust anyone who has a liquid breakfast."

So she'd observed what I had, that our supposedly sober prosecutor wasn't.

"Fair enough."

"Have you thought about the email I sent you?" Even with the full-time care and feeding of an infant, Casey had put together a comprehensive defense strategy, then sent me the same.

"Yes." I nodded. I'd read it twice and committed much to memory.

"Can you talk about Quinn and Parker? Based on what this written agreement is supposed to contain, both are up for investigation."

We didn't exactly go to breakfast. Instead, we got

coffees and muffins in the newly opened Starbucks in Key Tower. When Casey's phone pinged, she put down her nearly empty cup and read the notification.

"Let's go." Looking at me, she paused for a moment. The look in her eyes was one I'd tried to avoid. It wasn't pity exactly, but it wasn't raging desire, either. I couldn't decide what would make me comfortable given the circumstances we found ourselves in. She patted my forearm.

"Only if you're ready. You *can* walk away now. There is zero obligation to help out Long or Pope or the prosecutor's office. Or even—Justin—your fellow victims. Not if the personal cost to you is too high. So, go upstairs or go home?"

"I'd rather have immunity," I said.

"Then back to the ninth floor we go."

Casey gave the use-immunity agreement a good ten minutes of scrutiny. Only when she'd crossed out a few words, replaced them, initialed her changes, and passed it around for approval did she sign before giving it to me. Ignoring years of training in the place of nascent trust, I signed without perusal. Long signed on behalf of Pope, and both she and Casey tucked a fully executed copy into their respective portfolios.

"Where were you the night of January tenth?" Long directed the first question at me. This time, I knew she expected an answer.

"Home. Alone."

Casey leaned down to her messenger bag and

retrieved a small stack of papers. She slipped the first two across the table.

"This is Justin McPhee's internet data usage for the IP address assigned to his DSL account. Here's a printout of his browser history."

Goodness knows I'd left the Catholic church a long time ago, but I was thanking God right now that I'd kept my internet browsing clean that night.

"Long story short, he watched two episodes of *Mad Men*."

Dodds pointed to some lines that were covered with thick black marker. "What's that?"

"He also did legal research. In order to protect attorney-client privilege and attorney work product, those searches are redacted." The way Casey said the last almost dared them to challenge her. They didn't.

Long and Dodds both looked surprised when the conference room door opened. I turned to see Lori Pope come in. Suddenly I was glad that Casey hadn't operated on a handshake. They were serious about pinning the murder on someone. For now, that someone wouldn't be me.

"Justin. So glad you came in. Your help on this investigation would be invaluable." The county prosecutor grabbed my right hand with hers. Covered our clasped hands with her left hand. Held it a beat too long.

"Casey Cort." My attorney extended her own hand. Pope grabbed it and dropped it so quickly it was as if it hadn't happened.

Lori Pope sat at the table and scooted over so much as to push Long and Dodds away from the center. Classic mean girl move from a woman four decades out of her teens was odd to say the least. Made me glad I was solo.

"We just have a few questions about the night Sister Parker died as well as her relationships," Pope said.

"We've covered his whereabouts that night," Long interjected.

"Tell me about Sister Parker and Monsignor Quinn." Pope ignored her underlings. "How would you describe their relationship?"

"Cordial. They were adults. We were kids. Teenage boys. The nuance of relationships went over our heads." I didn't add that much of it went over my head now, exhibit one being the woman next to me who was the mother of my child but was treating me as client and friend.

"What about any other women?"

A flash of memory came and went with her question. Under the lens of adult scrutiny, I could see now how it was different than what I'd thought then.

"There was a nun back then, Sister Lozano. One time, Byron and I walked into the monsignor's office and she was sitting on his lap. She was wearing a dress, but like a shorter dress that ended at her knees or something, and not only was that weird, the short dress, but Byron said the monsignor had a hand up her skirt. When she saw us, Sister Lozano jumped off his lap and the two of them acted like they'd been looking at some religious book together. She was like, 'oh the letters are so tiny.' He didn't say anything at all, though it was like he was smiling but not really."

"What was Lozano's job?"

"I have no idea. Some nuns taught, though not as many in elementary. A lot did some kind of admin work. Answering phones. Making copies. Organizing and logistics."

"Did you ever know Lozano's first name?" Pope had grabbed Nicole Long's pad and was scribbling furiously.

"It was something kind of weird. Wait." I snapped my fingers as it came back to me. "It was the name of that pretty actress on that throwback show, *Wonder Years*. Danica. That's it. Sister Danica Lozano."

EIGHTEEN
BLAKE
FEBRUARY 8, 2009

The key fit smoothly into the lock. I was able to turn the metal with no resistance. A sigh of relief hadn't made it past my lips before it turned into a gasp with the hand that landed on my shoulder. I whipped around, and in the second before I saw who had touched me, I deeply regretted that my pacifist nature meant I'd eschewed my Second Amendment right to gun ownership.

"Logan? Loren, right?" I said to the detective. I damn well knew his name but wanted to give myself time to gather my bearings, push down the surge of adrenaline. He kept turning up unexpectedly. Whether he was a good penny or bad one was still to be determined.

"We met at Sister Angela Parker's crime scene. I was with Neil Walsh. Then we met again at Peter Parker's." He plainly laid out our brief acquaintance.

"Stalking me?"

"You're a pretty good investigator. Oddly one step ahead."

At one time in my life, I would have debated his use of odd. Nowadays, it didn't matter what anyone's opinion was. I worked for myself and made sure to get the story.

"Where is your partner?" Neil Walsh may haven't been a permanent fixture in homicide, but he was certainly the senior member of this partnership.

"Probably at the Zone Car." The westside establishment was the most popular of the cop bars. "It's a Sunday. He doesn't do weekends."

"Can I help you somehow?" I went on the offensive. On the surface, I didn't have much reason to be here, though I had permission. Half of being a good reporter, though, was acting as if I belonged anywhere I happened to be. He, on the other hand, would need a search warrant for entry.

Decidedly on the back foot, Logan sputtered, "Nicole Long gave me this address."

"The insurance broker on the first floor is closed today. There's no one living on the second floor."

"Is it a coincidence that you have a key to the property that Rivera claims to have been molested at some thirty-plus years ago?"

All that talking told me he didn't have a warrant. I had zero idea what he'd planned if I hadn't been here first, but I was dying to find out. So I slipped the shiny brass key from the lock. Pocketed it.

"We can either do a long, drawn-out dance, out here in

the cold," I said, shivering a little when wind tunneled through the alley, "or we can bottom line it so each of us can get on with our day. You go first."

"Has to be off the record."

"Of course." Cops were more often deep-background than first-paragraph quotes.

"Rivera is the only kid who Quinn assaulted in Cuyahoga County. Maybe the state of Ohio. Probably the United States."

Bingo.

It all made sense. Jurisdiction was the reason this case had vanished from the front page. Why Pope had stopped calling press conferences. Why Nicole Long had chosen to publicly gallivant in municipal court instead of stomping all over defendant rights in the secret chambers of the grand jury.

"And?" I probed for more. After all, I had the keys literally in my hand.

"I'm sure you know how it went down in court. So either we get enough evidence to bring to the grand jury, or this case goes up in smoke and Monsignor Quinn, like so many other priests, becomes another one who got away with years of awful crimes."

"Do you have a search warrant?" I knew the answer but needed to establish that I had the upper hand. Cops, whether it was true or not, always acted as if it were the other way around.

"Even the judges most friendly to prosecutors aren't eager to hand out a warrant based on fifteen-plus-year-old evidence. Maybe if there weren't any eyes on this case, but Pope put this on the front page. There's no way a judge is taking a risk like that. Ninety-nine percent of cases, no one gives a crap. On this one, Gordon Yarbrough would be the first to squawk. Every single judge is up for reelection whether it's in one year or six. None of them is going to risk it."

He was a smart one, who had a firm grasp on county politics. Not all of them were.

"Did you ask?"

"Put out feelers. The answer is no, without some concrete basis."

"So you were hoping someone lived here who, I don't know, kept decades-old evidence of a crime, where, in a breakfront?"

In TV detective shows, it was always that way. A cop rifled through a few drawers and the damning evidence fell out with socks or electric bills. Logan had to know better. Or maybe I did.

"More like an attic," Logan answered. "This Agent Mackenzie came over from Quantico. Told a group of us at some training that serial criminals were likely to keep trophies. Child molesters especially because it's a harder crime to commit. Even the ones who get good at it worry the supply will run out. They keep pictures, tapes, old clothes to relive moments. If someone were to tell us something like that existed, then we could use that to get a warrant on the rectory."

I was starting to realize that I'd just walked into this

scenario as the non-cop "someone" needed to possibly provide the basis for the theoretical warrant.

"Your idea?"

"Mine and Long's," Logan said. "Walsh wasn't having it, so I figured I'd pursue it on his day off."

It was a semisolid plan. Had to give him credit for that.

"Only hitch is that no one lives here." Which was where the plan failed. If he'd knocked and got let in and gotten permission to look around, that would have worked. If, on the other hand, he'd planned to lockpick his way into the building, that would have created a chain of custody problem that probably wouldn't have survived an evidentiary hearing. I'd sat through a few scoldings of a cop at the hands of a judge. The Fourth Amendment was no joke.

"How'd you get a key, then?" he finally asked. I knew he had to be curious.

"Owner."

"What were you going to do?"

"Go inside. Have a look around for background, atmosphere."

"That's it?"

"Maybe look for the kind of evidence you were talking about."

"What would it take for you to let me come in with you?" Logan asked.

That was the million-dollar question. I wish I'd known he were coming. If I had, I'd have prepared a long list of demands. I went for the obvious first.

"An exclusive interview."

"Of course," he agreed.

"That was too easy."

"We're on the same side here."

"And what side is that?"

"Truth, justice, and the American way." He parroted a popular line from *Superman*.

"Says the man without thick black glasses or a red cape."

At least he had the grace to smile sheepishly.

"Look." Logan spread his fleece-gloved hands apart. "Quinn is not only a bad guy, but a crafty one. He got parents to sign permission slips to take their children to South America to abuse them. He picked vulnerable boys. He only made a single mistake that we know of—Rivera. Maybe one mistake was two. If he had spiked brownies here, that couldn't have been a one-off event. It doesn't make sense, unless he was a pothead. And maybe he was or is, but I don't see it."

"There are a lot of priests with drinking problems. It's one of the other bases for reassignment." I wouldn't be surprised if illicit substance abuse was rampant in the clergy. The Catholic abuse scandal had revealed many priests had too much time and very little scrutiny. The solution to which was to pass them around from "treatment" to parish and back again on a kind of wobbly repeat.

"Alcohol is legal." Logan looked up and down the alley where we stood at the back door. Smiled. I couldn't decide if it was charming or wolfish. "It's cold out here. And while I'm very much enjoying our conversation, I'd like to continue it inside. So am I in or out?"

"What would you have done if I weren't here?"

"Called the insurance broker. See if they had an emergency key. There's always a backup plan..."

Since I couldn't think of a legitimate reason to say no, I put the key back in the lock and turned it. The door opened easily to a tall, narrow staircase. No real options except to go up the steps, so I did with Logan right behind. The key fitted in the second lock as easily as the first. All the shiny brass indicated both were new. Logan was with me all the way as if he were afraid I'd change my mind.

The wave of heat that enveloped me was a surprise. I'd thought an empty apartment would be cold. There was light as well, though upon further inspection, I could see timers between the lamps' plugs and the wall's sockets.

"In the tense negotiations down there, I forgot to ask how you got the key." Logan's smile was back. I had to wonder at his true motive. I'd never met a friendly cop.

"After the revelations in that preliminary hearing, I did a property search and found the owner."

"I thought newspapers always put the important information right up front. You're burying the lede."

"The headline," I started, then held up my hands and spread them apart slowly as if displaying inky black capital letters across a broadsheet. "Mary Elizabeth Parker is on the deed."

"What? She did have to take a vow of poverty, right?"

he asked, harkening back to our earlier conversation at Peter Parker's house when I told him that Quinn hadn't been subject to a Catholic priest's usual vow. I shrugged. Money and the church was a complicated matter in that the institution had a lot and the individuals had very little.

"She somehow got it from the previous owner."

"Who?" Logan's smile was gone, replaced by a deep well of curiosity and interest.

"None other than Monsignor Gregory Quinn."

"What in the hell is going on between these two? This is some serious three-dimensional chess. I don't get it." Logan shook his head. I was starting to think there wasn't much that he misunderstood. I liked smart cops. Wished there were more of them.

"I imagine your world is mostly crimes of passion and murders of criminals by criminals. Not much of a whodunit or whydunit challenge," I surmised.

"That's about the size of it. 'You looked at my girl-friend. I was drunk and got insulted in a bar. You took my stash or my corner.' Not the stuff of history books. Cases like this only come by once, maybe twice, in a cop's career."

"So says Neil Walsh."

"You heard that?" Logan furrowed his brow as if I had a listening device planted in the station.

"Sounded like something he'd say." I walked over to the cabinets in the kitchen area. I opened one, then another, then another. They were stocked. I almost looked over my shoulder as if Sister Parker or even Monsignor

Quinn was going to walk in at any minute even though I knew one was dead and the other had probably been warned to stay on the right side of the law.

"Does Quinn still have access to this place?" Logan asked, gesturing to the fresh-cut keys I still had in my hand.

"Until you asked that, I didn't think of it. I thought there would be cobwebs." The warmth and lights and food had me wondering what all had happened here in the last many years. "Let's split up," I offered. "You take the bedroom and bathroom. I'll stay in here."

It wasn't 1992, but I looked for pot brownies nonetheless. There weren't any, though all the other kinds of snacks were there. The super processed baked stuff that packed the front of any convenience store. Did Quinn have a sweet tooth? Did Parker? Or was Logan's hunch correct and there would be evidence that other young underage boys had come here. That Quinn had been sloppy.

On a table pushed right up to the exposed brick living room wall, there was a TV, flatter and bigger than what was probably there years ago. Wires came from the back to a DVD player. A player meant disks. A corner cabinet sat to the right. The top was open shelving with books. There were a few different Bibles: King James, New Revised Standard-Catholic edition, and two more—one in Latin, the other in Greek.

Interesting enough that I'd use it for background color when writing about this trip, but not relevant to the case. I skipped the rest of the books, which were no more than popular hardcovers and paperbacks from the last couple of decades. A mix of crime, romance, and literary fiction. Like the kind of general library you'd see at a bed-and-breakfast.

The doors on the cabinet below, when I first pulled at them, appeared to be not quite locked, didn't open fully. When I knelt down to examine the mechanism keeping me out, Logan appeared by my side.

"It's kid-proofed."

"What?"

The detective slipped his hand between the door and the back and pressed down on a tiny piece of plastic, and one door swung open. I repeated the gesture on the other side until the contents were exposed.

"My sister did this. Hides the lock so it's not ugly on the outside, but it's still a barrier for curious toddlers."

"And any visitors to this apartment who got too nosy, I guess." It was ingenious, actually. A locked drawer was way more suspicious. I got on my knees to get a closer look.

The DVD collection mirrored the books. *The Passion of the Christ* and *The Silent Witness* and *The Ten Commandments* and a bunch of other titles with religious covers were on the top shelf. The middle was filled with Blu-ray cases of popular films through the decades, including a DVD version of *Back to the Future* along with its sequels. I touched each plastic case and pulled a few out to check if the discs inside matched the box outside. They were legit. It wasn't like TV where a character would use a hollowed-out book to hide drugs or tiny treasures.

It was only then that I noticed there were some blank black disc cases in the back as well as smaller clear plastic cases. The discs in those were gold, the color of disks that were burned as opposed to bought. Pulling one out and waving it in the air so that the shiny surfaces caught the sunlight, I turned to the detective who was prowling through the rest of the furniture.

"I think this is what you're looking for," I said to Logan. He came over and leaned on his haunches.

"Do you want to put it in?"

"Not really."

There was a beat where we both laughed. Gallows humor. It had only been a few weeks, but I already missed being around people who could find humor in horror.

We scrounged until we found two remotes. I pressed at the buttons turning on the TV and DVD as well as choosing the right input and opening the tiny drawer with its recessed circle. Logan had found all the unlabeled disks, five in all. Three in plastic black cases and two in clear ones. I chose the first from a black case and slipped it in to the player. Waited for the laser reader to process the information from the disk.

The first was some Spanish language movie. Logan's glance toward me was perplexed.

"Probably burned it because of regional differences. The U.S. is region one. South America and Mexico are region four."

"Why do you think he'd bother?"

"Learning Spanish, would be my guess. The victims from up here probably aren't the only ones."

I took the remote and fast-forwarded through about fifty percent of the movie. There wasn't any secret content hidden on the second half.

"Next one."

Logan slipped in the second and third. The next two from the black cases were also movies. I wrote the titles on a pad to check later. Maybe for subversive themes, man-boy love, or something else. But honestly it just looked like run-of-the-mill foreign films.

"These look different." I pointed out the obvious about the other discs in clear cases. Then I took a moment to stand, stretch my legs, and look out the windows. The glare from the huge banks of snow reflected the sun. It was so bright outside while this apartment suddenly felt like it was shrouded in the darkness of the past.

"Ready?" Logan's gaze held empathy.

"I guess."

I wasn't ready.

While I loved my job, telling stories, sharing the truth that sometimes lay buried, this case was wearing on my soul. The boys who'd been victims. Sister Parker's story. Probably other people who remained unknown. A system that may not punish Quinn and letting him escape justice like so many men did for sexual assault. Especially when the victims were other men.

Logan opened the clear case and took out the first

unlabeled gold disk. It was dark purple on the silver side which signaled that it wasn't blank at all. I put a hand in front of my eyes the moment playback started. The idea of child molestation was one thing, actual video of it would be another. Possession of child pornography, even if it had been created outside of the U.S., would put Quinn behind bars for sure. I hoped it was there and not there all at the same time. The windows pulled my gaze from the screen. I dared move my hand.

Low murmurs came from the set. Still, I couldn't look. My hand went back to cover my eyes.

"It's not a child," Logan said, his hand on my forearm. I split open my fingers. It was two adults in a bedroom, presumably the one down the hall from where I stood. I tried to sort who they were or if I even knew them by sight.

I'd once run into the *Plain Dealer's* building guard at Tops market. He'd greeted me warmly, all the while I'd probably stared at him with a deer-in-the-headlights look.

Woody had stepped in to the awkward moment, done the black-guy handshake with the guard, introduced himself and asked where we knew each other from. Recognition dawned on me when the out-of-uniform security guard explained our connection. My ex-boyfriend hadn't been good for much, but he excelled at being charming.

When I'd gone to work on Monday, the guard was even nicer than he'd ever been. That was the last time I'd seen someone so far out of context. So while I stared at the two people on the screen engaging in sexual contact, it very slowly came to me that I was looking at a close up of Monsignor Quinn and his very erect penis with Sister Parker's mouth around the same.

"Oh, gosh." I picked up the remote again and fast-forwarded. From the fast-moving images of flesh on flesh, I gathered the two were having sex. There was little evidence at first glance that it wasn't consensual. "Put in the others."

Loren put in the second. It was Quinn, but a different adult woman. Same with the third. Without a habit or knowing who they were, it was impossible to tell if they were nuns or if they were consenting. But if they didn't come forward, there would be no way to know.

"Monsignor Quinn may be a horrible man," I said, "but I don't see a crime here."

"You gonna put them on blast?"

"How do you mean?" I asked. White people and urban slang. I couldn't imagine he meant that I'd put snippets of sex online, that a *Plain Dealer* reporter could do that.

"If you freeze the faces, you can publish them. Say the Cleveland detectives are looking for these people of interest."

"I...uh...the paper wouldn't do anything like that. No editor would approve it." I hated lying. It was getting harder to pretend by the day. My fear of being excluded from crime scenes and courts kept the deception going.

"But you could put it on your blog." Logan cut his eyes at me. Looked away.

The already warm room suddenly got much hotter.

"How—"

"I know you got laid off." Logan's voice was matter of fact, not damning at all.

"Oh. But you agreed—"

He held up a hand. Stopped my speech in its tracks.

"I read your work in the paper and on the blog. I think you're the real deal and that getting Quinn is important to you. I knew that before I agreed to anything here."

"I do believe in justice," I said. As corny as it sounds, it's what kept me on the crime beat.

"I think we're going to work together just fine, then. Real detective work is slow, methodical. But if we tackle this, I think Quinn will go down."

"Lori...um...hello." My greeting was one hundred percent awkward. I hadn't expected to see my boss. Not at night. Not at the end of the alley far from the crime scene tape.

"Glad you could make it," she said, and took a very slow and deliberate glance at her watch. In the warm February night, she wasn't wearing gloves. Her usually perfect manicure, wasn't. As subtly as I could, I looked her up and down. She wasn't quite disheveled, but she wasn't quite pulled together. Her pale pink double-breasted wool coat was looped over her crooked elbow. I'm sure if there had been a mirror, I didn't look much different. The Quinn case was wearing on us all.

"This has Monsignor Quinn's fingerprints all over it," Pope said.

"Have you...?" I thrust a thumb over my shoulder toward the homicide detectives.

"No." Her headshake was emphatic. "I think my presence would be disruptive. But I didn't want our office to miss out. If you hadn't been...able to come down, I'd have taken your place."

"Well, I think I should get on with it."

"I'm assuming that you'll report to me first thing in the morning with your plans for an indictment."

"You're so sure that the evidence will fall into place that quickly? On the boys and Sister Parker, he's been squirrely so far."

"Not this time. Not this goddam time..." Trailing off, Pope walked away and disappeared around a corner. Rattled, I power walked toward the lights and activity.

"This isn't how I thought we'd meet up again." I was trying for casual. The quaver in my voice may have given me away. Sealing my lips tight, I looked down at Loren Logan. The detective was leaning over something in the alley.

The same alley behind the same convent where Sister Angela Parker's life had come to an end just a month before. This time, it was a Sister Danica Lozano who'd shuffled off the mortal coil.

Looked like Logan had his eye on a rosary bead necklace with a large crucifix pendant. He lifted it with a pen and bagged it. Handed off the evidence to a tech. The white tarp that the coroner routinely used to cover bodies had been only partially pulled over the nun. Satisfied, Logan lifted and snapped the white plastic so that it lay like a sheet over unused furniture.

"Another dead nun," Logan said. He stood. He looked like he wanted to shake my hand. Maybe thought better of it and shoved his fist in his pocket.

I looked around for Neil Walsh. Didn't see him. Maybe the older detective had retired between the last case and this one. Wouldn't surprise me. Either way Logan seemed like he saw the cases the same way I did. Walsh was too quick to write off foul play. Kept his numbers up and his workload down.

"Murder this time?" I asked...hoped. Kept my virtual fingers crossed tight.

"Unless there's some suicide pact we don't know about, then yes. It's looking like it may be the last gasp of a desperate man."

"You suspect Quinn?" I worked hard to keep my voice neutral. He didn't need to know how good this could be for the murder case Pope and I were building. On the eternal scoreboard, double murder was worth about three times a regular crime.

I'd seen many a jury find a justification for homicide and nullify a crime, coming back with a not-guilty verdict. But when there were two dead bodies, it became a lot harder to find reasons for acquittal. It was the reason there was an evidence rule against introducing a defendant's prior crimes. Guilt by association was a powerful thing.

"He's not talking, which is his right, obviously. But no one else has anything to gain. Nuns by definition have a very short list of enemies."

"What would Quinn have to gain?" Logan asked, curiosity brimming just beneath the surface.

"I think these nuns were ready to talk."

"To protect their own hides?"

When it started to become clear that someone was going to prison, co-defendants scattered like rats on a ship, running to be the first to tattle, make a deal.

"Because Sister Parker at least was an accessory to his crimes." The other boys had stories similar to Rivera. Parker helped Quinn get what he wanted. The why I hadn't figured out. But I'd have offered her a deal in a heartbeat. Little fish were bait for the main catch.

"While they may have been accessories, they were victims as well."

"What are you saying?" Nothing about Parker taking children to an apartment and drugging them said "victim."

"I have reason to believe that Quinn regularly assaulted nuns."

"Reason to believe?" I was so confused. I knew that pedophiles were sometimes married but figured their primary attraction was to children. I'd never interviewed a pedo's wife who'd said their love life was normal. The women always knew something was off. Now I'd have to figure out how to tell a different kind of story to the jury. This case had veered so far from the straightforward, I wondered if I'd ever get back on the right path to conviction.

"Long story," Logan said with his voice lowered, "but I

have a source. Someone who showed me evidence that I wouldn't otherwise have access to."

"Confidential informant?"

"Something like that."

"How can we get that into court?" I was getting excited. Finally, *finally*, there was a path clearing that would lead to conviction.

"Another worry for another day. I think right now we need to focus on nailing down the elements. Motive is only for a jury."

He was right about that. A prosecutor never had to prove motive. But everyone, including jurors, wanted, *needed* a why. Otherwise people had difficulty making sense of something in their head that they themselves wouldn't do.

A jury of a defendant's peers would be a jury of criminals. The good voters of Cleveland weren't that corrupt, so they needed a little help to see something from the point of view of someone who was out to do evil.

"Well, I'll be damned!" The shout came from a technician.

Logan was up off his haunches and down the alley as fast as he could move without soiling the crime scene.

In block-heeled boots, I couldn't move quite as fast but eventually caught up.

Logan looked up at me. "We got him. Dollars to donuts, we have him." In his gloved hand, he held another evidence bag. In this one was a small white piece of plastic.

"What in the hell is that?" I'd been hoping for some kind of smoking gun. Not literally, but close.

"Part of a clerical collar."

"Next to a convent. How in the hell can we tie it to Quinn?"

Logan flipped the bag around. I had to lean down to see. On the back of the collar piece was a red-brown drop. Hope bubbled in my chest. I tamped it down.

"Blood?" My voice was neutral.

"Not ketchup."

"How?" I couldn't think of a way Lozano's blood could have gotten there. "The nun's blood on his collar, on the inside?"

"Not that. Better. We know she's dead. Now we know Quinn was here, if my hunch is right. And in answer to your question on how the blood got there, probably something as innocent as shaving."

Something as innocent as hair removal had put Quinn right into our crosshairs. I could feel it in my bones.

We had him.

"Put a rush on the DNA," I barked. "If you have any problems, call me. I've got Pope's backing on this one to make it the highest priority."

"Will do." Logan gave a mock salute.

"I'm going to have my own look around. Call me if anything comes up. I need to put together the paperwork. This time for two indictments for first-degree murder."

Logan went back to collecting evidence and talking to the techs. One day, hopefully not too far in the future, I'd be describing this crime scene to a jury. It was the warmest night in a long time and today's rain had tapered off, which meant that no one had to rush to collect evidence like the last time. I took myself to the far end of the alley. Looked up at the convent. The window from Parker's death hadn't been replaced. Plywood was nailed over the second-floor opening.

Two rooms down, light shone through the jagged glass panes and wood that remained where an intact window had been only hours before. Soon another square of plywood would join the first, giving the convent the look of an abandoned building. But with two murders, the second floor of the dormitory would remain a crime scene for some weeks more.

Even though my feet were roasting in my boots, I kept my pace slow as I swept my eyes in all directions. A glint of something caught my eye and made my heart rate surge. Careful not to attract attention, I took a step, then two, then three to the right. Making sure no one was watching me, I knelt as daintily as I could in heeled boots and a calf-length camel coat.

Two things struck my eye: a Cuyahoga County lapel pin and a shell-pink fingernail torn from a woman's hand. With a clean tissue from my pocket, I swept up both, wadded the Kleenex and stuffed it into my pocket. I was sure Quinn was on the hook and didn't need any stray evidence causing reasonable doubt.

TWENTY
BLAKE
FEBRUARY 13, 2009

Police officers, especially white ones, were not high on my list of people to trust. But Loren Logan had done me a solid. In addition to two deputy sheriffs and Monsignor Gregory Quinn, I was the only other person in the small hallway that would lead to the restricted elevator.

"Can I talk to you?" I asked of Quinn. Scooping my former employer would be a big feather in my cap.

"Who are you?" he asked. His scrutiny of me was cursory.

I gave him my name. "I'm a reporter. I'm here to get your side of the story. When you walk into that arraignment room, you're going to lose that chance. The rest of the press is going to paint you as an evil predator. Lump you in with all the other pedophile priests who have been out here victimizing innocent children all over the Catholic world for decades. I know you're not like that."

Honestly, I thought he was *exactly* like that. But every criminal was the hero of his own story. I'd bet both of my properties that Quinn somehow thought he wasn't guilty or was righteous in what he'd done. In all the years I'd covered the crime beat, they were all the same. No one woke up and said I'm a bad person who does bad things.

"I think my lawyer wouldn't like me talking to you."

That wasn't a good sign. I only had a few minutes to get him on my side before he thought better of talking to me.

"Look, let me bottom line this. I've worked at the *Plain Dealer* for nineteen years. I can't just print crap about you and get away with it. Or put lies on the internet like some bloggers do. But I do want to write a story about this whole case. So far, all I have is victim stories."

I knew my ethics might be in question with my inference that I still worked at the paper, but getting this story was more important than the outlet that broke it. I'd promised myself that, after this morning, I'd come clean from here on.

But I *was* different than some so-called journalists who'd risen up in this era of internet democratization. Plus, I truly only knew how to do ethical reporting. The scandals that knocked the plagiarists and cheaters like Jayson Blair and Jack Kelley from their pedestals kept me on the straight and narrow.

On top of all that, I knew a Quinn interview would make good reading. No *yes* and *no* answers for his type. Psychopaths, sociopaths, con men, and predators always talked far more than they should because they always thought they were the smartest men in the room.

"Victims?" Quinn asked, proving my point.

"I've talked to a couple of your former students. More importantly, I guess, I talked to Sister Parker's brother as well as Sister Mary Katherine Cortez."

"That's a blast from the past." The slight tick of his left eye was the only clue I'd disturbed his calm.

Doubling down, I said, "I think you're about to find out that jurors can be brutal. Cleveland's a Catholic city and so many are angry about what's gone on in Boston. In Chicago. In Ireland. Everywhere. They may take that anger out on you, if they can't see who you are. Hear your story outside of the bounds of the courtroom with all the evidence rules that will limit you to one-word answers or none at all."

Quinn turned toward his jailers. Held up his shackled hands. "How long do we have?"

"Fifteen minutes." As if there were some coordinated effort, the deputies walked away.

"Okay, I'll talk." Quinn clasped his fingers as if in prayer and nodded.

Of course he would talk. Manipulators always did. What they didn't realize is that they couldn't trick me the way they'd tricked other people. Everyone could get got, but I wasn't at the top of the list of those that could.

Twenty minutes later, interview recording and backup in my bag, and incredulity in my heart, I made my way up to the arraignment room.

The deal I'd struck with Quinn was that I couldn't publish until after the trial. Given the bombshell that he'd dropped on me, I was one thousand percent sure this man was either going to jail forever or was going to be the phoenix rising from the ashes. The tale he told left no middle ground.

The only question was whether a jury would buy his story or whatever tale Long could spin. Given the predilections of the head of major crimes, my money was on Quinn.

In a bored voice, Judge Cristina Sharp recited the charges.

"Gregory Quinn, you've been indicted by the grand jury of Cuyahoga County with two counts of aggravated murder in violation of Ohio Revised Code Section 2903.01. Ms. Long? Bond?"

"The constitution of the state of Ohio requires Mr. Quinn be held without bail as he's been charged with aggravated murder."

"Ms. Long, as you know that's upon indictment and initial detention. Now I have to decide whether his confinement should continue."

"I argue that it does, Your Honor," Long said.

"He's a priest for God's sake," Yarbrough interjected. "He's poor."

"But the Catholic church isn't," Long rebutted. Truer words were never spoken. The church had more wealth than most nations and remained the largest landowner in the world. It had used those funds to move priests to the Holy See where they were shielded from extradition.

"Either way, Your Honor, the state has the burden of proving that Quinn is a substantial risk to public safety," Yarbrough said. His voice was full of bombast. I could see how a jury could find him persuasive. I wondered what courtroom tricks Long would bring to the fight. "Then let's hear it, Your Honor. I want her to put in her proof," Yarbrough insisted.

"If it were only *one* murder, Your Honor, the state probably wouldn't fight bail," Long said by way of introduction. "But we have reason to believe that these murders were retaliation. The very worst kind of witness tampering."

"Against nuns?" Judge Sharp snapped her question, voice full of doubt.

"They were potential witnesses for the prosecution." This was a stretch. But who was going to protest these facts? Certainly not the nuns who were dead.

"This is news to me, Your Honor," Yarbrough said. He raised his hands above his shoulders so his palms faced the judge. The attorney's watch and ring glinted in the fluorescent light. Either was worth more than the car I'd parked in the affordable downtown lot ten blocks away.

"Your client couldn't share his plans to eliminate witnesses, counselor. It's the one thing that you'd have to report to the authorities. A big ol' exception to attorney-client privilege."

"He's not likely to flee, Your Honor."

"That's not the only thing to consider," Long said. "He's a risk to public safety. In addition to the issue of the murder of the two nuns, he's a known pedophile who has molested at least thirty different boys that we've identified. Research has shown that those who have a sexual preference can't—"

The judge cut her hand through the air, interrupting Long's argument.

"And the reason those charges aren't before me today? The sexual assaults against the boys...now men?"

"They're outside of the jurisdiction of the state of Ohio." I knew the prosecutor was being deliberately evasive. I wasn't sure if the judge had caught on.

"Is there another case pending in another state?"

"Not at this time, Your Honor."

I had to admire Long's ability to stop herself from overexplaining. Brevity was on her side.

Judge Sharp took in a deep breath. Surveyed the courtroom. I think she'd only just noticed how quiet everyone had become. The unusual number of reporters in the crowd. No judge would likely admit the press had influence over their decisions, but we did. Kept them accountable.

"I've heard enough," Sharp said. "Monsignor Gregory Quinn, you're going to be held without bond until trial. Your trial will take place within ninety days, minus time already served, as required by speedy trial laws, unless you and your lawyer waive time. Let me assign your case so that you can have that conversation with a different jurist." She slipped a letter opener through the judge stack, bound slips of paper that kept judicial assignments truly random. "The honorable Leroy Campbell. Next case."

The same two deputies from earlier surrounded Quinn and he went one way. The attorneys went the other. If I were a betting woman, I'd guess Quinn would live the remainder of his life in shackles. Somehow, it didn't feel quite like justice.

"What is that on your wrist?" my mom asked Krystyna. My younger sister lifted her wrist where a charm bracelet dangled. Too close to our faces, she swung it around so the lights glinted off the silver chain and red and green stone charms.

"Did you get that at the tween counter?" I asked as I pulled back from her. "I feel like I saw one of my juvenile clients with the same." I knew I was being mean, but I couldn't stop myself. When I was in a mood like this, I rarely showed up as my better self.

"Your clients shop at Tiffany?" she retorted, sounding like her twelve-year-old self, not that I sounded better as my fifteen-year-old doppelganger.

"Please tell me Iain didn't spend a lot of money on that?" I flicked a hand toward the bracelet.

"I didn't exactly look it up." She lifted an eyebrow,

which let me know she very much looked it up. "But I love it because he loves me."

I swallowed at the envy that clawed at my throat. I couldn't remember the last time someone had bought me something. Given me something that said they'd thought of me.

"Did you get something from Adrian?" I turned to my other sister to see what Valentine's Day had bestowed upon her.

"Not Adrian, but his parents did. They gave us babysitting vouchers along with the Entertainment book." The latter was a popular yearly bound volume of discounts on local dining and events.

"Oh, honey. You and Adrian deserve some date nights," our mother cooed at my sister. "Keeps a marriage together after you have kids. I should know."

"Mom. Dad killed himself," I blurted out before I could catch my bitter tongue. "I'm thinking he wasn't a fan of us or date nights."

"Justin Patrick McPhee! What in the hell is wrong with you? That's a horrible thing to say." I had to turn away from the hurt in my mother's eyes.

"But probably true." It was under my breath, but not quiet enough not to be heard by everyone at my mother's table.

"Your father did not kill himself because we had a bad dinner in Guarino's." My mother's open palm hit the wood table to emphasize her point.

"Was it because he didn't want to parent us, then? The

three of us too much?" I kept poking at the family's soft spots like a tongue worrying an infected tooth.

"We've been over this a hundred times. Your father's suicide wasn't anyone's fault but his own. It wasn't like it is today with a public service announcement and eight hundred number after every TV episode on suicide. He was probably wrestling with some mental health demons. His mom couldn't afford all the kids she had, so she did the best she could. Scraped up enough pounds to send him here from Ireland to be with a cousin and their family. I don't think they treated him well. He never said much. But he didn't take any of that out on you. He took it out on himself."

"But he left us." *Us* wasn't who got hurt, though. More quietly I said, "Left *me* to the mercy of anyone who wanted to do me harm." Monsignor Quinn would have surely left me alone if I had a dad around. Patrick McPhee didn't only kill himself. He put our intact family into the coffin along with himself.

Before we could go any deeper into that, my sister Stacey unmuted the TV that my mother had going in the background most of the day. It was *Sunday Chronicle*. I recited the show's tagline under my breath at the same time the host spoke it.

"Welcome to *Sunday Chronicle*. For the story behind the story. This week my guest is former *Plain Dealer* reporter-turned-blogger Blake Hardin Tatum and Father Michael Lynch." Reporter Victoria Greenlee turned from one camera to the other on her right. It zoomed in on her somber countenance. "For the last decade or more, revelations about priest abuse in the Catholic church have been coming at regular clip. From the Gilbert Gauthe case in 1985 to the *Boston Globe*'s Pulitzer Prize–winning reporting in 2002 until now, there have been a steady stream of accusations."

The host took a dramatic pause before she continued.

"Ten thousand victims. Four thousand priests. And now we have our own scandal right here in Cleveland. Monsignor Gregory Quinn was indicted this week and arraigned in Cuyahoga County court, not for abuse, but for *murder*. Blake Hardin Tatum, can you walk us through these most unusual charges for a Catholic priest?"

"Absolutely, Victoria. In the last few years, the church hasn't worked as hard to protect priests. There's less shuffling from parish to parish or moving them to the Holy See. It's not perfect by any means, but it's harder for pedophile priests to hide. The prosecutor's theory in this case is that the net was closing around Quinn. Charges for up to thirty-five boys were on the verge of being filed. As in many cases they were shoring up corroborating witnesses."

"Can you tell us what those are?" Greenlee asked Tatum. "Corroborating witnesses?"

"While a perfect justice system and jury would take a victim at their word, that's often not the case. Especially in sex crimes. In a case of 'he said, he said,' a skilled prosecutor will add witnesses to the roster. In rape they're rarely people who witnessed the crime, though they could be. They're usually people who knew about the incident at the time it happened or immediately thereafter. But this case is different."

"How so?"

"In this case, the nuns were also accomplices."

Even if Greenlee's gasp was inaudible on camera, her dramatic grasp at her throat was very visible.

"Was the prosecution alleging that nuns were complicit in these crimes against children?"

"Unfortunately. That's a hard pill for anyone, much less a jury, to swallow. Sister Angela Parker and Sister Danica Lozano were probably going to turn state's evidence."

"Are you saying they were going to testify *against* Monsignor Quinn?"

"Absolutely. I've interviewed a number of people involved in this case. And rather than face a trial or a jury of his peers for his alleged abuse, it's further alleged that Quinn murdered the nuns. Pushed them to their death from their convent windows. Permanently quieted them."

"It's called defenestration." Victoria Greenlee took another long pause for effect. "A word I never thought I'd use on the air. Father Lynch, what do you think of the charges against your fellow priest?"

"On behalf of the bishop and the archdiocese of Cleveland, I want to apologize to any of the victims who had been hurt as children. It's been a time of reckoning for the church."

I grabbed up the remote and muted the set.

"Why did you do that?" Stacey asked.

"He's got nothing to say. Just the standard non-apology."

"He sounded sorry," Mom said.

"That's his job. To sound sympathetic. If they were sorry, they'd actually do something."

"What would you have the church do? They can't change the past," my mother said, ever the church apologist.

Exhausted with all of it, I didn't want to fight anymore.

"Why did you call us here?" I asked instead. "There's no for sale sign outside. Are you pulling the house off the market? Are you and Beau going to stay?"

"Not exactly. Beau and I have talked, made some decisions. Now I want to discuss things with all of you." Mom did that thing where she looked us each in the eye in age order. "I want you to know that I don't have any favorites among the three of you. I love you all equally. I've worked very hard to give you everything you need, if not everything you want."

"Are you dying?" Stacey asked, her voice suffused with worry.

"Do you have some kind of disease?" Krystyna was next.

"Cancer?" I brought up the rear. I must have moved too much because Morro, who'd been quietly dozing, let out a soft woof.

"Stop." She held up a hand to quiet us. "I'm not dying!

Though I'm starting to think you want to put me in the grave next to your dad. Beau and I still want to go to Arizona. Planning on it either in March or October, depending."

"On what?"

"When Justin agrees to move in."

"Move in? Mom, I'm thirty-nine years old—nearly forty. I do not need to live with my mom. Nothing says unavailable hot mess better than 'I live with my mother.'"

If my mom wanted to couple me off so bad, she had to know "mama's boys" were a dealbreaker for most sane women.

"Not with me, Justin." She shook her head, hard. "Into the house."

"Are you leaving the house to him?" Krystyna asked. "Is that why you were talking about fairness?"

"No one is owed an inheritance," I said. It was something that I'd said to more than one client who'd planned their future based on their parents dying quietly in their collective sleep and leaving paid-off houses and six-figure bank accounts. I hated to burst their bubbles with all that could happen from extended hospital stays and elder care to spending down for Medicare.

"Easy for you to say," Stacey said. "Mom just offered you a house."

"I didn't say I was taking it," shot from my mouth.

"You girls both have spouses and houses. Justin needs a place where he can help raise baby Simon." Today was going to be nothing but metaphorical slaps in the face. I wasn't up for it.

"Mom. What are you talking about?" I returned her earlier death stare. "I told you that Casey's engaged to someone else. Living with him, I think. I have no claim on that baby. There's been no paternity or DNA test. There's been no conversation. I'm probably not even on the birth certificate." I'd lost a lot of sleep wondering if baby Simon's dad was listed as me, as him, or left blank. Not that an official document could displace DNA.

"Aren't you going to do something to change all that?" Mom asked. Sometimes it was as if she could see right through me to my heart. It was like when I was a kid and she knew what I wanted before I could even form a desire or the words to express it.

"I was thinking about it," I admitted. It was hard acknowledging the mistake I'd made out loud.

"So this will be part of it." Mom's voice was the very definition of earnest. "When you talk to her or her boyfriend or a judge, you can point out that you and that dog there"—Morro's ears perked up at the word for his species and his head lifted from where it was resting on my foot—"have a place to live with a room for a baby and a backyard. Your little apartment is adorable, but it's not really a place for a child."

The petulant teenager inside of me wanted to point out that I had plenty of clients who managed to—*had to* —raise kids plural in far lesser circumstances than my *adorable* apartment. But her offer had a certain ring to it.

Maybe when Quinn got his comeuppance for one of his many crimes. Maybe when this was all over and I could bury the past back in the deep memory well where it had been, I could build my own family. It was something I thought I'd never have, but suddenly I could see a future for myself that was different than getting old with no companionship except a series of dogs whom I outlived.

"How about this? I'll take the house." It was the most impulsive and probably the best decision I'd ever made. Then I turned to my sisters. "I'll pay each of you one-third of the value and it'll stay in the family."

TWENTY-TWO
NICOLE
MARCH 31, 2009

There were three things I knew for sure.

Monsignor Gregory Quinn had killed Sister Angela Parker.

Monsignor Gregory Quinn hadn't killed Sister Danica Lozano.

Monsignor Gregory Quinn was going to be convicted for both as long as I had breath in my body and the unsullied bar card in my wallet. It was the least I could do for the thirty-eight victims who wouldn't see justice here in Cuyahoga County where Quinn had hunted them. Preyed on them. Defiled them.

"Can you handle this?" Lori Pope walked into my office without so much as a knock or an invitation. Despite my promotion and the brass plate on the outside of my door, I didn't have the autonomy of my predecessor.

I patted my hand on a stack of folders that held

evidence, witness questions, and cases, which would be rebuttal to any arguments defense counsel made.

"I was working on this case all weekend with Dodds and all of the last two nights," I said. Then I opened my trial bag and started moving the stacks from my desk into the leather case.

"That's not what I meant."

I had a very good idea what she was getting at. I worked diligently to keep my eyes away from the insulated travel mug on my desk. I'd been to the coffee shop in Key Tower this morning. Asked the barista to leave space for cream. In the bathroom here, I'd topped up with Maker's Mark. I needed that courage, that fortitude to go to court and put this very guilty priest in jail. I'd never admit to that need under pain of death.

"Will I need to step in?" Pope wasn't going to beat around the bush this morning. No time.

"Between myself and Dodds, we have about a quarter of a century of experience. It's not a capital case, so I'm sure we have it well in hand."

"You've already botched the sex abuse case; this one has to be rock solid."

I'd taken the blame for Rivera. That was a Pandora's box whose lid was meant to stay shut tight. Everything was riding on these murder cases.

"Monsignor Quinn planned some thirty years in advance for this moment by raping young boys in another country," I said. "He's no different than sex tourists today who use money and power to their advantage."

"But he's a homegrown predator. We should be able to get him for that." I didn't challenge Pope on any of this. If he could have been prosecuted, he would have been. Under her obvious frustration, I knew she understood that. To satisfy the bloodlust of voters, we'd have to try this.

"Look. That's water under the bridge. Let's talk about today," I started, with the sole purpose of distracting her from my early failing in this case. "Sister Angela Parker's case will be mostly circumstantial," I explained. That meant all that had transpired around her before and after her death would be the evidence we used as there was no eyewitness or forensic evidence tying Quinn to her murder. "Sister Danica Lozano is the lynchpin in both cases. Our first task this morning will be to oppose Gordon Yarbrough's motion to sever the two cases."

"Think it's going to be an issue?" Pope was asking if Yarbrough was going to get this early win, make us try him for Parker's and Lozano's murders separately. I didn't want to promise anything. So much of being in a court-room was a roll of the dice. I wanted craps, but might come up snake eyes.

"The judge is Leroy Campbell."

"He's surprisingly prosecution friendly, coming from the outside as he did."

I didn't probe the "surprising" comment as I was a little afraid of what was behind it. Campbell was one of the few African American judges on the bench in Cuya-hoga County. While I'd revealed my background to

Dodds, I shared as little as possible with Pope. The county prosecutor was the kind of person who kept mental notes on everyone and used what she could where she could.

"Speaking of, I have to get up to his courtroom. The pretrial hearing is first thing. If it goes quickly, we may be able to pick a jury this morning."

I didn't wait to be excused. With my trial bag in one hand and my travel mug in the other, I made my way to courtroom 17-C. The judge was just coming into the courtroom as I scooted through the gallery to the prosecutor's table where Dodds had been holding down the fort.

After all the rising-for-the-judge rigmarole, we got down to business.

"What motions are pending before we call in the potential jurors?" Judge Campbell asked. His head swept between our table with Dodds and me and the defense table with Yarbrough and Quinn.

"Your Honor." Yarbrough stood. Buttoned his suit jacket. "Everything has been resolved except our motion to sever the charges."

"Right. You want the court to have two different trials for each indictment." I tried to interpret Judge Campbell's tone to prognosticate, but he gave up nothing.

"Absolutely, Your Honor," Yarbrough continued. "My client maintains that joinder of these two matters will prejudice both. While I understand the conservation of resources and saving the taxpayers money, my client's constitutional right to a fair trial weighs more heavily."

"Does the state of Ohio object?" Judge Campbell asked while looking at Dodds and me.

I stood. "We do, Your Honor."

"Mr. Yarbrough, it's your motion." Since our office opposed Quinn, his lawyer would have to convince the judge to grant his motion.

"Thank you, Judge Campbell," Yarbrough started. "On February eleven, the Cuyahoga County grand jury indicted my client on two counts of murder. The first victim is Sister Angela Parker also known as Mary Elizabeth Parker. The second is Sister Danica Lozano. She kept her baptismal name."

The defense attorney drew in a breath and stood taller, then continued.

"First, my client maintains that he is innocent of these charges lodged against him. Furthermore, trying the cases together because they are of a similar nature creates a great risk of prejudice to the defendant."

"So, counselor," Judge Campbell clarified, "you're suggesting that because each of the nuns was pushed from a window, and if the jury finds he killed one of them, it's likely that the jury will find him guilty of both." I sat forward as my stomach lurched a little because the judge was making the defense arguments for him. That was definitely a bad sign. I tried not to read too much into it. Kept myself from glancing toward Dodds to see if she was reading the same cues I was.

"Exactly, Your Honor," Yarbrough agreed.

"Ms. Dodds? Ms. Long? Which one of you is going to argue on behalf of the state?"

I stood again, cleared my throat, and moved around to the front of the prosecution table, my pad with all the bullet points I'd spelled out last night was gripped tight in my hand. After I took a quick glance at my notes one last time, I was ready.

"Your Honor, while I understand the defendant's points, Criminal Rule 8(a) allows joinder where the crimes are of the same or similar character.

"Here we have two nuns from the Immaculate Heart order who were pushed out of their convent window. Second, joinder is allowed where the crimes were part of a common scheme or plan. We're alleging that in the instant matter, Your Honor, the defendant killed two nuns who'd turned state's evidence, who were going to testify against him for a string of sex abuse crimes he'd committed.

"And it worked perfectly, Your Honor, because as of right now, we no longer have the evidence to charge him with a string of thirty-eight horrific crimes committed against dozens of minors, students at the school where he taught. But more importantly, Your Honor, you and I have a commitment to the taxpayers. Criminal trials are expensive and time-consuming. Two trials equal twice as much time. Inconvenience to witnesses. It's in everyone's best interests, even the defendant's to—"

"Your Honor, can we bring your attention to *State versus Echols*?" Yarbrough cut me off while fiddling with the buttons of his suit jacket. "While the conservation of judicial resources is one thing to consider, the right to a fair trial must prevail."

"*Echols* is a Hamilton County case," I pointed out. "It doesn't have precedence in Cuyahoga County." Each of the state's court of appeals had the right to determine law in that county, but no county had power over the other. Although one judge didn't turn a complete blind eye to another judge's rulings.

Judge Campbell raised his hand. We all fell silent.

"I'm going to go back to chambers to do some research. I'll return in a few minutes."

True to his word, Judge Leroy Campbell was back in the courtroom before my watch's minute hand moved from the six to the eight. After he rolled up his high-backed leather chair, he spoke.

"Counselors, I've had an opportunity to review the briefs submitted as well as consider the arguments put forth today. I'm not convinced that evidence of the Parker matter or Lozano matter would be admissible in the other case as that would be prejudicial under the evidence rules. For that reason, I'm granting Monsignor Quinn's motion to sever."

"Your Honor!" I jumped up so fast my coffee spilled all over the table. The smell of bourbon wafted under my nose. Pulled some tissues from my purse and tried to mop up the brown liquid. "Sorry. I'll tend to that later," I said while throwing daggers at Dodds.

She finally got the hint and pushed back and strode

from the courtroom. Presumably she was going to return with something absorbent.

Once recentered, I continued. "I ask you to reconsider. So many people have been seeking justice from the defendant. He has been committing crimes for more than three decades."

"Like everyone else in this county, and this state for that matter, I've heard about all the crimes of which Monsignor Quinn has been accused of." Campbell cleared his throat. "If any of that's true, it's a damned shame. But he's not standing trial for those charges in this here courtroom and is presumed innocent of every single one of them. It would be an abuse of my discretion to reverse my ruling."

Dodds was back with a wad of coarse paper towels. She worked efficiently to contain the mess. My colleague could fix the spill, but not the rest.

With a win in his pocket, Yarbrough took command.

"Your Honor, we're here and prepared for trial on both matters. The defendant is not the only one who wants speedy justice."

"I plan to start jury selection this afternoon. Miss Long, it's your choice as to whether to bring forward the Parker case or the Lozano case. Do you need time to consult with co-counsel or Ms. Pope?" I knew then that my boss had seen me blow it...again. I didn't dare turn around. It would shake what little confidence I had left.

"Lozano, Your Honor," I decided.

Judge Campbell banged his gavel.

"We're adjourned until one o'clock, when we'll start jury selection."

Dodds stood and walked over to Yarbrough, probably to talk witness lists.

Before I could pick up the papers from the desk or dispose of the soggy mess of pulp, Pope was on me.

"This is the second mess you've made of this case." She picked up a paper towel and smelled it. I could only hope the strong smell of coffee overrode that of Maker's Mark. "Is this what I think it is?" Pope asked. I had to wonder if she had the olfactory senses of a canine or if she were just making an educated guess. "Is this why you're fucking up, because you fell off the damned wagon?"

I moved my body so it was a barrier between the defense table and Pope. Shoved my hand into a deep pocket in the trial bag and pulled out Pope's lapel pin carefully preserved in an evidence bag I'd poached from a tech at Lozano's crime scene. She looked from it to the paper towels, then back to me. My boss didn't say a word, but she didn't have to. I knew she was backing down. Come this afternoon, I was trying the Lozano case.

TWENTY-THREE
BLAKE
APRIL 1, 2009

"Good morning, everyone. First, I want to thank you for making yesterday's jury selection swift and effective. It should always be this easy to seat twelve."

Judge Leroy Campbell was right about that. *Voir dire* in this case had been the fastest I'd ever seen in any felony matter. When I'd been breaking it down on my blog, I chalked up the non-adversarial nature of it to two diametrically opposed notions.

Cuyahoga County prosecutor Nicole Long was convinced that Quinn was as guilty as sin. While Monsignor Quinn was equally convinced of his own innocence. My readers were as divided. If the twelve folks in the jury box sorted out the same way, then Quinn was looking at acquittal. If he got off, I had a hard time seeing him being tried for the Parker murder or for any of the abuse cases. It was so much to rest on so little.

It was a few more minutes before the judge was done giving everyone a lay of the land and how he conducted trials in his courtroom. Interestingly, I'd really thought Campbell would be prosecution friendly, or at least lean a little that way. That was the gossip I'd heard from other reporters who'd sat in on felony trials over which he'd presided. Plus he was known to be heavy-handed in sentencing.

On the other hand, he wasn't a Catholic. As a matter of fact, he was on the membership roll of East View church, which leaned toward liberation theology. I clasped my hands together to try to squeeze out some of the anxiety. I wanted to be able to predict the future, but I'd have to wait and watch like every other person in this room with a stake in the outcome.

"Ms. Long, Ms. Dodds? Your opening statement?"

Long pushed back her chair slowly. Her straight black hair was bumped at the ends, a sharp contrast to the tight bun I'd usually seen her wearing. She smoothed down the calf-length sweater dress. It was an interesting choice. Wasn't as buttoned up, formal, or expensive as the suit her opposing counsel was wearing.

The dress and the buttery-soft tall boots made her look approachable. I had to wonder if she'd learned how to manage her look at her women's college or if it was something she'd been born into. It was money that made her look polished, I concluded. My own background was clearly more modest.

"Ladies and gentlemen of the jury, I have but a single

thing to prove to you," she started. Swept her hair behind her ears, adorned with simple gold studs. The whole thing made her look young and earnest. With the jurors' full attention on her, she continued. "Monsignor Gregory Quinn caused the death of Sister Danica Lozano. He did that with a prior plan. That's it. This case has but two elements to prove: that the priest over there executed a plan to kill this nun.

"The evidence will show that Lozano had the power to ruin the defendant's life. Knowing that she had that power to testify against him, to possibly implicate him in other crimes, the defendant sought to silence her. He did that by finding a way up to her room in the Immaculate Heart convent, then by pushing her out of her bedroom window to her death on the pavement of the alley below.

"Not only do we have a witness who saw him come to the convent, we have forensic evidence tying him to the crime. This is an open-and-shut case, at the end of which you will return a verdict of guilty."

The prosecutor took her seat. There was a beat as both the judge and Yarbrough snapped to attention. It was, I admit, the shortest opening statement I'd ever witnessed. The graver the charge, the heavier the sentence, the longer the statement usually. This one, though, was short but effective. Even I was nearly convinced that she'd present irrefutable evidence of guilt and we'd all be home thinking about something else by the weekend.

Nicole Long's abrupt ending had obviously caught the jurist by surprise. It took a moment before Judge Campbell asked Yarbrough if he wanted to make his opening argument now or save it for later.

"I'll reserve, Your Honor," the defense attorney said.

"Call your first witness." Judge Campbell's directive was aimed squarely at the prosecution table.

"Your Honor, we call Cleveland Police Detective Loren Logan to the stand." Nicole Long was standing up from her table and moving toward the lectern in the well of the courtroom. One of the tall, wood double doors opened, and a pale, hairy arm came around as a sheriff let Logan in, then shut it tight like a drum. It was a big deal to separate witnesses so they didn't hear each other's testimony. The cop took his chair where he made himself at home as if he were sitting in his living room.

Cops were almost always the first or second witnesses at a criminal trial. If the victim was alive, they were the first witness. In a murder trial, the victim couldn't speak for him or herself, of course. That was the job of a good homicide detective.

After Logan was sworn in and gave his name and job title, Long opened her leather portfolio. From my seat in the gallery's front row, I could see a yellow legal pad partially filled with black ink. While the prosecutor asked all the preliminary questions about his job and experience, I had a look at all the players.

Long's co-counsel, assistant prosecutor Valerie Dodds, was watching her colleague like a hawk. Yarbrough looked as cool as a cucumber. He was twirling a gold pen in his hands. His client was equally calm, despite facing a lifetime in prison. Quinn had a white pad in front of him, plain Bic pen poised over the paper.

"Can you tell the court what your work assignment was the night of February eighth of this year?" Long asked the detective.

"I was on call in homicide." Logan turned to the jury. He may have been a novice at homicide but not at testifying. He opened his hands and arranged his face in an open and welcoming way. Or that's how it appeared. I didn't know him well enough to tell if it was an act. Despite his fair treatment and the favor he'd done, there was something about him or me that left me undecided about his motives.

Logan continued, "If there was a suspicious death, I'd have to go to the scene and determine if an investigation will be necessary."

"Can you tell the jury what kinds of calls you typically receive?"

"I get a heads-up from dispatch when a death looks like it may have been an overdose, but the first officer to the scene isn't sure for some reason. Also when a body is found in an abandoned house or in a wooded area, we come and do a preliminary investigation."

"How often would you say that the cause of death is murder as opposed to an accident or something else non-nefarious?"

"Maybe two or three times a month? Just for me. There are way more calls than murders. I think that little old ladies end up watching true crime and court shows and somehow come to the conclusion that everything is a crime."

"How many homicides were there in the city of Cleveland in 2007?"

"One hundred thirty-four."

"So two and a half a week, or ten a month, of which you get about a few. Would that be a fair assessment?"

"Yes. I'm busy but not so much that I can't go out and make a thorough appraisal on suspicious deaths."

"Thank you for explaining all that, Detective Logan. Did you receive a call on February eight?"

"Yes, dispatch called us out to Immaculate Heart, indicating someone had died."

"And by 'us' who do you mean?"

"Detective Neil Walsh and myself."

I'd wondered what had happened to the senior detective. Usually the older and more experienced cop was the one to testify. The strategy to have Logan on the stand was odd. Maybe Walsh was a player to be named later or was holding on to some kind of explosive testimony. Either way, I ended my speculation and turned my attention back to Long and Logan.

"Was this your first call to the convent?" the prosecutor asked.

"Objection, Your Honor! Can we approach?"

Judge Campbell waved counsel forward. From my non-lawyer position back in the gallery, I didn't know the nitty-gritty of what they were discussing. But if I'd been a betting woman, I'd have guessed that they were discussing whether Long could bring in the other murder. When the trials had been severed, the ruling had dealt a blow to Long, and by extension Pope. Even I knew that a jury would, probably unfairly, deem Monsignor Quinn a murderer if there were two deaths, both similar.

After a long beat of whisper talking and whisper arguing, leading to whisper shouting, all unintelligible, Judge Campbell banged his gavel. "That's my ruling," was said into the mic. "Now everyone step back.

"Ms. Long. You may ask your question again."

"Was this the first time you were called out to the convent?"

"No, dispatch called me out on January tenth of this year."

"Why?"

"Another nun died under what the first cop on scene thought might be suspicious."

Yarbrough was like a bug-eyed beagle who was giving the stink-eye to judge and prosecutor, each only getting the scrutiny of one eye.

"Back to the night of the eighth of February. Did the death appear suspicious?"

"Yes."

"What was or were the bases upon which you made that suspicious-death determination?"

"First, because another nun had died in the same way in a short period of time. We have a saying in homicide, 'Once is an accident. Twice is a murder.'"

"Objection, Your Honor."

"The jury will disregard that last statement from the witness. Ms. Long?"

"What was another reason that you ruled the death suspicious?"

"Because she came from out of a window."

"And that doesn't happen often?" Long asked. I sat forward. My mom had warned me from sitting on our third-floor Cleveland Heights windowsill as a kid, scaring me with the idea of a hard head busting like a watermelon in a deadly fall.

"Not nearly as much as urban legend would have you believe. In the last year, about forty people, including twelve children, died that way in the U.S."

"That's less than a person per state per year."

"Yes, that's correct."

"How many cases have you been called to where someone's taken a fatal fall from a window?"

"Objection."

"Overruled, Mr. Yarbrough," the judge said. "I think you'd be more careful with your objections lest you call more attention to something you claim to want to minimize."

"In my career as a detective I've only been called to two fatalities resulting from a fall from a window."

"What else made this death one you moved from the suspicious category to the homicide category?"

"Evidence that Sister Lozano had come into contact with someone else before her death."

"What was that?"

"She'd attacked her attacker. Tried to defend herself. Pulled at his clothing."

"Ballsy. Didn't save her life, though. What evidence did you have of another person being there? In other words, what made you consider this a homicide as opposed to a suicide or an unfortunate accident?"

"On the ground near her," Logan explained, "we found a collar."

"What kind of collar?"

"It's called a clerical collar. That thing the priests wear around their neck so that everyone knows they're men of the cloth."

"Behind a convent and next to a church, a clerical collar doesn't seem all that uncommon. How many priests are there at the church?"

"Three."

Long let that sit for a bit. I wondered if the jury was as surprised as I was. Somehow I imagined the church parishes overrun with priests.

"Is that number high or low, if you know?"

"There's a large number of baby boomer priests who are now retiring. As long as Mass and Eucharist are covered, the number is perceived as sufficient."

"Who were the priests in residence at the time of Sister Lozano's death?"

"Father Octavio Carmona, Father Benedict Sosa, and Monsignor Gregory Quinn."

"Do you know why Quinn was living at the rectory at St. Stephen's and not at St. Ignatius?"

"No, just that he was."

Long was clever. She was getting in little, almost innocuous but not quite mentions that tied him to the crimes he'd been associated with in the news. The prosecution was playing it a little bit dirty. Judge Campbell was right, though. If Yarbrough kept objecting, the jury would think there was more to it or that the defendant was hiding something. I could only see the back of the attorney's head and the subtle shake he was making at Long's questions.

"After you found the collar, what made you think you could identify the owner?"

"There was blood on it."

That got the jury's attention.

"How did you know the blood wasn't that of the victim, Sister Danica Lozano?"

"Without DNA testing, we wouldn't, of course. But my job was to gather the evidence available and decide whether there was a suspicious death."

"Okay. What was it about the blood on the collar that aroused your suspicions?"

"That the blood was on the inside of the collar, not the outside."

"Thank you. Now, you said that there were at least three priests living at the St. Stephen's rectory."

"Yes."

"What caused you to eliminate the other two from your preliminary suspect list?"

"Both had alibis for the time in question."

"And what time was that?"

"Between seven thirty and seven forty-five."

"That's a very short timeline. Only fifteen minutes. How can you be sure it happened during that time?"

"Many neighbors called the police the minute they heard the victim screaming. We received seven 911 calls to dispatch between seven thirty-seven and seven fifty."

Long led Logan through a series of questions covering the more mundane parts of the investigation. Within forty-five minutes, though, she was done with the witness. Yarbrough was up and out of his chair before the prosecutor could claim hers.

"The defense can cross-examine after a ten-minute recess," Judge Campbell said as he interrupted Yarbrough's podium walk and blazer-button routine.

As people quickly left the gallery to use the few public toilets on each floor, I stood, stretched, then fleshed out my notes. Long had done a great job at pointing the finger toward Quinn. I had to wonder what facts a five-hundred-dollar-an-hour defense lawyer would spin to sow the seeds that would grow into a tree of reasonable doubt.

TWENTY-FOUR
NICOLE
APRIL 1, 2009

After the recess, Gordon Yarbrough waited a good two minutes for the courtroom to come to near complete silence. When anyone could hear a pin drop, he stalked to the podium without so much as a pad of paper or a single notecard. That move oozed confidence. Juries loved confidence. Made it TV dramatic, which was what they were all looking for no matter how many times the judge warned them that real-life trials were far more tedious.

I had to wonder if Yarbrough knew something I didn't. I tried not to look at Dodds or quake in my seat. During the break, I'd refilled my travel mug. Took a sip from there for fortification, to make it easier to face something else we may have overlooked.

"Mr. Logan, how long have you been in homicide?"

"I've been at the rank of detective for three years." It was a great answer that I hadn't even prepped him for.

Despite his inexperience in homicide, he was very charming on the stand. The jury hadn't looked away during his direct testimony or even now.

"Your Honor, it feels a little early in the trial to have this kind of evasion. Can you instruct the witness?"

"Detective Logan, for this trial to proceed smoothly, you'll need to answer exactly the question asked. Do you think that's something you can do?"

"Of course."

"Then can you please answer the single question Mr. Yarbrough has put before you?"

"I was assigned to homicide on the first of this year."

"Three months and a day, then," Yarbrough concluded. "Would that be an accurate representation of your experience investigating non-accidental deaths?"

"I guess so." His shrug was suitably self-effacing.

"Now that we've determined your *expertise*"— Yarbrough spread his hands expansively—"let's talk about the death of Sister Lozano."

Logan nodded. There wasn't the merest hint of annoyance on his face. I may have second-guessed a lot of decisions over the last months, but choosing Loren Logan over Neil Walsh as the horse I was going to bet on wasn't one of them.

"You said you'd found a clerical collar on the ground."

"Yes."

"Would you say that's unusual?"

"How do you mean?"

"How often have you seen a clerical collar on the ground like litter?"

"Never...I guess." Logan's shrug was "aw shucks" modest.

"How often have you walked the grounds of a church or convent?"

"Before these cases—"

"Your Honor..."

"Mr. Logan, Monsignor Quinn is solely facing a single charge today. I will not warn you again."

That last ruling was unfair. Yarbrough had opened the door, but I'd bide my time. Arguing over a tiny thing at this point in the case wouldn't get me any closer to conviction.

"I was asking you about clerical collars. Would you be surprised to find out that they've often been found lying about the grounds near religious institutions?"

"Maybe?"

"Would you believe me if I said that most collars are detached? Your Honor, may I present defense exhibits A, B, and C? And may I approach?"

"Go ahead." Judge Campbell waved permission.

Yarbrough provided me, then the judge with a copy of his exhibits, the stickers marking the letters sequentially. I paged through the documents, handed them to Dodds. They looked like internet listings for different types of paper or plastic clerical collars. The most expensive was $17.99. I'm not sure what I expected, but it was like looking behind the Wizard of Oz's curtain. Everything, including religious accessories, was a business.

"These are the three different collars that the church orders from clerical supply." To the judge, warding off what would have been my obvious objection, Yarbrough said, "I have a witness who can lay a foundation for this."

"Go ahead." Judge Campbell did more hand waving. I took it to mean, the judge wanted to get everything in front of a jury as fast and as clearly as possible. I could only hope he was as lenient when it was our turn.

"Can you have a look at these three collars?" With dramatic flair, Yarbrough spread out the three sheets as if they were playing cards and he were a Vegas dealer.

Logan picked up each one, glanced at it, then put them down in turn.

"Now, do any of these look like the collar you found?"

"No, but—"

"Did you question Monsignor Quinn?"

"No."

"So the only evidence you have that links him to the crime, that aroused suspicion in your mind, was the blood?"

"I guess."

"So in your months of experience"—Yarbrough used his fingers to air quote the word months—"you came to the conclusion that Sister Lozano's death wasn't a suicide, but was indeed a murder committed by my client based solely upon a collar?"

I put my coffee cup to my lips to keep my smile hidden

from the jury. Yarbrough had made a mistake. I could see from Logan's millisecond glance in our direction that he'd heard exactly what I had and was about to take down Quinn and Yarbrough.

"Not solely on the detachable collar, no. Also because of the suspicious death of Sister Angela Parker as well," Logan said so matter-of-factly that there was a long pause before Yarbrough caught on.

"Your Honor!" the defense attorney yelled from his spot behind the podium.

"You opened that door good and wide," Judge Campbell said.

The judge was right and Yarbrough decided to cut his cross-examination right there to save his client from any further damage.

"No further questions." Yarbrough sat and turned away from the jury, spoke in hushed tones with his client. Suddenly a conviction didn't seem so unlikely.

TWENTY-FIVE
JUSTIN
APRIL 3, 2009

call Garret McKenzie to the stand." Nicole Long turned toward the courtroom door with expectation.

A salt-and-pepper white dude came from the hall, through the gallery, and up to the stand. It was odd being on this side of the bar. I didn't have a list of witnesses or a preview of trial strategy. I had to watch it unfold in exactly the same manner as any juror or spectator.

Once you'd been behind the curtain, the audience was an uncomfortable place to be. I wasn't going anywhere, though. Quinn was not only guilty of the crimes he wasn't being charged with, I was sure he was likely guilty of murdering these nuns as well. There seemed to be nothing that he wouldn't do to escape responsibility.

After the witness was sworn, Long came to the podium. There wasn't much wobble in her step. Reassured me.

"Good morning. Can you share your job title and employer with the jury?"

"Supervisory Special Agent Garret McKenzie. I work for the Federal Bureau of Investigation."

"Commonly known as the FBI. Can you tell us the name of your department?"

"I work for the Behavioral Science Unit in Quantico, Virginia."

"The FBI's national headquarters?"

"Yes, that's correct."

"What is your focus?"

"Sexual predators." That revelation pushed me back in my seat. Somehow I hadn't seen the trial taking a turn in this direction. I couldn't imagine that Quinn had willingly subjected himself to psychiatric examination. Defendants usually didn't unless they were claiming they were not guilty by reason of insanity.

"Objection, Your Honor," Yarbrough shouted. "Relevance?"

"Ms. Long?"

"Motive, Your Honor," the prosecutor answered.

"I'll grant you some leeway," Judge Campbell allowed. "Please continue."

"Special Agent McKenzie." Long started by emphasizing his name. Any crime fan, true or fictional, would sit up straight for this one. I looked, and as expected, every member of the jury and the alternates had all eyes on the witness box. "Can you explain the difference between a child molester and a pedophile?"

"A pedophile is someone sexually attracted to children. A child molester is someone who acts on it."

"What's a situational child molester?"

"This is someone who doesn't prefer children...exactly. Rather how he chooses his victims is situational."

"What do you mean by situational?"

"If he has access to children, he predates on them. But this type, a situational predator, may also victimize others."

"Including adults?"

"The main trait in his victims isn't their age, but their vulnerability."

"How do you define that? Vulnerability?"

"Being young. Being female. Being poor. Having a lack of social support or protection."

"Do most victims have all the factors?"

"No, not all. But the more they have, the more likely they are to fall victim to a predator. It's why, for instance, children in foster care or jail are often the most vulnerable, followed by children who live in impoverished communities. Kids without either or both parents."

"Would a nun qualify as a likely victim?"

"Unfortunately, yes. Though their choices are voluntary, they're separated from their families at a relatively young age. They are by definition in poverty. And though they live in convents with other nuns, the massive reduction in their numbers has made them quite isolated."

"Is there a term for someone who victimizes the vulnerable?" Long asked. I had to wonder if the jury was getting all of this. Us lawyers, we loved experts. Bolded, underlined, and italicized everything we couldn't say. Juries were either utterly swayed or utterly bored. Even when I took a long moment to scrutinize the twelve in the box, I couldn't guess at what they were making of this FBI agent.

"A man like that is someone we term morally indiscriminate. He predates on those he can. What we find, though, is that they also lie, cheat, and steal throughout many areas of their life."

"Kind of an equal opportunity criminal, then?"

"Yes." McKenzie nodded in emphasis.

"If I were to tell you that someone who'd preyed on children and adults had effectively swindled someone out of their family home, would that fit?"

I looked at Yarbrough, waiting for the objection. He'd obviously decided to take Judge Campbell's advice to heart and not continue to draw attention to the misdeeds his client wasn't already on trial for.

"It would," Mackenzie affirmed.

"In earlier testimony, to which as a witness you weren't privy, we all heard from Sister Mary Katherine Cortez. To summarize for you, she testified that Monsignor Quinn had tried to coerce her into a sexual relationship. When she refused, he began preying on the now deceased Sister Angela Parker. Would this behavior be consistent with the situational child molester you mentioned a few moments ago?"

"Absolutely."

"I want to thank you, Special Agent McKenzie, for your willingness to come discuss this very difficult topic with us. I have one last question. Would a murder of a victim or victims to silence them be consistent with the psychological profile you've built for us today?"

"Yes." Special Agent McKenzie's nod was all solemnity and gravity. His gaze swept from the jury. He locked eyes with Quinn. "One hundred percent, it would."

"No further questions."

I couldn't see Long's face, as I was behind her in the gallery. But if I could, I knew it would hold a faint smirk of smug satisfaction. Unfortunately, I'd seen that up close and personal when going up against her in court.

Yarbrough was up and out of his seat before Long could scoot hers toward the table.

"Special Agent McKenzie, I'll make this easy for you. Not waste your or the jury's time. Get you back to Quantico with your research papers and boundless theories. I only have one question. Have you at any time during this case or in any capacity interviewed my client, Monsignor Gregory Quinn?"

"No, I have not."

"No further questions."

TWENTY-SIX

NICOLE

"Ms. Long? Ms. Dodds?" Judge Leroy Campbell looked pointedly in our direction. He was asking what our next step in *Ohio versus Quinn* was going to be.

It hadn't been a particularly splashy presentation, but we'd done our jobs over the last week to present incontrovertible evidence of the elements of the case.

A murder had occurred in the city of Cleveland, in the county of Cuyahoga. The aggravated charge was warranted by Quinn's preplanning. The priest's motive had been to shut up a woman who could have ended his career and curtailed his freedom with her possible testimony about his nefarious deeds across so many years and the abuse of so many victims.

"The prosecution rests, Your Honor," I said, my eyes on the jury.

Judge Campbell turned to opposing counsel. "Mr.

Yarbrough?"

"I'll waive an opening, Your Honor. I'd like to call my first witness."

If my side-eye to Dodds could have been interpreted in English, it would have said: What in the ever-loving hell was Yarbrough pulling? I veered wildly between worrying I'd watch this case go down in flames along with what was left of my career and whether the defendant was so cowed that Quinn was walking himself into jail sans handcuffs.

Judge Leroy Campbell waved his hand at Yarbrough's abdication as if to say, "it's your circus."

Out loud for the record, the judge said, "Go ahead."

"I call Monsignor Gregory Quinn to the stand." Gordon Yarbrough's voice boomed with confidence.

I traded a look with Dodds. Both of us pulled our legal pads closer, got our pens poised and ready. Obviously, Quinn was a known quantity and on the witness list. A defendant always was. Despite that, the number of times the man or woman on trial was called to the stand was virtually zero.

If the defendant did the crime and their attorney knew that, they couldn't ethically support their client's right to testify and more than likely lie on the stand. Ninety-nine point nine percent of the time, the defendant had done the crime but wanted to say otherwise.

This had to be the first time I *actually* knew, *really* knew, a defendant was innocent. There would be zero barrier to his testimony. Other than his guilt for the bevy of other crimes, of course. If I were the monsignor's defense attorney, I'd probably have kept him off the stand for that reason alone. Though, to be frank, Quinn had little to lose.

As the priest practically sauntered to the stand, I had to admit he had a certain charisma or what the kids today would call swagger. It had been the same for the head of New Day megachurch, Seth Collins. He'd roamed the campus as if he were anointed and untouchable. My mind wandered from Quinn's swearing in and back to FBI Special Agent Garret Mackenzie's testimony.

For nine days, I'd wondered if I'd somehow made a convenient victim in the same way the boys and nuns had been for Quinn. But if the statistics were true and eighty-one percent of women and forty-three percent of men were victims of some kind of sexual abuse...maybe we were all victims. I shook the crap from my head and turned my eyes back to the witness stand. In order to get the conviction, I needed to get my mind out of the past and back in the game.

"Can you please state your name for the record?" Yarbrough asked his client.

"Gregory Samson Quinn," he said. I was once again left wondering at the Old Testament middle name. It was so not Catholic. I hadn't quite grown up in the bosom of the church, but traditions were...traditions.

"What is your job?"

"I was appointed by Bishop Kollie to be the pastor at St. Stephen's church."

"When was your appointment?"

"September of last year."

"Do you have a say in your appointments?"

"Not exactly. I go where I'm appointed. At seventy, I'm grateful the Church still finds that I can be of service."

These were the most words I'd heard Quinn speak. He was just so disarming with his big hands open in supplication and his "aw shucks" demeanor. I had to wonder if it was how he was on a daily basis or whether he was taking pointers from Loren Logan. Either way, it was working. The jury at first tensed when he took the stand, relaxed when Quinn didn't have obvious claws and fangs.

"What are your duties?" Yarbrough asked his neutered client. He'd stepped aside from the podium. The defense counsel had shoved his hands in his pockets. He paced in front of the judge head down as if he were listening very hard.

"Give religious instruction to the faithful," Quinn started. "Administer sacraments, manage parish property, and watch over the moral conduct of the parishioners. I say Mass on Sundays and Wednesdays and administer the holy sacrament."

Moral conduct? I wanted to cough bullshit into my closed fist. That would have been unprofessional. I took a fortifying sip of my morning brew instead.

"And you live at the parish?"

"It's easier to be close to where I work."

"Who else lives with you...in the parish?"

"The assistant pastor and our emeritus parochial

vicar."

I felt like I needed a primer in Catholic hierarchy. I'd thought pastors were only Protestants and vicars a remnant of the Church of England.

"How old are they?" Yarbrough asked. Quinn was a team player. Before he'd establish his own innocence, he was going to get his roommates off the hook. It was the same process of elimination that Walsh, Logan, and I had made. Old men without a grudge were hardly the best suspects.

"The assistant is sixty-six I believe. The other is eighty-two."

"Is it fair to say that you're all getting up there in years."

"Yes, well." Quinn chuckled. "Speaking for myself, I can say that I'm not ready for the alternative."

Several jurors were unable to hold back their own smiles.

"I mean no disrespect with this question, but are the three of you fully able to care for yourselves, or do you need...assistance?"

"It has been the parish tradition to rely on the kindness and devotions of the Sisters of the Immaculate Heart."

"What do they do for you?"

"Ours is a traditional arrangement," Quinn hedged. Even at seventy, he knew that traditional gender roles had changed outside of the church.

"What does that mean?" Yarbrough asked.

"They cook and serve breakfast and dinner. They organize laundry. Washing and dry cleaning, I expect. They keep the rectory tidy. Those kinds of things."

Dodds and I shared a look that spoke volumes about patriarchy and misogyny. So much of women's domestic labor that went unnoticed and unappreciated.

"Would you say that you have regular interactions with the Immaculate Heart nuns?"

"Yes."

"Before the deaths of Parker and Lozano, who else lived and worked in the convent?"

"Sister Anne Holmes and Sister Ida Patrick."

"A total of four nuns and three priests, then."

"Yes. That's it."

"How well would you say you knew the nuns?"

"I'd known Sister Parker from Boston when we were both in religious training. Sister Lozano worked as an administrator at St. Ignatius along with Parker. I didn't really know the other two, Sister Holmes and Sister Patrick, until I moved from Ignatius to here."

"You just met Holmes and Patrick?"

"Not exactly. I'm nearly one hundred percent sure I'd met them at some gathering over the years. But there are dozens of clergy and nuns at so many different times who often move around taking different assignments. I couldn't pinpoint exactly when over my last fifty years."

"Fair enough," Yarbrough concluded. "You're on trial today for the aggravated murder of Sister Danica Lozano. Are you responsible for her death?"

Every one of the jurors and alternates lasered in on the defendant waiting for a denial or a *Perry Mason* or *Matlock* moment.

"No. I did not kill her, did not push her to her death. I would never—"

Yarbrough's "cut it" hand movement was so quick, so subtle, I think the jury missed it. But I didn't. So far Quinn's attorney had not suborned perjury. Quinn buffered by overconfidence was probably going to say something like he would never murder anyone. Yarbrough needed to shut that door way tight, otherwise on cross-examination I'd have walked through it with the other bag of evidence I'd gathered for the other case where he indeed was guilty.

"Can you tell us what happened the night of her death? In your own words, of course."

I knew the omission of Lozano's name was purposeful. In most murder cases, there were no end of people to testify about the rich life of a victim cut short by violence. Lozano had a solitary life of devotion that hadn't played on the jury's heartstrings like I'd hoped.

"It was a Sunday, which is our busiest day of the week. It's not a day of rest for us," Quinn said, as if he were Joe Lunchbox and not an exalted member of the church.

"What do you normally do on Sunday?" Yarbrough asked, as if the monsignor were tasked with all sorts of duties beyond putting on shiny satin robes and waving incense.

"The nuns serve breakfast. Usually on weekdays it's

oatmeal or some kind of porridge. Sundays are special. They feed us a lot to get us fortified for the day."

"What was breakfast on February eight, if you remember?"

"Of course I recall. Everything from that day will be etched in my memory forever. They'd made waffles. Someone had gifted us a Belgian waffle maker for Christmas. We were all big fans of it. Served it with warm syrup and bananas. Bacon as well."

"What time did you eat?"

"Six."

Jurors grimaced. Probably no one's idea of a funday Sunday.

"First Mass is at eight. After breakfast, we all went over to the church. Got ready in the sacristy."

"Just the priests?"

"Nuns aren't allowed in. And the tradition of altar boys has kind of gone away."

I could see Yarbrough's and Quinn's eyes both skitter sideways. Less said about that practice, the better, I thought.

"How long are you at church?"

"As soon as we're dressed, we take confession. It's only on a half hour on Wednesdays and Sundays before Mass. Eight o'clock is English Mass. At nine I do the rosary. Nine thirty is Latin Mass. Then a second English Mass at eleven thirty."

"Do you get a bathroom break?" Yarbrough asked. I

wondered if it was an attempt at levity or just humanizing men whom had been treated like gods on earth.

"Before the second English Mass, we get a break."

"After that?"

"I change my clothes and usually join in a potluck in the basement. I talk to all the parishioners that need communion, in the other sense, counsel, company. Often it goes well into the afternoon. Maybe four or five or so, depending. If there are a lot of older parishioners there, I end up talking about illnesses, holding their hands and blessing them."

"What happened next that day?" Yarbrough asked to pull the defendant back to the timeline.

"I went back to the rectory. Relaxed for a bit. I usually read a little fiction, maybe watch some TV. Then we usually have dinner. It's early on Sunday."

"Why?"

"Give the sisters some rest on the day of rest."

"Do you remember dinner?"

"Pot roast, I think. It's usually something like that from the Crock-Pot."

"What time was dinner done?" Yarbrough was subtly building a timeline supporting his client's innocence. It was good defense work.

"Around seven or so."

"Then what happened?"

"I asked Sister Holmes why Sister Lozano wasn't downstairs. Danica usually serves on Sunday."

"What did she say about Sister Lozano's whereabouts?"

"Sister Holmes didn't really know." Quinn's face morphed into one of concern.

"What did you do?"

"I went upstairs to check on Danica...Sister Lozano."

"Do priests usually go into the convent's living areas?"

"Usually?" Quinn shrugged. "It's not like a college dorm where we're visiting back and forth all the time. But if we want to talk or check on someone who's sick, it's not unheard of."

"You went upstairs?"

"Yes, I knocked on her door and she invited me in."

"Did she know it was you?"

"I can't say. I didn't announce who I was, just knocked."

"Then what happened?"

"I went in. She was sitting on her bed, rosary spilling through her fingers. I asked how she was."

I had to admit that Quinn was good at painting a verbal picture. In my mind's eye, I was in the room with him. Probably the same for the jurors.

"What did she say?" Yarbrough asked his client.

Dodds looked like she was going to stand up and object. I put a stiff hand on her arm. There was no way Lozano's words were being offered for the truth of what she was saying. Whatever Quinn was going to utter would fit into one of the hearsay objections. Yarbrough wasn't that careless.

"Danica said that she was thinking of leaving the church and her vows. I sat down next to her. Asked her if she was tired from the end-of-the-year work. Was she sick, or was she ready to step back from service, maybe try a different placement."

"Why those questions?"

"Because she wasn't old, exactly. In her mid to late forties, if I had to guess."

"What did you say to her?"

"I tried to counsel her to seek out answers from prayer. She stood, went to look out the window. Turned back to me. I stood too. She said prayer and counsel weren't enough. She thought she may want more out of life. She grabbed my arms and was shaking with so much emotion, it drained her. When she got weak, I tried to prop her up. I think that's when she may have grabbed at my collar. Or it slipped and I pulled it off. Anyway, she waved me off. Said she wanted to be alone. I took the hint and left."

"When you walked out of Sister Lozano's room at the convent, she was alive?"

"Very much so."

"What time do you think it was?"

"Seven fifteen."

"Why so precise?"

"The quarter-hour chime went on the grandfather clock in their lounge. It's different at quarter after, half past, and quarter till."

Like seeing the rosary beads, I could hear the elaborate clock's distinctive chime.

"Where did you go then?"

"Back to the rectory."

"Right away?"

Quinn shook his head. Flapped open his suit jacket for effect.

"I took a quick walk around the block. The buildings were hot. It was fifty degrees that day after being twenty the day before. We don't have modern thermostats. We have to turn the steam down at the radiators. In the meantime, the rectory stays hot. I just wanted to get some cold air."

"Did you see anyone?"

"Someone walking a dog. A couple of kids dragging sleds through slush. Maybe a couple of single people. A man walking home. A woman going to the store or something."

"Why did you think the man was going home?"

"I'd seen him before that night. Plus I saw him walk up to a house and use a key to open the door."

"And the woman?"

"She had a shopping bag, like an empty canvas one you see at West Side Market and her purse."

"Where do you think the woman was going to shop?" Yarbrough asked, as if Sunday night in Cleveland was the most ridiculous time to try to shop. Unfortunately, he was not wrong. Cleveland made New Orleans look like New York City in comparison.

"I hadn't thought of it," Quinn said with a touch too much guile for my taste.

"Objection," I jumped up. "Relevance."

"Alternate theory, Your Honor."

"Go ahead," Judge Campbell permitted.

I took a big sip of my cooling drink, both coffee and bourbon more bitter than they were when Quinn had started testifying. An alternate theory might just be the truth.

"Is there anywhere to shop within walking distance of the church?"

Quinn took a moment as if searching through all the possible sundry-acquisition options. I wanted to cough another bullshit into my hand. He'd just admitted that he was served a home-cooked breakfast, lunch, and dinner. That nuns cleaned for him. I didn't imagine he had the faintest idea of how and where to acquire the ingredients that made up the meals he ate.

"Not really. I mean there's West Side Market, but that's a good thirty-minute walk. Also it's not open on Sunday night."

"What else?" Yarbrough asked in what was clearly carefully crafted testimony.

"Nothing really. Cleveland's not a city like New York or Boston. Especially on Sunday evening, most everything is closed."

"What did this woman look like?"

"Blonde? She had a hat on that looked like someone had sprinkled confetti on it, with a pom-pom. Pink coat. I didn't think too much more about her. I turned around and went back to the rectory."

"You're very observant."

"It's a big part of my job. Keeping an eye on people. Making sure everyone is okay. Remembering many names and faces."

Yarbrough nodded, satisfied with the explanation.

"Then what happened?"

"I went to my room. Changed into my lounge clothes. I was washing up in the bathroom when I heard a scream. I pulled on tennis shoes and ran outside. Didn't see anything, anyone. Went back in, but then there were sirens. They got louder and closer. I put on my coat this time. Went out back instead of front. There she was…" Quinn trailed off. Swallowed enough that his Adam's apple bobbed above his collar. Then he continued, "Sister Danica lying in the alley. Her body was all out of…just wasn't normal." Quinn shuddered.

"What did you do then?"

"Went to my room. Prayed for her salvation. Prayed the rosary. Offered solace to Sister Holmes and Sister Patrick."

"Did the police come in?"

"They took out the nuns to talk to them. I'm not sure about the other priests. I told the cops I was going to exercise my constitutional right to remain silent. Then I called you."

He was one smart priest. No one would say it out loud, but if every defendant exercised that right, there'd be far less prisoners incarcerated.

TWENTY-SEVEN
BLAKE
APRIL 8, 2009

I looked between the jury and the defendant. The fourteen in the box, twelve and two alternates, were awake, paying attention. Somewhat a rarity for a trial, even one as salacious as this. Most of any trial was dull and juries got bored.

Despite all their eyes being open, they had a collective poker face. I couldn't tell at all if they were on Team Quinn or Team Lozano. From a not-so-stealth glance at my watch, I could see that Quinn had already been on the stand for half an hour. I wondered if Yarbrough was going to turn it over to Long for cross-examination or if he had more up his sleeve.

A defendant on the stand was an all or nothing, tightrope-walking moment in a murder case.

"When you called me, what did I tell you?" Yarbrough asked. He wasn't done.

"You told me, sir, that I needed to come clean. That I needed to tell my own story in my own words."

Tingling started somewhere in my body. Did I have the scoop of the century or had I been played by Quinn or Logan or Yarbrough or all three? With that one admission from Quinn, no one was asleep. I found myself scooting to the hard-lipped edge of the wooden bench. I wasn't the only reporter or lawyer or victim or wayward spectator who was leaning forward, eyes and ears wide open for the truth.

"Where were you born?"

"Worcester." He pronounced the city as if it were spelled like the last name of Bertie Wooster from a P.G. Wodehouse story. "It's a city in central Massachusetts," Quinn said.

"Big family?"

Quinn gave another disarming shrug.

"Typical Irish American family of that generation. There were five of us. I had two older brothers, one older sister, and one younger sister. I was number four."

"Your parents?"

"My dad worked on the line manufacturing barbwire at National Steel and Wire. My mother stayed at home with us." I could hear the accent then. He mostly did a good job at hiding the worst of the central Massachusetts vowel mangling.

"When did you decide to become a priest?" Yarbrough started to lead his client down the path of creating empathy in the jury. When a client was facing life in prison or the death penalty, giving a jury or judge any reason to lower a sentence or find him not guilty was paramount. No one wanted to put someone they liked or felt sympathy for behind bars or into a chair to be killed by a lethal drug cocktail.

"There's that Catholic saying that every family has to give one to the convent or priesthood." About half the jurors nodded in recognition. "My parents didn't actually say that flat-out...but my mother not-so-gently suggested that it may be the best place for a kid like me." Quinn's voice got very soft on those last three words. Everyone, including Long and Dodds, leaned forward a little more.

"Monsignor Quinn, what did your mother mean when she said, 'a kid like you'?"

Quinn's hands came up, his large palm and fingers meeting to cover his face. Yarbrough was quiet. The judge was quiet. Quinn didn't speak...until he did.

"I was called sensitive. I was called a sissy. What I was...am...is a homosexual." He paused again. "My mother said that the world of the mid-fifties wasn't a place for a man like me. Our local parish priest in Worcester had said I would be accepted, that I wouldn't be lonely."

"You knew you had to take a vow of chastity, though, right?"

"I was seventeen. Controlling what I thought were unnatural urges seemed like something I could do in a community where others had made the same choice. I kind of thought there would be checks and balances. That maybe there was some lessons from God that would change who I was. Maybe I was naïve, but it was 1957. There'd been no Stonewall. There'd been no Harvey Milk."

Since I'd heard all of this before, I was able to watch everyone's reactions. They were eating it up. Since Proposition 8 in California, the tide was turning on the discourse around homosexuality. Even in Ohio. Cuyahoga County was a blue county in a sea of red.

"But you were ultimately unable to control it?" Yarbrough asked, his voice dripping with sympathy.

"It's so complicated... The short answer is no."

"How is it...complicated?"

"I was not the only gay Catholic to make the decision to become a priest. I met my first...lover the first month I was there. At seminary I was like new blood in the water of a sea of sharks. At least three different priests propositioned me before I even started classes. I was equal parts repulsed and compelled and didn't think I could say no."

"Were you a willing and consenting participant, or did you see yourself as a victim?"

"I was seventeen, eighteen, nineteen. I don't know if I can truly answer that question."

"Were you a victim to anyone else?"

Quinn closed his eyes for a long moment. When he opened them, they were glassy. A man of a certain age trying to keep tears at bay. I could see that even from my perch some twenty feet away.

"This is hard to talk about," Quinn said, his voice hoarse with emotion.

"Do you need a minute?" Judge Campbell asked.

Quinn shook his head. Raked his hands through his sparse hair and over the liver spots on his pate that gave away his age. Cleared his throat.

"I'll repeat the question," Yarbrough started. "Were you ever a victim?"

"Objection, Your Honor!" Dodds stood. "Relevance. He's on trial for murder. He is *not* the victim here."

"And there's where you're wrong, Ms. Dodds. Monsignor Quinn, though this is very hard for him, is about to disclose the true nature of his relationship with the victim. I would say it's very relevant," Yarbrough argued to Dodds and the court.

Judge Campbell banged his gavel to end the argument between counsel. "Overruled!"

"Sister Lozano blackmailed me into an affair," rushed from Quinn's lips before either the prosecution, judge, or defense attorneys could debate any further.

A collective gasp rose from the gallery. Several jurors covered their mouths to unsuccessfully hide their reactions.

"Are you telling us that there was extortion?"

"I'm not a lawyer. My training was in the spiritual, so I'm not exactly sure of the definition of extortion."

I had to wonder if they'd rehearsed that because it was a perfect opening for Yarbrough to steer the jury in a way judges rarely allowed.

"The non-legal, dictionary definition is getting something or coercing someone to do something by force or by threat." I was surprised there was no interjection from the judge or the prosecution. Everyone, including the court, had a stake in how Quinn's behavior was interpreted. "Would that describe what happened?" Yarbrough asked.

"Yes." Quinn's nod was brief. The monsignor held his head down for a long second. Not looking at his counsel or the jury until Yarbrough posed the next question.

"What was the threat?"

The priest looked past everyone toward the door. "Sister Danica...she was going to expose that fact that I was...that I am a...that I'm..." He swallowed, paused, swallowed again. "A homosexual. Gay."

"Is that all?"

"No."

"What else did she threaten you with?"

"That she would tell the archdiocese that I had sex with some boys from school. Get me sent away from here."

"Sex?" Yarbrough's raised eyebrow was a nod to the coercion that happened with abuse victims. "You were charged with sexual assault."

"Those charges were dropped."

"Why do you think that was?"

"Objection," Dodds called out.

"Sustained."

"When you say sex," Yarbrough continued as if the objection had never happened, "do you mean it was consensual?"

Quinn nodded.

"You have to speak aloud."

"Yes. Some boys go to all-boys schools for the same

reasons that gay men go into the seminary. They hide out there. But if I've learned anything over the years, it's that sexual urges can't be ignored as easily as people speak the word abstinence."

"Do you regret what you did?"

"Yes. I do. Of course, I do. I regret if anyone was hurt by my actions. It's been explained that while everyone said yes to me, the power differential may have colored their responses. I now know I may have acted in a way that made my students feel uncomfortable. No matter when the attraction between us sprung up or how close we got, I always made sure the kids were over sixteen. Many were even eighteen. The age of consent. The age they're legal adults."

"You never had sex with anyone underage?"

"No. No. I would never. I don't like children. I'm just a man attracted to other males. It's a sin what I did with Sister Lozano, but not a crime."

Either Gregory Quinn was a misunderstood gay man born at the wrong time and place or a brilliant sociopath. After all my years on the crime beat, I was amazed that I was having a hard time telling the difference.

"Have you sought any kind of...counseling?"

"I've confessed my sins. The other priests have followed the 1986 Catechism that says the LGBTQ community are welcome as long as we vow chastity."

"And Sister Lozano?"

"I didn't kill her because of her...blackmail...or extortion as you called it. Even if I were that kind of person, there was no need."

"Why is that?"

"I'm seventy years old. She wasn't interested in me in that way anymore."

"Why?"

"Because I was...I am...impotent. It had always been hard completing the act with her. I'd had to use the little blue pill to help out. After a bout of angina, my heart couldn't take it.

"As I recommitted myself to the church, to my vows, it became impossible for me to...perform. She was older too. I was no longer at St. Ignatius and had stopped seeking out companionship from the student body.

"It was a kind of unspoken agreement that kept us from doing any more harm to each other. We were on good terms that night when she was talking about leaving the church and I was trying to convince her to recommit like I had.

"I'm just so sorry that she's dead. That she chose to take her own life or someone chose to end it for her. I'm not sure what happened, but she was alive when I left her room. I've done some regrettable things in my life. But the death of Sister Danica Lozano? That wasn't me."

"I know this was hard for you, but everyone here appreciates your honesty." Yarbrough turned to the prosecution table. "Your witness."

Casey Cort's grip on my arm was like a vise. She knew me well. That viselike grip was the *only* thing that kept me from standing up like I was in a bad television drama and calling out the lies that Monsignor Quinn had told.

I wasn't gay.

I did not consent.

I was a victim of clergy abuse, not his erstwhile teenage lover.

With my eyes, I pleaded with Casey not to believe what this pathological liar was spouting. She leaned in very close to my ear. So close, I could feel her warm breath, but no one else would hear a word she said.

"I know your truth, Justin. I know you. You've been through this. I've been through this. A defendant will say whatever they need to say to stay out of jail. Remember this is Yarbrough's job. Let's just hope that Long can do *her* job and put this bastard behind bars."

It was only then that I was able to relax the tiniest bit. Shake her hand from my arm and grasp her hand in mine. I had to wonder why I'd run away from her for so long when this felt so good and so right.

"Monsignor Quinn, I'm assistant county prosecutor Nicole Long. I'm going to ask you about some of the things you testified about as well as the night of the murder of Sister Danica Lozano. Do you need a break before I begin?"

"No. I'm ready to finally share the truth I was unable to before."

Long held to her authoritative stance, but a close observer who'd seen her in court before would have known, like I did, that Quinn's statement had put her on the back foot. She laid her yellow pad on the podium. Took another page, probably Dodds's notes and put it beside. She took a long sip of water and a deep breath.

"Monsignor Quinn, are you saying that every sexual relationship that you've had since you took vows of celibacy was consensual?"

"A sin, not a crime." I noticed that he didn't answer and she didn't press it.

"Did you kill Sister Danica Lozano to hide the fact that you've raped her repeatedly over the last twenty years?"

"No. I told you that she was the one who coerced me."

"Did you kill Sister Lozano to hide your crimes against dozens of boys?"

"All within the age of consent. I liked these boys.

Loved many of them. We satisfied our sinful urges together."

"How many years were you intimate with her?"

"Since nineteen ninety-six or so. She'd been at the school about a year and a half by then."

"Long enough for her to learn about your activities."

"Yes, long enough for her to decide that she could prey on me."

"Or the other way around?"

"How do you figure that?"

"Yesterday, our office received a journal from Sister Ida Patrick." Long held up an embossed green leather notebook about eight inches square.

"Objection!" Yarbrough was up and on his feet in an instant. "Your Honor, this smells of straight-up prosecutorial misconduct."

"May we approach?" That was Dodds. She was up and out of her seat, ready to shut down any discussion that the prosecution had misled defendant, judge, or jury. Gone were the days that juries took the word of cops and prosecutors as gospel. It was progress, but of the kind that was making Long's case harder than it would have been even a decade earlier.

"Do you really think the prosecution just came across it yesterday?" Casey asked me as the judge held his hand over the mic and counsel argued at the bench out of earshot of the jury.

"For their sake, I hope so," I said. "Even if it was day before yesterday, they'd have to establish some kind of chain or have handwriting analysis to make sure the victim truly wrote it."

"You're right. Let's see."

Judge Campbell took his hand off the microphone, waved counsel back to the table, then turned to the jurors.

"Due to some specific rules of evidence that I am required by law to honor, Monsignor Quinn's testimony will be suspended. Two witnesses will testify about the journal you heard about. Then Ms. Long will continue her cross-examination."

He called a brief recess, probably to allow Long to produce said witnesses she'd need to prove chain of custody of the journal.

"What in the hell?" I said.

"The wheels are about to come off this thing." We looked at each other and smiled a little. Surprise was an anathema to a well-tried case. When it happened, though, it was a sight to behold. As an old woman came up through the gallery, I realized I hadn't thought about Quinn or what happened during my high school years for a solid five minutes. It had been glorious. Atheist that I was, I prayed for a future free of memories of Quinn.

"The prosecution calls Sister Ida Patrick," Long announced. I wondered if Long and Dodds had had the nun on ice. They must have anticipated the pushback of new evidence and the need to establish its provenance.

Trials hardly ever surprised anyone: the lawyers, the judges, the gallery. How anyone ever sat through a trial on CourtTV, I couldn't figure, if I as a lawyer found it mind-numbing. Today was different. As the nun was sworn in, I got ready, because for once, I had no idea what was next.

"Sister Patrick, how long have you lived in the Immaculate Heart convent?"

"Thirty years."

"Were you there when sister Danica Lozano took up residence?"

"Yes."

"How long had she been there, then?"

"Since the mid-nineties. I don't remember the date exactly. The church has papers, though."

Long held up the journal she'd showed to Quinn earlier. "Do you recognize this?"

"It's Sister Danica's journal."

"How do you know that?"

"She often had it with her. I once asked her about it. With the leather cover, I'd thought it a thumb Bible. I love tiny personal Bibles. They were often received when the person was a child. Some have beautiful original illustrations. When I asked about it, Sister Lozano corrected me, told me it was a journal."

"Did you ever see her write in it?"

"Not that I can recall."

"How did the journal come to be in the possession of my office, that of the county prosecutor?"

"Sister Holmes came to me yesterday morning. Said she thought Quinn was going to get away with it, that—"

"Objection!" Yarbrough was on his feet.

"Overruled." Judge Campbell had his gavel in hand, ready for a fight.

"Can I continue?" Sister Patrick said, looking between the judge and Long for permission.

"Yes, please tell us what Sister Holmes said."

"That he was going to get away with murder. That Sister Danica couldn't speak for herself, but maybe her journal could."

"What did you do after you spoke with Sister Holmes?"

"I called that detective—Logan—to ask him if we could go into her room because that yellow crime scene tape was still up. He put me on hold, but came back and said yes. Leaving it up had been an oversight on their part. I ripped it down and went in. Our rooms are sparse. A bed. A dresser. A closet. A desk. I opened the desk drawer and it was there along with a pen that looked special."

"Special, how?"

"It had a crown on it. Kind of silly, I know. A student brought it back from a trip to London. Got it at Harrods."

"Then what did you do?"

"Got the pen and the journal. Put them in a Ziploc bag like you see on TV. Brought it to your office. Sister Holmes said I should give it to you or that negro girl...sorry... African American woman over there. The other prosecutor."

"Is that what happened?"

"Yes, I gave it to her."

"Thank you, Sister Patrick, for what you've done for

your fellow sister in Christ. Oh, wait, one last question. Did you read any of the journal before you gave it over to assistant prosecuting attorney Dodds?"

When Sister Patrick's face went tomato red, I shared a quick smile with Casey. I wanted to think maybe one day we'd laugh over this guileless nun.

"There's no crime if you did," Long said.

"When I was on the bus on the way over, I took it out of the bag. I was wearing gloves the entire time. I skimmed the first ten pages or so, but then I closed it. Put it back."

"Why?"

"It felt too personal."

"Did the passages you…uh…skimmed have any theme? Anything in common."

"She wrote about harassment and abuse from Monsignor Quinn."

Before Yarbrough was fully up out of his chair in protest, Long pinned him with her eyes.

"That's all. Your witness."

"Sister Patrick, do nuns typically keep diaries or journals?" Yarbrough rushed forward, blurted his question as if he could obliterate what had just spilled from her mouth.

"Typically? I can't say. We've been encouraged to keep notes of significant times in our spiritual journal, if we're so inclined."

"Do you keep a journal?"

"No."

"Why not?"

"I was never much good with writing or school. I'm a good cook, though. That's how I serve at Immaculate Heart."

Even from my seat in the gallery, I could see Yarbrough reconsider his plan of treating Sister Patrick like she was part of some vast criminal conspiracy. Anything even remotely antagonistic would come across like he'd kicked a puppy.

Point to Long.

"No further questions."

"We call Burl Bower to the stand," Long announced.

A guy about my age came to the stand. It was the first time I'd seen anyone in a bolo tie in years.

"I know you're thinking of Vernon Dinwiddie," Casey whispered through her cupped hand to my ear. It immediately brought to mind the African American lawyer who'd once been famous for his civil rights work before turning to moneymaking as a private attorney. He was famous for the string ties and metal-tipped-collar, embroidered cowboy shirts and his near monopoly on black plaintiffs on the county's east side.

I had to cover my mouth so my laughter didn't get me tossed out for inappropriate conduct. Campbell seemed like he'd be that kind of judge. Preliminaries concluded, Nicole Long asked, "Can you tell us your area of expertise?"

"Objection, Your Honor. He hasn't been qualified as an expert yet per Rule 702."

Judge Campbell rubbed at his lightly stubbled jaw.

"Sustained. Ms. Long, can you refrain from calling your witness's area of specialty an area of expertise?"

"I will, Your Honor. Mr. Bower, can you please tell the jury and the court where you went to school and what training you've had in handwriting and forensic ink analysis."

For a good five minutes, Bower explained his schooling, a degree in criminal justice from John Jay, as well as a string of classes, trainings, and certifications, some at the FBI on handwriting, thermal desorption, gas chromatography, and mass spectrometry as it applied to chemical analysis of ink.

"Thank you for that exhaustive explanation of your background and expertise." Long paused as if waiting for an objection. Yarbrough wasn't that stupid. When the defense attorney remained quiet, she turned back to Bower. "Specifically, what are your job duties?"

"I analyze handwriting and sometimes ink to determine the provenance and age of writings."

"Provenance?"

"Who owned it. Who wrote it."

"Did Ms. Dodds call you on April eight and ask you to analyze this journal I'm holding?"

"Yes. I signed for it, picked it up, and took it back to my lab. Then I visited Detective Loren Logan, who by that time had gathered other evidence of the victim's handwriting from Immaculate Heart and St. Ignatius."

"Such as?"

"School forms she'd completed before computers

became standard. Lists she'd made, like shopping and to-dos."

"Can you explain the process by which you decide something you know belongs to a person can help you determine if another writing belongs to her?"

"Handwriting, in many ways, is like a fingerprint. Although people often do change how they write over time or can alter how they write for the short term—think trying to complete a form legibly or fit a lot of words into a small space, writing a large check for example. Or being sick or hungry and the hand shakes."

"Got it. Can you describe the twelve characteristics of writing?"

Bower went on for about a half hour describing, in some detail, the ways in which each person's handwriting was unique. Long and he then had a lengthy discussion on the age and qualities of ink, paper, and acid, and the use of high-end machines to determine the same.

"So, long story short," Long summarized, "you would feel comfortable concluding that the victim, Sister Danica Lozano, is the author of the journal and that the writing was contemporaneous with the dates she used for each entry."

"Yes. In most cases, there's not this volume of material for comparison. In this case, I'm one hundred percent certain."

"Thank you, Mr. Bower. Your witness."

Sometime in the last forty-five minutes or so, Yarbrough must have decided that fighting this wasn't going to benefit his client in the least. While Bower had been testifying about gas chromatography and mass spectrometry, he'd been reading and underlining photocopied journal pages. When he was done with one, he'd pass it to Quinn. They continued that way for the duration of the expert's testimony. From the look on his face, the defense was going to have a bigger problem than provenance.

"No questions, Your Honor."

"Will you stipulate that Danica Lozano was the author of the journal in question?"

"Yes."

"Any hearsay objections?"

"Your Honor, I've had an opportunity to read the evidence presented so very late in this trial process. What is the purpose—"

"Let me stop you there. Ladies and gentlemen of the jury, I think the bailiff has some treats from Dairy Queen. We have some business to take care of in here and I wouldn't want them to melt."

With the promise of sweets, the jurors were up and out of their seats in seconds. Judge Campbell had just secured at least fourteen votes for his next reelection campaign.

"Mr. Yarbrough?"

"This is hearsay, plain and simple. Ms. Long is going to offer this journal asserting the truth of what is written. While we all know courts prefer live testimony and Lozano is dead, this does not mean her statements about the defendant should be admitted in court. There's no exception here. The results will be highly prejudicial."

Campbell held up a hand. Spent ten minutes skimming, flipping, and reading his own Xeroxed copy of the journal. My hands itched to have my own copy, but I wasn't a party to the case and had to get my information the same way as everyone else.

"Ms. Long?"

"First, under 803, this is not hearsay. This is clearly a present sense impression, a writing made right after an event is admissible unless the declarant was untrustworthy. I'd love to hear Mr. Yarbrough talk about the trustworthiness of a nun, Your Honor. Even if this could in some far-off bizarro world be considered hearsay, then it would be admissible because the defendant can't kill the witness, then claim we can't hear their testimony."

"I'm inclined to let it in. Let's let the jurors enjoy their treats. We'll reconvene tomorrow at ten o'clock."

TWENTY-NINE
NICOLE
APRIL 9, 2009

"As I was saying yesterday morning when I started this examination, Sister Danica Lozano kept a diary or journal of sorts. Were you surprised to discover that?"

I'd recalled Monsignor Gregory Quinn to the stand the moment the trial reconvened. I was fortified. I was caffeinated. I was ready to put a nail into the defendant's coffin. It was truly going to be his metaphorical funeral.

"No, I guess. Many of us often document our spiritual journey or keep notes on various aspects of our lives."

"Do you keep one?"

"Nope. Writing things down has never been my thing."

"I imagine it wouldn't have been." I hadn't been able to resist taking a potshot. I could practically feel my co-counsel's eyes boring into my back. I tried to telegraph telepathically that I'd behave from here on out.

"Objection."

"Sustained. Counselor, I'm already granting you some leeway, please let's get to the questions you want to cross the defendant on."

"In front of you is a photocopy of relevant pages of Sister Danica Lozano's journal. It's not the entire journal. That has been furnished to the court and your counsel. I have highlighted some relevant portions that I want to ask you about. Do you understand?"

"Yes."

"Your Honor, these are marked with the relevant exhibit numbers." I handed copies of the same curated pages with highlights to the judge while Dodds gave another to the court reporter and Gordon Yarbrough. "Monsignor Quinn, can you please read the passage dated January thirty-one, 1996?"

"'Bless me, Father, for I have sinned. I have been placed at St. Ignatius in the school's administrative office since the year started in September. I just saw a copy of some correspondence between Monsignor Gregory Quinn, who is very important here, and a priest in Guatemala, Padre Geraldo Morales. They were talking about having sex with boys. I know I should report them to the bishop, but I'm not ready to leave this post. I could be moved back to San Antonio. I can't go back there. I can't have another abortion. I don't want the priests there to touch me ever again.'"

"Is that first sentence familiar to you?"

"It's what parishioners say at the start of confession."

"Did you write to a Father Morales about sex with boys?"

"As I said earlier, I'm a gay man. I only had sex with those who were at the age of consent. There weren't many I could confide in. Anyone who shared my...orientation became a friend."

"By orientation do you mean, likes to have sex with children?"

"Objection."

"Overruled."

"He told me he was gay. I didn't ask questions about what he did."

"Then what was the letter about?"

"It was probably about having privacy. The kids stayed in barracks-type dorms. There was no privacy for consensual relations."

"Can you read the next highlighted entry from April one, 1996?"

"'Bless me, Father, for I have sinned,'" the priest read haltingly, hesitantly. "'Monsignor Quinn came to my room tonight. I don't know why he was in the convent. I thought it was Sister Parker knocking on my door, but I was wrong. He came in. Told me that he was attracted to me. That he thought we should have a relationship. I reminded him of his vow of celibacy and mine of chastity. He laughed in a way that gave me the creeps. He laughed just like the priests in San Antonio.'"

"You testified that in your first encounters with Sister Lozano, she'd coerced or blackmailed you into a relationship by threatening to reveal your encounters with boys at the school. Which is the truth: what she wrote at the time it happened, or what you've testified to some thirteen years later?"

"I was telling the truth. Am."

"Okay, let's look at this entry from the fifth of May. Can you please read?"

"'Bless me, Father, for I have sinned. I snuck out to Planned Parenthood in Cleveland Heights. On the other side of town from here. They gave me birth control pills. I don't think the monsignor will continue to take no for an answer. I can't have another abortion. I think the pills are a lesser sin.'"

"That supports my case. She got the pills as part of her plan to blackmail me." His excuse sounded weak, pathetic.

"Can you read the June sixteenth entry?"

"'Bless me, Father, for I have sinned. After second Mass, Monsignor Quinn came to my room. He put my chair under the doorknob. He told me that if I gave him head, he wouldn't do anything else to me. It was the lesser of the two sins.'"

"Do you recall that day or evening?"

"Yes, just differently. She left a note for me requesting I come to her room. She told me that she was going to the bishop unless..."

"Unless what, she got to give you a blow job?"

"Objection!"

"To what? My terminology? Excuse me. Monsignor

Quinn, is it your testimony that she coerced you into fellatio?"

"No. That's not what happened!"

"Did you save the note she sent you requesting your presence in her room?"

"No, I didn't think I'd need it."

"Can you read this passage from some three years later, in August 1999?"

"'Bless me, Father, for I have sinned. I had a miscarriage. One of the sisters found my pills and threw them away. Monsignor Quinn didn't care. He went ahead even though I told him I could get pregnant. Planned Parenthood gave me something called Norplant this time.'"

"Were you aware of a miscarriage?"

"Yes. She blamed me for it. I'd tried wearing a condom, but she'd insisted on going bare."

"Can you turn the page to the passage dated April fifteen, 2001?"

Quinn looked down. Shook his head. Didn't open his mouth.

"Can you please read that entry?"

"'Bless me, Father, for I have sinned. Monsignor Quinn brought another priest with him tonight. They held me down and took turns. I'm still bleeding. I told Mother Superior that I can't serve because I have the flu.'

"This didn't happen. This isn't a journal. This is fiction made out of whole cloth. I would never have brought someone else. She doesn't even name anyone because that person doesn't exist."

I didn't need to do much work by way of questions. Quinn was digging his own grave.

"Please read the entry from September sixteen, 2001."

"Your Honor. This is crazy. How can we rely on this writing from a dead woman? How do we even know if she wrote it? I wouldn't be surprised if someone else came up with this. The same person who framed me for this murder," Quinn objected. He turned his pleading eyes on the judge.

"Your Honor, can you please instruct the witness," I requested.

"The admission of this evidence has already been decided by the court. Please read from the section the prosecutor asked about."

"'Bless me, Father, for I have sinned. I told Monsignor Quinn if he continued his visits, I would go to the bishop with what I knew about his relations with the boys at school. He laughed.'"

"And April ten, 2005."

"'Bless me, Father, for I have sinned. I showed Monsignor Quinn my list of all the boys he'd ever molested. I told him things were different now. The church wouldn't protect him. He would go to jail.'"

"Were you afraid of going to jail?" I asked the monsignor.

"Yes, of course," he said. Straightened up. Looked less like a condemned man. "Homosexuals have been persecuted for millennia. That's why I did whatever she wanted."

"November twenty-six, 2006, please."

"'Bless me, Father, for I have sinned. Monsignor Quinn came after not being here for a year and a half. I told him I wasn't joking about the list. He said he'd found someone else anyway. He told me if I ever talked to the bishop or anyone at the archdiocese, he'd kill me.'"

"Did you threaten her life?"

"This is so twisted." He let the sheet fall to the floor. I left it there as the next passage was on a different piece of paper. "Never."

"Can you read the last highlighted passage from January eleventh of this year?"

"'Bless me, Father, for I have sinned. I heard them arguing. I heard her scream. I saw Monsignor Quinn run back to the rectory. I told the police I knew nothing. May Sister Parker be in peace in the hands of God.'"

"Objection!" Yarbrough practically had steam coming from his ears. "That's about the Parker matter, not this case before the court."

"What that was, Your Honor, was motive. No further questions."

THIRTY
NICOLE
APRIL 10, 2009

"Your Honor, it's Friday," Gordon Yarbrough said when we'd reconvened after a short lunch break.

"Yes, I'm so glad we've all agreed to the Gregorian calendar," Judge Campbell deadpanned. "Do you have a point?"

"I have no further witnesses. I anticipate the same of the prosecution. That means we'll give closing arguments, jury instruction, and deliberation will start."

Judge Campbell continued to run his courtroom as if Yarbrough hadn't made his implied request.

"Ms. Long, Ms. Dodds, will the state of Ohio have further witnesses?"

"No, Your Honor."

"What's your assertion, Mr. Yarbrough?"

"That if we give the case to the jury on Friday, they'll

rush to judgment. Because they want to be done before the Easter holiday."

"Mr. Yarbrough, I'd agree with you if this were Christmas or Thanksgiving where the court would be closed on weekdays. But there's no difference between a regular Sunday or Easter Sunday as the court will be closed. We've talked about the efficient use of court resources. I see no reason to send them home early. We will have them deliberate until four thirty. Any questions?"

"No, Your Honor," Yarbrough and I said in unison.

"I'll call in the jury. You'll make your arguments. I'll give instruction and start deliberation. Step back."

Today my coffee was just that...a strong Ethiopian brew. I took several sips and let the heat and caffeine work their way through my body as the jury made their way to their chairs.

"Again, I want to thank you for your service. I'm going to ask you a question, but I ask that you raise your hand rather than answering out loud," Judge Campbell instructed. "Do any of you have airline tickets for flights that leave this afternoon? If yes, raise your hand."

The jurors' badges shifted as they all looked at each other, but no one raised their hand.

"Does anyone have plans to leave before five o'clock today to drive to a faraway destination for the weekend?"

They all shifted again looking at each other, but no hands came up. The judge cast a meaningful glance toward Yarbrough.

"If there are no further witnesses, then we'll move to the part of the trial known as closing arguments. Legal procedure determines the order. Monsignor Quinn's counsel will go first. The prosecutor for the state of Ohio will go last. Mr. Yarbrough, you may begin."

"Ladies and gentlemen of the jury, I'm going to say something I wouldn't normally admit. My client is misguided. This is no excuse, but he was born and raised in a different time and a different era. It wasn't safe to 'come out,' and be an 'out and proud' gay man. He took well-meaning advice and joined the clergy.

"From then on, he engaged in consensual relationships. He was propositioned by older men and women when he first got to seminary. When he matured, he sought out mutually fulfilling and consensual relationships. Does he now realize there was a power differential? Yes. I think in our ever-evolving world, we know that people should seek partnerships from those they're equal with. But we can't go back. Monsignor Quinn didn't rape children. I wanted to get that out of the way even though those are not the charges today.

"He's on trial for the aggravated murder of Sister Danica Lozano. My client unequivocally denies he committed that crime. He testified before you that their relationship, despite a rocky beginning, had changed. They were no longer intimate. They were coworkers and friends of sorts. They were all rattled by Sister Parker's murder.

"He checked on Sister Lozano, then took a walk. After

he left the grounds, the victim was pushed from the window. There were other people around. A woman in a pink coat specifically. Someone unfamiliar in the neighborhood with no real purpose for being near the convent. My client was with Lozano, but he left. When he last saw her, she was alive.

"Monsignor Gregory Quinn is an honest man. He's an innocent man. The only reasonable verdict in this case is one of not guilty. Thank you."

"Ms. Dodds? Ms. Long?"

"'The Lord knoweth how to deliver the godly out of temptations, and to reserve the unjust unto the day of judgment to be punished.' Peter chapter two, verse nine. Ladies and gentlemen of the jury, today is that day," I said. I was known for my Bible verses in court. Never had I worked so hard to choose the right one.

"Monsignor Gregory Quinn is a predator," I continued, my voice loud and clear. "He preyed on innocent boys. All his excuses about the age of consent are just that...excuses. He's a crafty criminal who made sure he couldn't be held responsible for his crimes. He intimidated nuns. You heard it directly from her journal. He coerced her. He raped her. When she pushed back. When she threatened to expose him, he killed her. It's that simple.

"This man, this predator needs to be stopped. The church didn't do it. The nuns couldn't do it. Only the twelve of you will be able to once and for all put this man behind bars. There is no reasonable doubt. The only verdict you can return is one of guilty. Guilty of the aggravated murder of Sister Danica Lozano."

"Thank you, counselors, for your excellent work on this most difficult matter. First, I'm going to dismiss our two alternates. Thank you."

Two jurors got up from the end of the box and left through the back of the courtroom. Judge Campbell gave them a long list of instructions.

"Any questions?" Judge Campbell asked the jurors. None were forthcoming.

"I know that it's Friday afternoon, but I want to stress that a man's life and freedom are on the line. There is no hurry to reach a verdict. If you can't agree before four thirty, you get to go home, enjoy a weekend with your family and friends, and come back for further deliberation next week. A rush to judgment would be unfair to the defendant and contrary to justice."

Despite the judge's admonition, the jury was back in less than two hours.

"You've reached a verdict?"

"We have, Your Honor," the foreperson said officiously. She handed the jury slip to the bailiff, who handed the same to the judge. He read the verdict, poker face in full force, then turned it back to the foreperson.

"What say you?"

"We find the defendant...guilty."

THIRTY-ONE
JUSTIN
APRIL 10, 2009

"There's nothing healthy on the menu, but I'll pay."

"If there ever was a comfort food day, it's today."

I buried my face in the menu. I'm not sure if it was adrenaline or what, but I was having a hell of a time sitting here across from Casey. More than anything, I wanted to run away. Go home. But I couldn't stand the idea of being alone there. Even with Morro.

"Did you ever go to those...meetings with the other St. Ignatius guys? Do you think they'll be satisfied with the verdict?"

I shook my head. "Don't know." I didn't say anything about the meetings. I wasn't a joiner. Wasn't a group I wanted to be a part of.

"The mandatory sentence is life in prison. The sentencing hearing will only be a formality in this case."

"I'm just glad it's done. I know some prosecutors like to go after defendants already in prison. The sitting ducks they can pile life sentences on. I don't see that here. The prosecutor's office barely pulled this one out. It'll be case closed. You and the other guys can move on. Maybe you can share that with them."

I nodded again, then gave the server my order of loaded nachos and a so-called Dublin mule. The latter of which I hoped was a mix of enough strong alcohol to make sleep come easy.

Casey had a salad and a virgin drink. I glanced at her breasts and immediately looked away. My sisters were sober when they were nursing. Probably the same for her.

"I thought I was going to walk home from here, but maybe you could give me a ride since you're not drinking. If you don't have to rush, that is."

"It's covered. Whatever you need."

"I'm moving."

"Where? I thought you loved that apartment."

"My mom is selling me her house. She's moving to Arizona."

"No more Cleveland winters? Good for her. Won't she miss the grandkids?"

"That's the reason for the house."

The food arrived quickly. I was both famished and full at the same time. I pushed my plate to the side, which earned me a side-eye from the waitress until I took a big slug of my drink, which assured the server that I had my priorities straight.

Casey had taken her utensils from the cloth napkin, which adorned her lap. She had knife and fork poised above the laden greens.

"I don't follow. What does you moving have to do with your sisters' kids?"

"I want to be involved in Simon's life."

"One year and three months ago."

"What's that?"

"That's when I needed to hear you say this."

I could only shrug, take another big sip of the mule.

"You're saying words, Justin, but I don't know what any of that means. I came to you that Christmas, heart in my hand. You walked out of the door without a glance back, without a second thought."

"I—"

"Congratulations! You must be relieved that Quinn's behind bars." Lori Pope approached our table, the front woman of an entourage of three. Valerie Dodds and Nicole Long brought up the rear.

"Thanks, I guess. I'm glad that he's behind bars, for the rest of his life. New victims will be spared."

"I suppose. You owe me big-time. I had to pull this case out of the fire more than once."

"Congratulations on your win," Casey said, to break up the awkwardness Pope was spreading.

"Let me buy you a drink," Pope offered. Before I could say anything, she'd made herself comfortable on one of the barstools at the bar-height four-top. Dodds and Long shared a brief look before Dodds took the last stool and

Long went in search of another to drag over. The server, seeing that her tip had likely tripled, was back over in a heartbeat adding another mule to the order. Pope ordered a tequila for herself. Dodds said something about not drinking and Long, who'd probably had her fair share of alcohol already, demurred as well.

"Party pooper," Pope directed at Dodds. The drinks arrived quickly and Pope threw back her shot. "I'll leave partying to you younger folk. You all can rest easy tonight knowing that each and every one of you did the right thing in this case."

Pope left. A long moment of awkward silence followed.

"Didn't expect to see you here." Casey was bolder once Pope had vacated the premises. "Figured Farro House was safe and you guys would be at the Side Bar."

"Pope insisted we come here and buy you a drink."

A shudder went through me that I tried hard to hide. The prosecutor was like that. Showing up when you least expected, like the time she'd accosted me and Morro at the park to ask me to help out in the Quinn matter. Or the time she'd showed up with Sister Parker during our last trial. She wouldn't last forever. No elected official did.

"If you don't mind, Casey and I have some work stuff to discuss."

Dodds and Long took the hint. Lifted their glasses, coats, and purses and found another table on the other side of the large restaurant. It was happy hour and getting louder by the moment. Enough to give us privacy for the discussion I needed to have with Casey.

"Shouldn't we have tried to make nice?"

"I can't do both right now, think about work and think about the future."

"What do you want, Justin? When you thought of this dinner or whatever in your head, how did you see it going?"

I shook my head as if I didn't have a clue. Then I thought about everything for a long moment. If I didn't go for broke now, I'd have another year or years of regret against me.

"It was one year, three months, and seventeen days, Casey. That's when you told me you loved me and wanted to make a family with you, me, and Simon. It was Christmas Day in 2007 when I walked out of the door having told you I didn't have feelings for you. That the white-picket-fence future you had in mind couldn't happen, at least not with me."

"Excellent recap." Casey Cort wasn't giving me an inch. Fair enough.

"I wasn't lying to you. I was lying to myself. I love you. I'm in love with you. I want us to do this thing called life together. Mom gave me the house. I have a backyard and a dog."

"Why did you change your mind?"

"I thought I wasn't good enough for you. That if you knew the truth about me, that if anyone knew the truth about me, that if I admitted the truth to myself, I'd never be husband or partner material."

"Ron loves me. No, that's not it...Ron stepped up when you wouldn't. He didn't run. There were no caveats."

My behavior was indefensible. What she said wasn't wrong. But I knew she and I belonged together.

"A surfeit of suitors."

Casey glared at me, but there wasn't anger behind it. I could see she was trying not to laugh. It didn't work. Once I started, she couldn't help herself. We were nearly falling off our chairs. Once again, the server who'd been coming our way swerved and pivoted, leaving us alone. I'd have to leave a big tip for the meal we'd never finish.

"What am I going to do with you, Justin Patrick McPhee?"

"Marry me."

A tear rolled down her cheek. She wiped it away with her left hand, the one wearing a glittery engagement ring I hadn't put there. She shook her head, but didn't say no. For the first time in my nearly forty years, I could see a future where I was happy to be me.

THIRTY-TWO
BLAKE
APRIL 11, 2009

"Um, I didn't give you my address," I said to Loren Logan. Yet there he was, standing on my front porch knocking on my door. At least he wasn't in uniform. Didn't want my tenants or new neighbors thinking I was bringing trouble to this neighborhood, which was already precariously balanced between poverty and gentrification.

"I know and I'm sorry."

"You looked me up in the DMV database?"

"That would be a misuse of power. I called 411. You still have a land line."

"You could have called that number, given me a heads-up." A chance to let it go to voicemail and put him off until I wanted to deal with him. Like next month or something.

"Look. I'm sorry for coming over like this, uninvited. But I was up half the night thinking about some things and wanted to talk to you."

"Me?"

"Are you going to invite me in?" His question bordered on rude. But he was vibrating under his skin. Needed to talk to someone. The woman who'd been raised to put men's feelings first, relented.

"Are you carrying a gun?" I asked. I thought he was honorable. I might even trust him, but firearms scared the hell out of me.

"Yes." He nodded. Lifted his fleece-lined shirt. A shoulder holster and gun were over a thermal that molded to his body. I stepped back from the heat that emanated from him. Pointed behind him toward the street.

"Then you're going to need to put that in your car."

Logan didn't blink. Instead, he turned around and went to a newer red Nissan SUV parked at the curb, opened the trunk, fiddled around for a moment or two, closed it, and came back.

"Unarmed." Logan held up his hands so that his empty palms faced me in a "don't shoot" manner.

"I don't believe in guns, so you're safe."

"Don't believe in them? Like someone doesn't believe in Santa Claus?"

"Don't believe the Second Amendment meant that our country should have more guns than people. But I was raised to not talk politics with strangers."

"Can this stranger come in?"

I finally moved back from the door. Gestured to the stairs behind me. "I'm on the second floor."

I turned and walked up the stairs to the landing,

turned and walked the second bit. My apartment door wasn't quite closed as I'd thought I'd run down, turn a solicitor away, then come back up.

"You moved recently?"

I'd unpacked all my stuff in the first weeks of the new year after the move. The stack of boxes by the door was stuff that Woody had left behind. Not wanting to get into that, I just nodded.

"Without the salary and health insurance from the paper, I had to scale down. Fortunately, this was available right away, so I moved over."

"Looks like you're comfortable already."

I did not want to discuss my furniture or paint choices. It was already uncomfortable enough. I pushed that aside for a moment and reached for my home training.

"Would you like something to drink? I have coffee, iced tea, water." While I was talking, I walked to the kitchen. Logan followed. The cop wasn't overly big or intimidating, but I was a little on edge nonetheless. I sliced some lemon poppyseed bread and laid the slices on a plate. Poured sweet tea into two glasses. Handed him a glass, then took the bread and my own glass to the small round high-top table I used in the morning. There were two matching chrome-trimmed diner stools. I gestured for him to sit opposite mine.

Before I could hand him a fork, he picked up the bread and took a bite of half the slice.

"This is really good," he said before he swallowed.

"It's quick bread. Had a craving this morning." Truthfully I was glad to share. I was finding myself eating what would have been Woody's portion of treats.

"It's the perfect blend of tart and sweet and moist. Your secret?"

"Lemon yogurt."

I watched him finish the slice and help himself to another two. Only after he ate those and finished the tea did he ask, "Was that okay? Skipped breakfast."

"It's fine. I'm going to guess that you're not at my house at noon on Saturday to discuss secrets of baking. What's up?"

He was quiet for a long moment. It was only in that pause that I saw he was as discomfited as I was. A second later, an awareness of Logan as a man thrummed through my body. Jesus. I had to hope he wasn't here to ask me out on a date or something. I didn't know how I would say no to that one. Grateful for my journalism training that kept me from filling uncomfortable silences, I waited.

"Off the record."

I nearly sighed in relief that we were talking about work. I was getting too old to be thinking about dating and relationships.

"Of course. I'm not exactly taking notes here," I said. This time, I was the one to hold up my empty hands.

"There are some discrepancies...um...I want to look into some convictions," stuttered from his lips.

"You think someone was wrongfully convicted?" I asked.

"Yes?" His answer was more question than affirmation.

"I'm not a mind reader. Let's just say this is a confidential conversation between friends and not cop and journalist." I'd made that offer hundreds of times. People wanted to talk but didn't want to face the consequences of what they were about to set in motion. "Okay? What's going on?"

"I think Lori Pope has some wrongful convictions that have come out of her office."

I tried not to show how underwhelmed I was with his statement. True believers were always surprised by reality.

"I think that could be said of every prosecutor in America. The Innocence Project didn't end after a single case. It spread like a virus to a lot of states."

"It's more than that." His hands clapped the tabletop. "I think she's set up defendants."

"Framed them? You're talking more than run-of-the-mill prosecutorial misconduct?" For the first time since he'd walked in the door, he had my full attention.

"It started with this woman, Tia Wetzel. She was framed by some bad cops. She's got the Ohio Innocence Project out of Cincinnati on her case."

"Big guns, then." These clinics didn't take every case that walked through the door. They were looking for reasons for exoneration, and usually found them.

"Case came across my desk before I moved to homicide. There was something about Quinn's case that reminded me of the Wetzel one."

I itched to get my notepad and pen. But I could take notes later. For now, I needed to dig into what he wanted from me.

"Are you saying Quinn's not a killer?"

"Quinn killed Parker. I'm sure of that. But I don't think he killed Danica Lozano."

"Can you prove it?"

"I'm surely going to try."

I sat back. Looked out the window at my neighbors working on a car. Another walked by with an ugly terrier pulling at a leash. I pulled my attention back into the room. Looked Logan me in the eye.

"How does your command feel about that?"

"I haven't exactly run that one up the flag pole. It's an off-the-books sort of thing."

"So why are you here? It's not for the lemon poppyseed bread, which you didn't know was on the menu."

He smiled. Mimicked a chef's kiss before he answered.

"I want your help. You were a step ahead of me this whole time. I need someone with your smarts and tenacity."

I wanted to ask what was in it for me, but I knew. I'd have material for my blog and podcast. My Quinn article, with the "gay man seeks consensual sex" angle, had only gone up this morning, and between the time I'd put the bread in the oven and taken it out, I'd gotten a ping on my phone that I was at eighty percent of my server capacity. I'd had thousands of visitors in less than an hour.

My body felt like a magnet flipping polarity—equal parts compulsion and repulsion.

"You could lose your job," I warned. I didn't have a job to lose.

"Let me worry about me. You in?"

The universe hadn't put me in Logan's path for me to take the easy way out.

"Tell me what you have," I said. "Let's see where it leads."

ABOUT THE AUTHOR

Aime Austin is the author of the Nicole Long & Casey Cort Legal Thriller Series. She practiced family and criminal law in Cleveland, Ohio for several years.

When Aime isn't writing, she's hosting her podcast A Time to Thrill, raising her son, or traveling between Budapest and Los Angeles.

To hear about Aime's latest books first, and to be eligible for member only giveaways, sign up for the exclusive New Release Mailing List here: http://ebooks.buzz/aimenews.

Reviews are gold to authors! If you've enjoyed this book, please consider rating it and reviewing it at your favorite retailer or bookish site.

To connect with Aime Austin

www.aimeaustin.com

aime@aimeaustin.com